SNAFU ON VENUS

"I gather that you were sent here, in answer to my message?"

"Certainly," Matt said.

"Thank heaven for that—even if you guys were stupid enough to stumble right into it. Now tell me—how many are there in the expedition. This is going to be a tough nut to crack."

"This *is* the expedition, right in front of you."

"*What?* This is no time to joke. I sent for a regiment of marines, equipped for amphibious operations."

"Maybe you did, but this is what you got. What's the situation?"

Burke seemed dazed. "It's no use," he said. "It's utterly hopeless."

"What's so hopeless? The natives seem friendly, on the whole. Tell us what the difficulty was, so we can work it out with them."

"Friendly!" Burke gave a bitter laugh. "They killed all of my men. They're going to kill me. And they'll kill you too. . . ."

Space Cadet

Robert A. Heinlein

'A Del Rey Book

BALLANTINE BOOKS • NEW YORK

For William Ivar Bacchus

A Del Rey Book
Published by Ballantine Books

ISBN 0-345-30631-7

This edition published by arrangement with
Charles Scribner's Sons

Manufactured in the United States of America

First Ballantine Books Edition: September 1978
Second Printing: December 1981

Cover art by Darrell Sweet

CONTENTS

TERRA BASE

"TO MATTHEW BROOKS DODSON," the paper in his hand read, "greetings:

"Having successfully completed the field elimination tests for appointment to the position of cadet in the Interplanetary Patrol you are authorized to report to the Commandant, Terra Base, Santa Barbara Field, Colorado, North American Union, Terra, on or before One July 2075, for further examination.

"You are cautioned to remember that the majority of candidates taking these final tests usually fail and you should provide—"

Matt folded the paper and stuck it back in his belt pouch. He did not care to think about the chance of failure. The passenger across from him, a boy about his own age, caught his eye. "That paper looks familiar, you a candidate too?"

"That's right."

"Well, shake! M' name's Jarman—I'm from Texas."

"Glad to know you, Tex. I'm Matt Dodson, from Des Moines."

"Howdy, Matt. We ought to be about there—" The car sighed softly and slowed; their chairs rocked to meet the rapid deceleration. The car stopped and their chairs swung back to normal position. "We *are* there," Jarman finished.

The telescreen at the end of the car, busy a moment before with a blonde beauty demonstrating Sorkin's Super-

Stellar Soap, now read: TERRA BASE STATION. The two boys grabbed their bags, and hurried out. A moment later, they were on the escalator, mounting to the surface.

Facing the station a half mile away in the cool, thin air stood Hayworth Hall, Earth headquarters of the fabulous Patrol. Matt stared at it, trying to realize that he was at last seeing it.

Jarman nudged him. "Come on."

"Huh? Oh—sure." A pair of slidewalks stretched from the station to the hall; they stepped onto the one running toward the building. The slidewalk was crowded; more boys streamed out of the station behind them. Matt noticed two boys with swarthy, thin features who were wearing high, tight turbans, although dressed otherwise much like himself. Further down the walk he glimpsed a tall, handsome youth whose impassive face was shiny black.

The Texas boy hooked his thumbs in his belt and looked around. "Granny, kill another chicken!" he said. "There's company for dinner. Speaking of that," he went on, "I hope they don't wait lunch too long. I'm hungry."

Matt dug a candy bar out of his pouch, split it and gave half to Jarman, who accepted it gratefully. "You're a pal, Matt, I've been living on my own fat ever since breakfast—and that's risky. Say, your telephone is sounding."

"Oh!" Matt fumbled in his pouch and got out his phone. "Hello?"

"That you, son?" came his father's voice.

"Yes, Dad."

"Did you get there all right?"

"Sure, I'm about to report in."

"How's your leg?"

"Leg's all right, Dad." His answer was not frank; his right leg, fresh from a corrective operation for a short Achilles' tendon, was aching as he spoke.

"That's good. Now see here, Matt—if it should work out that you aren't selected, don't let it get you down. You call me at once and—"

"Sure, sure, Dad," Matt broke in. "I'll have to sign off— I'm in a crowd. Good-by. Thanks for calling."

"Good-by, son. Good luck."

Tex Jarman looked at him understandingly. "Your folks always worry, don't they? I fooled mine—packed my phone in my bag." The slidewalk swung in a wide curve preparatory to heading back; they stepped off with the crowd, in front of Hayworth Hall. Tex paused to read the inscription over the great doorway. "*Quis custodi*— What does it say, Matt?"

"*Quis custodiet ipsos custodes.* That's Latin for: Who will watch the guardians?"

"You read Latin, Matt?"

"No, I just remember that bit from a book about the Patrol."

The rotunda of Hayworth Hall was enormous and seemed even larger, for, despite brilliant lighting at the floor level, the domed ceiling gave back no reflection at all; it was midnight black—black and studded with stars. Familiar stars— blazing Orion faced the tossing head of Taurus; the homely shape of the Dipper balanced on its battered handle at north-northeast horizon; just south of overhead the Seven Sisters shone.

The illusion of being outdoors at night was most persuasive. The lighted walls and floor at the level at which people walked and talked and hurried seemed no more than a little band of light, a circle of warmth and comfort, against the awful depth of space, like prairie schooners drawn up for the night under a sharp desert sky.

The boys caught their breaths, as did everyone who saw it for the first time. But they could not stop to wonder as something else demanded their attention. The floor of the rotunda was sunk many feet below the level at which they entered; they stood on a balcony which extended around the great room to enclose a huge, shallow, circular pit. In this pit a battered spaceship lurched on a bed of rock and sand as if it had crash-landed from the mimic sky above.

"It's the *Kilroy*—" Tex said, almost as if he doubted it.

"It *must* be," Matt agreed in a whisper.

They moved to the balcony railing and read a plaque posted there:

USSF Rocket Ship *Kilroy Was Here*
FIRST INTERPLANETARY SHIP

From Terra to Mars and return—Lieut. Colonel
Robert deFries Sims, Commanding; Captain Saul
S. Abrams; Master Sergeant Malcolm MacGregor.
None survived the return landing. Rest in Peace.

They crowded next to two other boys and stared at the
Kilroy. Tex nudged Matt. "See the gash in the dirt, where
she skidded? Say, do you suppose they just built right over
her, where she lay?"

One of the other two—a big-boned six-footer with tawny
hair—answered, "No, the *Kilroy* landed in North Africa."

"Then they must have fixed it to look like where she
crashed. You a candidate too?"

"That's right."

"I'm Bill Jarman—from Texas. And this is Matt Dodson."

"I'm Oscar Jensen—and this is Pierre Armand."

"Howdy, Oscar. Glad to know you, Pierre."

"Call me Pete," Armand acknowledged. Matt noticed that
he spoke Basic English with an accent, but Matt was unable
to place it. Oscar's speech was strange, too—a suggestion of
a lisp. He turned back to the ship.

"Imagine having the guts to go out into space in a cracker
box like that," he said. "It scares me to think about it."

"Me, too," agreed Oscar Jensen.

"It's a dirty shame," Pierre said, softly.

"What is, Pete?" Jarman demanded.

"That their luck didn't hold. You can see it was an almost perfect landing—they didn't just crash in, or there
would have been nothing left but a hole in the ground."

"Yeah, I guess you're right. Say, there's a stairway down,
over on the far side—see it, Matt? Do you suppose we could
look through her?"

"Maybe," Matt told him, "but I think we had better put
it off. We've got to report in, you know."

"We had all better check in," agreed Jensen. "Coming,
Pete?"

Armand reached for his bag. Oscar Jensen pushed him aside and picked it up with his own. "That's not necessary!" Armand protested, but Oscar ignored him.

Jarman looked at Pierre. "You sick, Pete?" he asked. "I noticed you looked kind of peaked. What's the trouble?"

"If you are," put in Matt, "ask for a delay."

Armand looked embarrassed. "He's not sick and he'll pass the exams," Jensen said firmly. "Forget it."

"Sho', sho'," Tex agreed. They followed the crowd and found a notice which told all candidates to report to room 3108, third corridor. They located corridor three, stepped on the slideway, and put down their baggage.

"Say, Matt," said Tex, "tell me—who was Kilroy?"

"Let me see," Matt answered. "He was somebody in the Second Global War, an admiral, I think. Yeah, Admiral 'Bull' Kilroy, that sounds right."

"Funny they'd name it after an admiral."

"He was a flying admiral."

"You're a savvy cuss," Tex said admiringly. "I think I'll stick close to you during the tests."

Matt brushed it off. "Just a fact I happened to pick up."

In room 3108 a decorative young lady waved aside their credentials but demanded their thumb prints. She fed these into a machine at her elbow. The machine quickly spit out instruction sheets headed by the name, serial number, thumb print, and photograph of each candidate, together with temporary messing and rooming assignments.

The girl handed out the sheets and told them to wait next door. She abruptly turned away.

"I wish she hadn't been so brisk," complained Tex, as they went out. "I wanted to get her telephone code. Say," he went on, studying his sheet, "there's no time left on here for a siesta."

"Did you expect it?" asked Matt.

"Nope—but I can hope, can't I?"

The room next door was filled with benches but the benches were filled with boys. Jarman stopped at a bench which was crowded by three large cases, an ornate portable

11

refresher kit, and a banjo case. A pink-faced youth sat next to this. "Your stuff?" Tex asked him.

The young man grudgingly admitted it. "You won't mind if we move it and sit down," Tex went on. He started putting the items on the floor. The owner looked sulky but said nothing.

There was room for three. Tex insisted that the others sit down, then sat down on his bag and leaned against Matt's knees, with his legs stretched out. His footwear, thus displayed, were seen to be fine western boots, high-heeled and fancy.

A candidate across from them stared at the boots, then spoke to the boy next to him. "Pipe the cowboy!"

Tex snorted and started to get up. Matt put a hand on his shoulder, shoving him back. "It's not worth it, Tex. We've got a busy day ahead."

Oscar nodded agreement. "Take it easy, fellow."

Tex subsided. "Well—all right. Just the same," he added, "my Uncle Bodie would stuff a man's feet in his mouth for less than that." He glared at the boy across from him.

Pierre Armand leaned over and spoke to Tex. "Excuse me—but are those really shoes for riding on horses?"

"Huh? What do you think they are? Skis?"

"Oh, I'm sorry! But you see, I've never seen a horse."

"What?"

"*I* have," announced Oscar, "in the zoo, that is."

"In a *zoo?*" repeated Tex.

"In the zoo at New Auckland."

"Oh—" said Tex. "I get it. You're a Venus colonial." Matt then recalled where he had heard Oscar's vaguely familiar lisp before—in the speech of a visiting lecturer. Tex turned to Pierre. "Pete, are you from Venus, too?"

"No, I'm—" Pete's voice was drowned out.

"Attention, please! Quiet!" The speaker was dressed in the severely plain, oyster-white uniform of a space cadet. "All of you," he went on, speaking into a hand amplifier, "who have odd serial numbers come with me. Bring your baggage. Even numbers wait where you are."

"Odd numbers?" said Tex. "That's me!" He jumped up.

Matt looked at his instructions. "Me, too!"

The cadet came down the aisle in front of them. Matt and Tex waited for him to pass. The cadet did not hold himself erectly; he crouched the merest trifle, knees relaxed and springy, hands ready to grasp. His feet glided softly over the floor. The effect was catlike, easy grace; Matt felt that if the room were suddenly to turn topsy-turvy the cadet would land on his feet on the ceiling—which was perfectly true.

Matt wanted very much to look like him.

As the cadet was passing, the boy with the plentiful baggage plucked at his sleeve. "Hey, mister!"

The cadet turned suddenly and crouched, then checked himself as quickly. "Yes?"

"I've got an odd number, but I can't carry all this stuff. Who can I get to help me?"

"You can't." The cadet prodded the pile with his toe. "*All* of this is yours?"

"Yes. What do I do? I can't leave it here. Somebody'd steal it."

"I can't see why anyone would." The cadet eyed the pile with distaste. "Lug it back to the station and ship it home. Or throw it away."

The youngster looked blank. "You'll have to, eventually," the cadet went on. "When you make the lift to the school ship, twenty pounds is your total allowance."

"But— Well, suppose I do, who's to help me get it to the station?"

"That's your problem. If you want to be in the Patrol, you'll have to learn to cope with problems."

"But—"

"Shut up." The cadet turned away. Matt and Tex trailed along.

Five minutes later Matt, naked as an egg, was stuffing his bag and clothes into a sack marked with his serial number. As ordered, he filed through a door, clutching his orders and a remnant of dignity. He found himself in a gang refresher which showered him, scrubbed him, rinsed him, and blew

13

him dry again, assembly-line style. His instruction sheet was waterproof; he shook from it a few clinging drops.

For two hours he was prodded, poked, thumped, photographed, weighed, X-rayed, injected, sampled, and examined until he was bewildered. He saw Tex once, in another queue. Tex waved, slapped his own bare ribs, and shivered. Matt started to speak but his own line started up.

The medicos examined his repaired leg, making him exercise it, inquired the date of the operation, and asked if it hurt him. He found himself admitting that it did. More pictures were taken; more tests were made. Presently he was told, "That's all. Get back into line."

"Is it all right, sir?" Matt blurted out.

"Probably. You'll be given some exercises. Get along."

After a long time he came into a room in which several boys were dressing. His path took him across a weighing platform; his body interrupted electric-eye beams. Relays closed, an automatic sequence took place based on his weight, height, and body dimensions. Presently a package slid down a chute and plunked down in front of him.

It contained an undergarment, a blue coverall, a pair of soft boots, all in his size.

The blue uniform he viewed as a makeshift, since he was anxious to swap it for the equally plain, but oyster white, uniform of a cadet. The shoes delighted him. He zipped them on, relishing their softness and glovelike fit. It seemed as if he could stand on a coin and call it, heads or tails. "Cat feet"—his first space boots! He took a few steps, trying to walk like the cadet he had seen earlier.

"Dodson!"

"Coming." He hurried out and shortly found himself thrust into a room with an older man in civilian clothes.

"Sit down. I'm Joseph Kelly." He took Matt's instruction sheet. "Matthew Dodson . . . nice to know you, Matt."

"How do you do, Mr. Kelly."

"Not too badly. Why do you want to join the Patrol, Matt?"

"Why, uh, because—" Matt hesitated. "Well, to tell the

truth, sir, I'm so confused right now that I'm darned if I know!"

Kelly chuckled. "That's the best answer I've heard today. Do you have any brothers or sisters, Matt?" The talk wandered along, with Kelly encouraging Matt to talk. The questions were quite personal, but Matt was sophisticated enough to realize that "Mr. Kelly" was probably a psychiatrist; he stammered once or twice but he tried to answer honestly.

"Can you tell me now why you want to be in the Patrol?"

Matt thought about it. "I've wanted to go out into space ever since I can remember."

"Travel around, see strange planets and strange people—that's understandable, Matt. But why not the merchant service? The Academy is a long, hard grind, and it's three to one you won't finish, even if you are sworn in as a cadet—and not more than a quarter of the candidates will pass muster. But you could enter the merchant school—I could have you transferred today—and with your qualifications you'd be a cinch to win your pilot's ticket before you are twenty. How about it?"

Matt looked stubborn.

"Why not, Matt? Why insist on trying to be an officer of the Patrol? They'll turn you inside out and break your heart and no one will thank you for your greatest efforts. They'll make you over into a man your own mother wouldn't recognize—and you won't be any happier for it. Believe me, fellow—I know."

Matt did not say anything.

"You still want to try it, knowing chances are against you?"

"Yes. Yes, I think I do."

"Why, Matt?"

Matt still hesitated. Finally he answered in a low voice. "Well, people look up to an officer in the Patrol."

Mr. Kelly looked at him. "That's enough reason for now, Matt. You'll find others—or quit." A clock on the wall suddenly spoke up:

"Thirteen o'clock! Thirteen o'clock!" Then it added thoughtfully, "I'm hungry."

"Mercy me!" said Kelly. "So am I. Let's go to lunch, Matt."

II

ELIMINATION PROCESS

MATT'S INSTRUCTIONS told him to mess at table 147, East Refectory. A map on the back of the sheet showed where East Refectory was; unfortunately he did not know where Matt was—he had gotten turned around in the course of the morning's rat race. He ran into no one at first but august personages in the midnight black of officers of the Patrol and he could not bring himself to stop one of them.

Eventually he got oriented by working back to the rotunda and starting over, but it made him about ten minutes late. He walked down an endless line of tables, searching for number 147 and feeling very conspicuous. He was quite pink by the time he located it.

There was a cadet at the head of the table; the others wore the coveralls of candidates. The cadet looked up and said, "Sit down, mister—over there on the right. Why are you late?"

Matt gulped. "I got lost, sir."

Someone tittered. The cadet sent a cold glance down the table. "You. You with the silly horse laugh—what's your name?"

"Uh, Schultz, sir."

"Mister Schultz, there is nothing funny about an honest answer. Have you never been lost?"

"Why— Well, uh, once or twice, maybe."

"Hm . . . I shall be interested in seeing your work in astrogation, *if* you get that far." The cadet turned back to Matt. "Aren't you hungry? What's your name?"

"Yes, sir. Matthew Dodson, sir." Matt looked hurriedly at

16

the controls in front of him, decided against soup, and punched the "entrée," "dessert," and "milk" buttons. The cadet was still watching him as the table served him.

"I am Cadet Sabbatello. Don't you like soup, Mr. Dodson?"

"Yes, sir, but I was in a hurry."

"There's no hurry. Soup is good for you." Cadet Sabbatello stretched an arm and punched Matt's "soup" button. "Besides, it gives the chef a chance to clean up the galley." The cadet turned away, to Matt's relief. He ate heartily. The soup was excellent, but the rest of the meal seemed dull compared with what he had been used to at home.

He kept his ears open. One remark of the cadet stuck in his memory. "Mr. van Zook, in the Patrol we never ask a man where he is from. It is all right for Mr. Romolus to volunteer that he comes from Manila; it is incorrect for you to ask him."

The afternoon was jammed with tests; intelligence, muscular control, reflex, reaction time, sensory response. Others required him to do two or more things at once. Some seemed downright silly. Matt did the best he could.

He found himself at one point entering a room containing nothing but a large, fixed chair. A loudspeaker addressed him: "Strap yourself into the chair. The grips on the arms of the chair control a spot of light on the wall. When the lights go out, you will see a lighted circle. Center your spot of light in the circle and keep it centered."

Matt strapped himself down. A bright spot of light appeared on the wall in front of him. He found that the control in his right hand moved the spot up and down, while the one in his left hand moved it from side to side. "Easy!" Matt told himself. "I wish they would start."

The lights in the room went out; the lighted target circle bobbed slowly up and down. He found it not too difficult to bring his spot of light into the circle and match the bobbing motion.

Then his chair turned upside down.

When he recovered from his surprise at finding himself hanging head down in the dark, he saw that the spot of light

17

had drifted away from the circle. Frantically he brought them together, swung past and had to correct.

The chair swung one way, the circle another, and a loud explosion took place at his left ear. The chair bucked and teetered; a jolt of electricity convulsed his hands and he lost the circle entirely.

Matt began to get sore. He forced his spot back to the circle and nailed it. "Gotcha!"

Smoke poured through the room, making him cough, watering his eyes, and veiling the target. He squinted and hung on grimly, intent only on hanging onto that pesky circle of light—through more explosions, screaming painful noise, flashing lights, wind in his eyes, and endless, crazy motions of his chair.

Suddenly the room lights flared up, and the mechanical voice said: "Test completed. Carry out your next assignment."

Once he was given a handful of beans and a small bottle, and was told to sit down and place the bottle at a mark on the floor and locate in his mind the exact position of the bottle. Then he was to close his eyes and drop the beans one at a time into the bottle—if possible.

He could tell from the sound that he was not making many hits, but he was mortified to find, when he opened his eyes, that only one bean rested in the bottle.

He hid the bottom of his bottle in his fist and queued up at the examiner's desk. Several of those lined up had a goodly number of beans in their bottles, although he noted two with no beans at all. Presently he handed his bottle to the examiner. "Dodson, Matthew, sir. One bean."

The examiner noted it without comment. Matt blurted out, "Excuse me, sir—but what's to keep a person from cheating by peeking?"

The examiner smiled. "Nothing at all. Go on to your next test."

Matt left, grumbling. It did not occur to him that he might not know what was being tested.

Late in the day he was ushered into a cubbyhole containing a chair, a gadget mounted on a desk, pencil and paper, and framed directions.

"If any score from a previous test," Matt read, "appears in the window marked SCORE, return the starting lever to the position marked NEUTRAL to clear the board for your test."

Matt found the window labeled "SCORE"; it had a score showing in it—"37." Well, he thought, that gives me a mark to shoot at. He decided not to clear the board until he had read the instructions.

"After the test starts," he read, "a score of '1' will result each time you press the lefthand button except as otherwise provided here below. Press the lefthand button whenever the red light appears provided the green light is not lighted as well except that no button should be pressed when the righthand gate is open unless all lights are out. If the righthand gate is open and the lefthand gate is closed, no score will result from pressing any button, but the lefthand button must nevertheless be pressed under these circumstances if all other conditions permit a button to be pressed before any score may be made in succeeding phases of the test. To put out the green light, press the righthand button. If the lefthand gate is not closed, no button may be pressed. If the lefthand gate is closed while the red light is lighted, do not press the lefthand button if the green light is out unless the righthand gate is open. To start the test move the starting lever from neutral all the way to the right. The test runs for two minutes from the time you move the starting lever to the right. Study these instructions, then select your own time for commencing the test. You are not permitted to ask questions of the examiner, so be sure that you understand the instructions. Make as high a score as possible."

"Whew!" said Matt.

Still, the test looked simple—one lever, two pushbuttons, two colored lights, two little gates. Once he mastered the instructions, it would be as easy as flying a kite, and a durn sight simpler than flying a copter!—Matt had had his copter license since he was twelve. He got to work.

First, he told himself, there seems to be just two ways to

make a score, one with the red light on and one with both lights out and one gate open.

Now for the other instructions— Let's see, if the lefthand gate is not closed—no, if the lefthand gate *is* closed—he stopped and read them over again.

Some minutes later he had sixteen possible positions of gates and conditions of lights listed. He checked them against the instructions, seeking scoring combinations. When he was through he stared at the result, then checked everything over again.

After rechecking he stared at the paper, whistled tunelessly, and scratched his head. Then he picked up the paper, left the booth, and went to the examiner.

That official looked up. "No questions, please."

"I don't have a question," Matt said. "I want to report something. There's something wrong with that test. Maybe the wrong instructions sheet was put in there. In any case, there is no possible way to make a score under the instructions that are in there."

"Oh, come, now!" the examiner answered. "Are you sure of that?"

Matt hesitated, then answered firmly, "I'm sure of it. Want to see my proof?"

"No. Your name is Dodson?" The examiner glanced at a timer, then wrote on a chart. "That's all."

"But— Don't I get a chance to make a score?"

"No questions, please! I've recorded your score. Get along —it's dinner time."

There were a large number of vacant places at dinner. Cadet Sabbatello looked down the long table. "I see there have been some casualties," he remarked. "Congratulations, gentlemen, for having survived thus far."

"Sir—does that mean we've passed all the tests we took today?" one of the candidates asked.

"Or at least won a retest. You haven't flunked." Matt sighed with relief. "Don't get your hopes up. There will be still fewer of you here tomorrow."

"Does it get worse?" the candidate went on.

Sabbatello grinned wickedly. "Much worse. I advise you

all to eat little at breakfast. However," he went on, "I have good news, too. It is rumored that the Commandant himself is coming down to Terra to honor you with his presence when you are sworn in—if you are sworn in."

Most of those present looked blank. The cadet glanced around. "Come, come, gentlemen!" he said sharply. "Surely not all of you are that ignorant. You!" He addressed Matt. "Mister, uh—Dodson. You seem to have some glimmering of what I am talking about. Why should you feel honored at the presence of the Commandant?"

Matt gulped. "Do you mean the Commandant of the Academy, sir?"

"Naturally. What do you know about him?"

"Well, sir, he's Commodore Arkwright." Matt stopped, as if the name were explanation.

"And what distinguishes Commodore Arkwright?"

"Uh, he's blind, sir."

"Not blind, Mr. Dodson, not blind! It simply happens that he had his eyes burned out. How did he lose his eyesight?" The cadet stopped him. "No—don't tell them. Let them find out for themselves."

The cadet resumed eating and Matt did likewise, while thinking about Commodore Arkwright. He himself had been too young to pay attention to the news, but his father had read an account of the event to him—a spectacular, single-handed rescue of a private yacht in distress, inside the orbit of Mercury. He had forgotten just how the Patrol officer had exposed his eyes to the Sun—something to do with transferring the yacht's personnel—but he could still hear his father reading the end of the report: "—these actions are deemed to be in accordance with the tradition of the Patrol."

He wondered if any action of his would ever receive that superlative distinction. Unlikely, he decided; "duty satisfactorily performed" was about the best an ordinary man could hope for.

Matt ran into Tex Jarman as he left the mess hall. Tex pounded him on the back. "Glad to see you, kid. Where are you rooming?"

"I haven't had time to look up my room yet."

"Let's see your sheet." Jarman took it. "We're in the same corridor—swell. Let's go up."

They found the room and walked in. Sprawled on the lower of two bunks, reading and smoking a cigarette, was another candidate. He looked up.

"Enter, comrades," he said. "Don't bother to knock."

"We didn't," said Tex.

"So I see." The boy sat up. Matt recognized the boy who had made the crack about Tex's boots. He decided to say nothing—perhaps they would not recognize each other. The lad continued, "Looking for someone?"

"No," Matt answered, "this is the room I'm assigned to."

"My roommate, eh? Welcome to the palace. Don't trip over the dancing girls. I put your stuff on your bed."

The sack containing Matt's bag and civilian clothes rested on the upper bunk. He dragged it down.

"What do you mean, his bed?" demanded Tex. "You ought to match for the lower bunk."

Matt's roommate shrugged. "First come, first served."

Tex clouded up. "Forget it, Tex," Matt told him. "I prefer the upper. By the way," he went on, to the other boy, "I'm Matt Dodson."

"Girard Burke, at your service."

The room was adequate but austere. Matt slept in a hydraulic bed at home, but he had used mattress beds in summer camp. The adjoining refresher was severely functional but very modern—Matt noted with pleasure that the shower was installed with robot massage. There was no shave mask, but shaving was not yet much of a chore.

In his wardrobe he found a package, marked with his serial number, containing two sets of clothing and a second pair of space boots. He stowed them and his other belongings; then turned to Tex. "Well, what'll we do now?"

"Let's look around the joint."

"Fine. Maybe we can go through the *Kilroy*."

Burke chucked his cigarette toward the oubliette. "Wait a sec. I'll go with you." He disappeared into the 'fresher.

Tex said in a low voice. "Tell him to go fly a kite, Matt."

"It'ud be a pleasure. But I'd rather get along with him, Tex."

"Well, maybe they'll eliminate him tomorrow."

"Or me." Matt smiled wryly.

"Or me. Shucks, no, Matt—we'll get by. Have you thought about a permanent roomie? Want to team up?"

"It's a deal." They shook hands.

"I'm glad that's settled," Tex went on. "My cellmate is a nice little guy, but he's got a blood brother, or some such, he wants to room with. Came to see him before dinner. They chattered away in Hindustani, I guess it was. Made me nervous. Then they shifted to Basic out of politeness, and that made me more nervous."

"You don't look like the nervous type."

"Oh, all us Jarmans are high strung. Take my Uncle Bodie. Got so excited at the county fair he jumped between the shafts of a sulky and won two heats before they could catch him and throw him."

"Is that so?"

"My solemn word. Didn't pay off, though. They disqualified him because he wasn't a two-year-old."

Burke joined them and they sauntered down to the rotunda. Several hundred other candidates had had the same idea but the administration had anticipated the rush. A cadet stationed at the stairway into the pit was permitting visitors in parties of ten only, each party supervised by a cadet. Burke eyed the queue. "Simple arithmetic tells me there's no point in waiting."

Matt hesitated. Tex said, "Come on, Matt. Some will get tired and drop out."

Burke shrugged, said, "So long, suckers," and wandered away.

Matt said doubtfully, "I think he's right, Tex."

"Sure—but I got rid of him, didn't I?"

The entire rotunda was a museum and memorial hall of the Patrol. The boys found display after display arranged around the walls—the original log of the first ship to visit Mars, a photo of the take-off of the disastrous first Venus expedition, a model of the German rockets used in the Second Global War, a hand-sketched map of the far side of the Moon, found in the wrecked *Kilroy*.

They came to an alcove the back wall of which was filled by a stereo picture of an outdoor scene. They entered and found themselves gazing, in convincing illusion, out across a hot and dazzling lunar plain, with black sky, stars, and Mother Terra herself in the background.

In the foreground, life size, was a young man dressed in an old-fashioned pressure suit. His features could be seen clearly through his helmet, big mouth, merry eyes, and thick sandy hair cut in the style of the previous century.

Under the picture was a line of lettering: *Lieutenant Ezra Dahlquist, Who Helped Create the Tradition of the Patrol—1969-1996.*

Matt whispered, "There ought to be a notice posted somewhere to tell us what he did."

"I don't see any," Tex whispered back. "Why are you whispering?"

"I'm not—yes, I guess I was. After all, *he* can't hear us, can he? Oh—there's a vocall"

"Well, punch it."

Matt pressed the button; the alcove filled with the first bars of Beethoven's Fifth. The music gave way to a voice: "The Patrol was originally made up of officers sent to it by each of the nations then in the Western Federation. Some were trustworthy, some were not. In 1996 came a day shameful and glorious in the history of the Patrol, an attempted *coup d'état*, the so-called Revolt of the Colonels. A cabal of high-ranking officers, acting from Moon Base, tried to seize power over the entire world. The plot would have been successful had not Lieutenant Dahlquist disabled every atom-bomb rocket at Moon Base by removing the fissionable material from each and wrecking the triggering mechanisms. In so doing he received so much radiation that he died of his burns." The voice stopped and was followed by the Valhalla theme from *Götterdämmerung*.

Tex let out a long sigh; Matt realized that he had been holding his own breath. He let it go, then took another; it seemed to relieve the ache in his chest.

They heard a chuckle behind them. Girard Burke was leaning against the frame of the alcove. "They go to a lot of trouble to sell it around here," he remarked. "Better watch it, me lads, or you will find yourselves buying it."

"What do you mean by that? Sell what?"

Burke gestured toward the picture. "That. And the plug that goes with it. If you care for that sort of thing, there are three more, one at each cardinal point of the compass."

Matt stared at him. "What's the matter with you, Burke? Don't you want to be in the Patrol?"

Burke laughed. "Sure I do. But I'm a practical man; I don't have to bamboozled into it by a lot of emotional propaganda." He pointed to the picture of Ezra Dahlquist. "Take him. They don't tell you he disobeyed orders of his superior officer—if things had fallen the other way, he'd be called a traitor. Besides that, they don't mention that it was sheer clumsiness that got him burned. Do you expect me to think he was a superman?"

Matt turned red. "No, I wouldn't expect it." He took a step forward. "But, since you are a practical man, how would you like a nice, practical punch in the snoot?"

Burke was no larger than Matt and a shade shorter, but he leaned forward, balanced on the balls of his feet, and said softly, "I'd love it. You and who else?"

Tex stepped forward. "I'm the 'who else.'"

"Stay out of this, Tex!" Matt snapped.

"I will not! I don't believe in wasting fair fighting on my social inferiors."

"Stay out, I tell you!"

"Nope, I want a piece of this. You slug him and I'll kick him in the stomach as he goes down."

Burke looked at Jarman, and relaxed, as if he knew that the fighting moment was past. "Tut, tut, gentlemen! You're squabbling among yourselves." He turned away. "Goodnight, Dodson. Don't wake me coming in."

Tex was still fuming. "We should have let him have it. He'll make your life miserable until you slap him down. My Uncle Bodie says the way to deal with that sort of pimple is to belt him around until he apologizes."

"And get kicked out of the Patrol before we're in it? I let him get me mad, so that puts him one up. Come on—let's see what else there is to see."

But Call-to-Quarters sounded before they worked around to the next of the four alcoves. Matt said good night to Tex at his door and went inside. Burke was asleep or shamming. Matt peeled off his clothes, shinnied up into his bunk, looked for the light switch, spotted it, and ordered it to switch off.

The unfriendly presence under him made him restless, but he was almost asleep when he recalled that he had not called his father back. The thought awakened him. Presently he became aware of a vague ache somewhere inside him. Was he coming down with something?

Could it be that he was homesick? At his age? The longer he considered it the more likely it seemed, much as he hated to admit it. He was still pondering it when he fell asleep.

III

OVER THE BUMPS

THE NEXT MORNING Burke ignored the trouble they had had; he made no mention of it. He was even moderately cooperative about sharing the 'fresher. But Matt was glad to hear the call to breakfast.

Table 147 was not where it should be. Puzzled, Matt moved down the line until he found a table marked "147-149," with Cadet Sabbatello in charge. He found a place and sat down, to find himself sitting next to Pierre Armand. "Well! Pete!" he greeted him. "How are things going?"

"Glad to see you, Matt. Well enough, I guess." His tone seemed doubtful.

Matt looked him over. Pete seemed—"dragged through a

knothole" was the phrase Matt settled on. He was about to ask what was wrong when Cadet Sabbatello rapped on the table. "Apparently," said the cadet, "some of you gentlemen have forgotten my advice last night, to eat sparingly this morning. You are about to go over the bumps today—and ground-hogs have been known to lose their breakfasts as well as their dignity."

Matt looked startled. He had intended to order his usual lavish breakfast; he settled for milk toast and tea. He noticed that Pete had ignored the cadet's advice; he was working on a steak, potatoes, and fried eggs—whatever ailed Pete, Matt decided, it had not affected his appetite.

Cadet Sabbatello had also noticed it. He leaned toward Pete. "Mister, uh—"

"Armand, sir," Pete answered between bites.

"Mr. Armand, either you have the digestion of a Martian sandworm, or you thought I was joking. Don't you expect to be dropsick?"

"No, sir."

"No?"

"You see, sir, I was born on Ganymede."

"Oh! I beg your pardon. Have another steak. How are you doing?"

"Pretty well, on the whole, sir."

"Don't be afraid to ask for dispensations. You'll find that everyone around here understands your situation."

"Thank you, sir."

"I mean it. Don't play 'iron man.' There's no sense in it."

After breakfast, Matt fell in step with Armand. "Say, Pete, I see why Oscar carried your bag yesterday. Excuse me for being a stupe."

Pete looked self-conscious. "Not at all. Oscar has been looking out for me—I met him on the trip down from Terra Station."

Matt nodded. "I see." He had no expert knowledge of interplanetary schedules, but he realized that Oscar, coming from Venus, and Pete, coming from one of Jupiter's moons, would have to change ships at the artificial satellite of Earth called Terra Station, before taking the shuttle rocket down.

It accounted for the two boys being well acquainted despite cosmically different backgrounds. "How do you feel?" he went on.

Pete hesitated. "As a matter of fact, I feel as if I were wading in quicksand up to my neck. Every move is an effort."

"Gee, that's too bad! Just what is the surface gravity on Ganymede? About one-third 'g' isn't it?"

"Thirty-two per cent. Or from my point of view, everything here weighs three times as much as it ought to. Including me."

Matt nodded. "As if two other guys were riding on you, one on your shoulders, and one on your back."

"That's about it. The worst of it is, my feet hurt all the time. I'll get over it—"

"Sure you will!

"—since I'm of Earth ancestry and potentially just as strong as my grandfather was. Back home, I'd been working out in the centrifuge the last couple of earth-years. I'm a lot stronger than I used to be. There's Oscar." Matt greeted Oscar, then hurried to his room to phone his father in private.

A copter transport hopped Matt and some fifty other candidates to the site of the variable acceleration test—in cadet slang, the "Bumps." It was west of the base, in the mountains, in order to have a sheer cliff for free fall. They landed on a loading platform at the edge of this cliff and joined a throng of other candidates. It was a crisp Colorado morning. They were near the timberline; gaunt evergreens, twisted by the winds, surrounded the clearing.

From a building just beyond the platform two steel skeletons ran vertically down the face of the two-thousand-foot cliff. They looked like open frames for elevators, which one of them was. The other was a guide for the testing car during the drop down the cliff.

Matt crowded up to the rail and leaned over. The lower ends of the skeleton frameworks disappeared, a dizzy distance below, in the roof of a building notched into the sloping floor of the canyon. He was telling himself that he hoped the engineer who had designed the thing knew what he was doing when he felt a dig in the ribs. It was Tex. "Some roller coaster, eh, Matt?"

"Hi, Tex. That's an understatement if I ever heard one."

The candidate on Matt's left spoke up. "Do you mean to say we ride down that thing?"

"No less," Tex answered. "Then they gather the pieces up in a basket and haul 'em up the other one."

"How fast does it go?"

"You'll see in a mom— Hey! *Thar she blows!*"

A silvery, windowless car appeared inside one guide frame, at its top. It poised for a split second, then dropped. It dropped and dropped and dropped, gathering speed, until it disappeared with what seemed incredible velocity— actually about two hundred and fifty miles per hour—into the building below. Matt braced himself for the crash. None came, and he caught his breath.

Seconds later the car reappeared at the foot of the other framework. It seemed to crawl; actually it was accelerating rapidly during the first half of the climb. It passed from view into the building at the top of the cliff.

"Squad nine!" a loudspeaker bawled behind them.

Tex let out a sigh "Here I go, Matt," he said. "Tell mother my last words were of her. You can have my stamp collection." He shook hands and walked away.

The candidate who had spoken before gulped; Matt saw that he was quite pale. Suddenly he took off in the same direction but did not line up with the squad; instead he went up to the cadet mustering the squad and spoke to him, briefly and urgently. The cadet shrugged and motioned him away from the group.

Matt found himself feeling sympathetic rather than contemptuous.

His own test group was mustered next. He and his fellows were conducted into the upper building, where a cadet explained the test: "This test examines your tolerance for high acceleration, for free fall or weightlessness, and for violent changes in acceleration. You start with centrifugal force of three gravities, then all weight is removed from you as the car goes over the cliff. At the bottom the car enters a spiraling track which reduces its speed at deceleration of three gravities. When the car comes to rest, it enters the ascending tower; you make the climb at two gravities, dropping to one gravity, and momentarily to no weight, as the car reaches the top. Then the cycle is repeated, at higher accelerations, until each of you has reacted. Any questions?"

Matt asked, "How long is the free fall, sir?"

"About eleven seconds. We would increase it, but to double it would take four times as high a cliff. However, you will find this one high enough." He smiled grimly.

A timid voice asked, "Sir, what do you mean by 'react'?"

"Any of several things—hemorrhage, loss of consciousness."

"It's dangerous?"

The cadet shrugged. "What isn't? There has never been any mechanical failures. Your pulse, respiration, blood pressure, and other data are telemetered to the control room. We'll try not to let you die under test."

Presently he led them out of the room, down a passage and through a door into the test car. It had pendulum seats, not unlike any high-speed vehicle, but semi-reclining and heavily padded. They strapped down and medical technicians wired them for telemetering their responses. The cadet inspected, stepped out and returned with an officer, who repeated the inspection. The cadet then distributed "sick kits"—cloth bags of double thickness to be tied and taped to the mouth, so that a person might retch without inundating his companions. This done, he asked, "Are you all ready?" Getting no response, he went out and closed the door.

Matt wished that he had stopped him before it was too late.

For a long moment nothing happened. Then the car seemed to incline; actually, the seats inclined as the car started to move and picked up speed.

The seats swung back to the at-rest position but Matt felt himself getting steadily heavier and knew thereby that they were being centrifuged. He pressed against the pads, arms leaden, legs too heavy to move.

The feeling of extra weight left him, he felt his normal weight again, when suddenly that, too, was taken from him. He surged against the safety belts.

His stomach seemed to drop out of him. He gulped and swallowed; his breakfast stayed down. Somebody yelled, "We're falling!" It seemed to Matt the most unnecessary statement he had ever heard.

He set his jaw and braced himself for the bump. It did not come—and still his stomach seemed trying to squirm its way out of his body. Eleven seconds? Why, he had been falling more than eleven seconds already! What had gone wrong?

And still they fell, endlessly.

And fell.

Then he was forced back against the pads. The pressure increased smoothly until he was as heavy as he had been just before the drop. His abused stomach tried to retch but the pressure was too much for it.

The pressure eased off to normal weight. A short while later the car seemed to bounce and momentarily he was weightless, while his insides grabbed frantically for anchorage. The feeling of no weight lasted only an instant; he sagged into the cushions.

The door was flung open; the cadet strode in, followed by two medical technicians. Someone yelled, "Let me out of here! Let me out of here!" The cadet paid no attention but went to the seat in front of Matt. He unstrapped the occupant and the two medical assistants carried him out. His head lolled loosely as they did so. The cadet then went to the candidate who was kicking up the fuss, unstrapped him, and stepped back. The boy got up, staggered, and shuffled out.

"Anyone need a fresh sick kit?" There were muffled responses. Working swiftly, the cadet helped those who needed it. Matt felt weakly triumphant that his own kit was still clean.

"Stand by for five gravities," commanded the cadet. He

made them answer to their names, one by one. While he was doing so another boy started clawing at his straps. Still calling the roll, the cadet helped him free and let him leave. He followed the lad out the door and shut it.

Matt felt himself tensing unbearably. He was relieved when the pressure took hold—but only momentarily, for he found that five gravities were much worse than three. His chest seemed paralyzed, he fought for air.

The giant pressure lifted—they were over the edge again, falling. His mistreated stomach revenged itself at once; he was sorry that he had eaten any breakfast at all.

They were still falling. The lights went out—and someone screamed. Falling and still retching, Matt was sure that the blackness meant some sort of accident; this time they would crash—but it did not seem to matter.

He was well into the black whirlpool of force that marked the deceleration at the bottom before he realized that he had come through without being killed. The thought brought no particular emotion; breathing at five gravities fully occupied him. The ride up the cliff, at double weight dropping off to normal weight, seemed like a vacation—except that his stomach protested when they bounced to a stop.

The lights came on and the cadet re-entered the room. His gaze stopped at the boy on Matt's right. The lad was bleeding at his nose and ears. The candidate waved him away feebly. "I can take it," he protested. "Go on with the test."

"Maybe you can," the cadet answered, "but you are through for today." He added, "Don't feel bad about it. It's not necessarily a down check."

He inspected the others, then called in the officer. The two held a whispered consultation over one boy, who was then half led, half carried from the test chamber. "Fresh sick kits?" asked the cadet.

"Here," Matt answered feebly. The change was made, while Matt vowed to himself never to touch milk toast again.

"Seven gravities," announced the cadet. "Speak up, or stand by." He called the roll again. Matt was ready to give up, but he heard himself answer "ready" and the cadet was gone before he could make up his mind. There were only six of them left now.

It seemed to him that the lights were going out again, gradually, as the weight of his body built up to nearly a thousand pounds. But the lights "came on" again as the car dropped over the cliff; he realized dully that he had blacked out.

He had intended to count seconds on this fall to escape the feeling of endless time, but he was too dazed. Even the disquiet in his middle section seemed remote. Falling—falling—

Again the giant squeezed his chest, drained the blood from his brain, and shut the light from his eyes. The part that was Matt squeezed out entirely. . . .

"How do you feel?" He opened his eyes, saw a double image, and realized dimly that the cadet was leaning over him. He tried to answer. The cadet passed from view; he felt someone grasping him; he was being lifted and carried.

Someone wiped his face with a wet, cold towel. He sat up and found himself facing a nurse. "You're all right now," she said cheerfully. "Keep this until your nose stops bleeding." She handed him the towel. "Want to get up?"

"Yes, I think so."

"Take my arm. We'll go out into the air."

Out on the loading platform Matt sat in the sunshine, dabbling at his nose and regaining his strength. He could hear sounds of excitement from the rail behind each time the car dropped. He sat there, soaking in the sun and wondering whether or not he really wanted to be a spaceman.

"Hey, Matt." It was Tex, looking pale and not too sure of himself. There was a blood stain down the front of his coverall.

"Hello, Tex. I see you've had it."

"Yeah."

"How many g's?"

"Seven."

"Same here. What do you think of it?"

"Well—" Tex seemed at a loss. "I wish my Uncle Bodie could have tried it. He wouldn't talk so much about the time he rassled the grizzly."

There were many vacant seats at lunch. Matt thought about those who had gone—did they mind being "bumped out," or were they relieved?

He was hungry but ate little, for he knew what was ahead that afternoon—rocket indoctrination. He had looked forward to this part of the schedule most eagerly. Space flight! Just a test jump, but the real thing nevertheless. He had been telling himself that, even if he failed, it would be worth it to get this first flight.

Now he was not sure; the "bumps" had changed his viewpoint. He had a new, grim respect for acceleration and he no longer thought drop-sickness funny; instead he was wondering whether or not he would ever get adjusted to free fall. Some never did, he knew.

His test group was due in Santa Barbara Field at fourteen-thirty. He had a long hour to kill with nothing to do but fret. Finally it was time to go underground, muster, and slidewalk out to the field.

The cadet in charge led them up to the surface into a concrete trench about four feet deep. Matt blinked at the sunlight. His depression was gone; he was anxious to start. On each side and about two hundred yards away were training rockets, lined up like giant birthday candles, poised on their fins with sharp snouts thrusting against the sky.

"If anything goes wrong," the cadet said, "throw yourself flat in the trench. Don't let that get your goat—I'm required to warn you.

"The jump lasts nine minutes, with the first minute and a half under power. You'll feel three gravities, but the acceleration is only two gravities, because you are still close to the Earth.

"After ninety seconds you'll be travelling a little faster than a mile a second and you will coast on up for the next three minutes for another hundred miles to an altitude of about one hundred fifty miles. You fall back toward the earth another three minutes, brake your fall with the jet and ground at the end of the ninth minute.

"A wingless landing on an atmosphere planet with gravity as strong as that of Earth is rather tricky. The landing will be radar-robot controlled, but a human pilot will stand by and check the approach against the flight plan. He can take over if necessary. Any questions?"

Someone asked, "Are these atomic-powered ships?"

The cadet snorted. "These jeeps? These are chemically powered, as you can see from the design. Monatomic hydrogen. They are much like the first big rockets ever built, except that they have variable thrust, so that the pilot and the passengers won't be squashed into strawberry jam as the mass-ratio drops off."

A green signal flare arched up from the control tower. "Keep your eyes on the second rocket from the end, on the north," advised the cadet.

There was a splash of orange flame, sun bright, at the base of the ship. *"There she goes!"*

The ship lifted majestically, and poised for an instant, motionless as a hovering helicopter. The noise reached Matt, seemed to press against his chest. It was the roar of an impossibly huge blowtorch. A searchlight in the tower blinked, and the ship mounted, up and up, higher and faster, its speed increasing with such smoothness that it was hard to realize how fast it was going—except that the roar was gone. Matt found himself staring straight at the zenith, watching a dwindling artificial sun, almost as dazzling as Sol himself.

Then it was gone. Matt closed his mouth and started to look away when his attention was seized by the ice trail left as the rocket sliced its way through the outer atmosphere. White and strange, it writhed like a snake with a broken back. Under the driving force of the many-hundred-miles-an-hour winds of that far altitude it twisted visibly as he watched.

"That's all!" the cadet shouted. "We can't wait for the landing."

They went underground, down a corridor, and entered an elevator. It went up right out of the ground and into the air, supported by a hydraulic piston. It mounted close by the side of a rocket ship; Matt was amazed to see how large it was close up.

The elevator stopped and its door let down drawbridge fashion into the open hatch in the rocket's side. They trooped across; the cadet raised the bridge and went down again.

They were in a conical room. Above them the pilot lay in his acceleration rest. Beside them, feet in and head out, were acceleration couches for passengers. "Get in the bunks!" shouted the pilot. "Strap down."

Ten boys jostled one another to reach the couches. One hesitated. "Uh, oh, Mister!" he called out.

"Yes? Get in your couch."

"I've changed my mind. I'm not going."

The pilot used language decidedly not officerlike and turned to his control board. "Tower! Remove passenger from number nineteen." He listened, then said, "Too late to change the flight plan. Send up mass." He shouted to the waiting boy, "What do you weigh?"

"Uh, a hundred thirty-two pounds, sir."

"One hundred and thirty-two pounds and make it fast!" He turned back to the youngster. "You better get off this base fast, for if I have to skip my take-off I'll wring your neck."

The elevator climbed into place presently and three cadets poured across. Two were carrying sandbags, one had five lead weights. They strapped the sandbags to the vacant couch, and clamped the weights to its sides. "One thirty-two mass," announced one of the cadets.

"Get going," snapped the pilot and turned back to the board.

"Don't blow your tubes, Harry," advised the cadet addressed. Matt was amazed, then decided the pilot must be a cadet, too. The three left, taking with them the boy; the hatch door shut with a *whish.*

"Stand by to raise!" the pilot called out, then looked down

to check his passengers. "Passengers secure, nineteen," he called to the tower. "Is that confounded elevator clear?"

There was silence as the seconds trickled away.

The ship shivered. A low roar, muffled almost below audibility, throbbed in Matt's head. For a moment he felt slightly heavy, the feeling passed, then he was pressed strongly against the pads.

Matt was delighted to find that three gravities were not bad, flat on his back as he was. The minute and a half under power stretched out; there was nothing to hear but the muted blast of the reactor, nothing to see but the sky through the pilot's port above.

But the sky was growing darker. Already it was purple; as he watched it turned black. Fascinated, he watched the stars come out.

"Stand by for free fall!" the pilot called out, using an amplifier. "You'll find sick kits under each pillow. If you need 'em, put 'em on. I don't want to have to scrape it off the port."

Matt fumbled with heavy fingers under his head, found the kit. The sound of the jet died away, and with it the thrust that had kept them pinned down. The pilot swung out of his rest and floated, facing them. "Now look, sports —we've got six minutes. You can unstrap, two at a time and come up for a look-see. But get this: Hang on tight. Any man who starts floating free, or skylarking, gets a down check." He pointed to a boy. "You—and the next guy."

The "next guy" was Matt. His stomach was complaining and he felt so wretched that he did not really want the privilege offered—but his face was at stake; he clamped his jaws, swallowed the saliva pouring into his mouth, and un-strapped.

Free, he clung to one strap, floating loosely, and tried to get his bearings. It was curiously upsetting to have no up-and-down; it made everything swim—he had trouble focusing his eyes. "Hurry up there!" he heard the pilot shout, "or you'll miss your turn."

"Coming, sir."

"Hang on—I'm going to turn the ship." The pilot unclutched his gyros and cut in his precessing flywheels. The ship turned end over end. By the time Matt worked his way to the control station, moving like a cautious and elderly monkey, the rocket was pointed toward Earth.

Matt stared out at the surface, nearly a hundred miles below and still receding. The greens and browns seemed dark by contrast with the white dazzle of clouds. Off to the left and right he could see the inky sky, stabbed with stars. "That's the Base, just below," the pilot was saying. "Look sharp and you can make out Hayworth Hall, maybe, by its shadow."

It did not seem "just below" to Matt; it seemed "out"—or no direction at all. It was disquieting. "Over there—see? —is the crater where Denver used to be. Now look south— that brown stretch is Texas; you can see the Gulf beyond it."

"Sir," asked Matt, "can we see Des Moines from here?"

"Hard to pick out. Over that way—let your eye slide down the Kaw River till it strikes the Missouri, then up river. That dark patch—that's Omaha and Council Bluffs. Des Moines is between there and the horizon." Matt strained his eyes, trying to pick out his home. He could not be sure— but he did see that he was staring over the bulge of the Earth at a curved horizon; he was *seeing* the Earth as round. "That's all," ordered the pilot. "Back to your bunks. Next pair!"

He was glad to strap a belt across his middle. The remaining four minutes or so stretched endlessly; he resigned himself to never getting over space sickness. Finally the pilot chased the last pair back, swung ship jet toward Earth, and shouted, "Stand by for thrust—we're about to ride 'er down on her tail!"

Blessed weight pressed down on him and his stomach stopped complaining. The ninety seconds of deceleration seemed longer; it made him jumpy to know that the Earth was rushing up at them and not be able to see it. But at last there came a slight bump and his weight dropped suddenly to normal. "Grounded," announced the pilot, "and all in one piece. You can unstrap, sports."

Presently a truck arrived, swung a telescoping ladder up to the hatch, and they climbed down. On the way back they passed a great unwieldy tractor, crawling out to retrieve the rocket. Someone stuck his head out of the tractor. "Hey! Harry—why didn't you land it in Kansas?"

Their pilot waved at the speaker. "Be grateful I didn't!"

Matt was free until mess; he decided to return to the observation trench; he still wanted to see a ship land on its jet. He had seen winged landings of commercial stratosphere rockets, but never a jet landing.

Matt had just found a vacant spot in the trench when a shout went up—a ship was coming in. It was a ball of flame, growing in the sky, and then a pillar of flame, streaking down in front of him. The streamer of fire brushed the ground, poised like a ballet dancer, and died out. The ship was down.

He turned to a candidate near him. "How long till the next one?"

"They've come in about every five minutes. Stick around."

Presently a green flare went up from the control tower and he looked around, trying to spot the ship about to take off, when another shout caused him to turn back. There again was a ball of fire in the sky, growing.

Unbelievably, it went out. He stood there, stupefied—to hear a cry of "Down! Down, everybody! Flat on your faces!" Before he could shake off his stupor, someone tackled him and threw him.

He was rocked by a sharp shock, on top of it came the roar of an explosion. Something snatched at his breath.

He sat up and looked around. A cadet near him was peering cautiously over the parapet. "Allah the Merciful," he heard him say softly.

"What happened?"

"Crashed in. Dead, all dead." The cadet seemed to see him for the first time. "Get back to your quarters," he said sharply.

"But how did it happen?"

"Never mind—this is no time for sightseeing." The cadet moved down the line, clearing out spectators.

39

IV

FIRST MUSTER

MATT'S ROOM WAS EMPTY, which was a relief. He did not want to see Burke, nor anyone. He sat down and thought about it.

Eleven people—just like that. All happy and excited and then—*crrump!*—not enough left to cremate. Suddenly he himself was back up in the sky— He broke off the thought, trembling.

At the end of an hour he had made up his mind that the Patrol was not for him. He had thought of it, he realized, through a kid's bright illusions—*Captain Jenks of the Space Patrol, The Young Rocketeers*, stuff like that. Well, those books were all right—for kids—but he wasn't hero material, he had to admit.

Anyhow, his stomach would never get used to free fall. Right now it tightened up when he thought about it.

By the time Burke returned he was calm and, if not happy, at least he was not unhappy, for his mind was at rest.

Burke came in whistling. He stopped when he saw Matt. "Well, junior, still here? I thought the bumps would send you home."

"No."

"Didn't you get dropsick?"

"Yes." Matt waited and tried to control his temper. "Didn't you?"

Burke chuckled. "Not likely. I'm no groundhog, junior. I—"

"Call me 'Matt.' "

"Okay, Matthew. I was going out into space before I could walk. My old man builds 'em, you know."

"I didn't know."

"Sure. 'Reactors, Limited'—he's chairman of the board. Say, did you see the fireworks out at the field?"

"You mean the ship that crashed?"

"What else? Quite a show, wasn't it?"

Matt could feel himself coming to a slow boil. "Do you mean to stand there and tell me," he said quietly, "that you regard the deaths of eleven human beings as 'quite a show'?"

Burke stared at him. Then he laughed. "I'm sorry, old fellow. I apologize. But it actually didn't occur to me that you didn't know."

"Didn't know what?"

"But you weren't supposed to know, of course. Relax, son—no one was killed. You were framed."

"Huh? What are you talking about?"

Burke sat down and laughed until he had tears. Matt grabbed him by the shoulder. "Cut that out and talk."

The other candidate stopped and looked up. "Honest, I rather like you, Dodson—you're such a perfect country cousin. How do you feel about Santa Claus and the Stork?"

"Talk!"

"Haven't you caught on to what they've been doing to you ever since you checked in?"

"Doing what?"

"War of nerves, man. Haven't you noticed some tests were too easy—too easy to cheat in, that is? When you went over the bumps, didn't you notice that they let you take a good look at the drop before you made it? When they could just as easily have kept you inside where it wouldn't worry you?"

Matt thought about it. It was an enticing notion—he could see how some of the things he had not understood would fit in to such a theory. "Go on."

"Oh, it's a good gag—it cleans out the weak sisters and it cleans out the stupes, too—the guys so dumb that they can't resist an invitation to cheat, never dreaming that it might be booby-trapped. It's efficient—a Patrol officer has to be smart and fast on his feet and cool-headed. It keeps from wasting money on second-raters."

"You just called me dumb and yet I got by."

"Of course you did, junior, because your heart is pure." He laughed again. "And I got by. But you'll never make a Patrolman, Matt. They've got other ways to get rid of the good, dumb boys. You'll see."

"Okay, so I'm dumb. But don't call me junior again. What's this got to do with the ship that crashed?"

"Why, it's simple. They want to eliminate all the dead-wood before swearing us in. There are candidates with cast-iron stomachs who don't get upset by the bumps, or anything. So they send up a ship under robot control—no pilot, no passengers—and crash it, just to scare off those who can be scared. It's a darn sight cheaper than training just one cadet, if he doesn't pay off in the long run."

"How do you know? Have you got inside information on it?"

"In a way, yes. It's a logical necessity—those ships *can't* crash, unless you crash 'em on purpose. I *know*—my old man makes them."

"Well—maybe you're right." Matt dropped the matter, unsatisfied but lacking basis for further argument. It did convince him of one thing, however—spacesickness or not, come what may, he resolved to hang on as long as Girard Burke did, and at least twenty-four hours longer!

His table at dinner that night was numbered "147, 149, 151 & 153." There was room enough to seat the survivors.

Cadet Sabbatello looked them over pleasantly. "Congratulations, gentlemen, on having lasted it out. Since you will be sworn in tonight, when next we meet it will be in a different status." He grinned. "So relax and enjoy your last meal of freedom."

In spite of no effective breakfast and little lunch, Matt found himself unable to eat much. Girard Burke's interpretation of the tests and what they meant troubled him. He still intended to take the oath, but he had an uneasy feeling

that he was about to take it without knowing what it signi-
fied—what the Patrol really was.

When the meal broke up, on sudden impulse he followed
the cadet in charge of the table out. "Excuse me—Mr.
Sabbatello, could I speak to you privately, sir?"

"Eh? I suppose so—come along." He led Matt to his own
room; it was exactly like Matt's. "Now what is it?"

"Uh—Mr. Sabbatello, that crash today: was anybody
hurt?"

"Hurt? It killed eleven people. Don't you call that 'hurt'?"

"Are you sure? Is it possible that it was a drone and
nobody was inside?"

"It's possible, but it's not the case. I wish it were—the
pilot was a friend of mine."

"Oh—I'm sorry. But I had to know, for sure. You see, it's
very important to me."

"Why?"

Matt sketched out Burke's version of what had happened,
without giving Burke's name. As he talked, Sabbatello
showed more and more annoyance. "I see," he said, when
Matt was done. "It is true that some of the tests are
psychological rather than overt. But this matter of the crash
—who fed you that nonsense?"

Matt did not say anything.

"Never mind. You can protect your informant—it won't
matter in the least in the long run. But about the crash—"
He considered. "I'd give my word of honor to you—in fact
I do—but if you accept the hypothesis your friend holds,
then you won't pay any attention to my sworn word." He
thought a moment. "Are you a Catholic?"

"Uh, nossir." Matt was startled.

"It doesn't matter. Do you know who Saint Barbara is?"

"Not exactly, sir. The field—"

"Yes, the field. She was a third-century martyr. The
point is that she is the patron saint of all who deal with
high explosives, rocket men among others." He paused.

"If you go over to the chapel, you will find that a mass
is scheduled during which Saint Barbara will be asked to

43

intercede for the souls of the men who were lost this afternoon. I think you realize that no priest would lend his office to any such chicanery as your friend suggests?"

Matt nodded solemnly. "I see your point, sir. I don't need to go to the chapel—I've found out what I needed to know."

"Fine. You had better hightail it and get ready. It would be embarrassing to be late to your own swearing in."

First Muster was scheduled for twenty-one o'clock in the auditorium. Matt was one of the first to arrive, scrubbed and neat and wearing a fresh coverall. A cadet took his name and told him to wait inside. The floor of the hall had been cleared of seats. Above the stage at the far end were the three closed circles of the Federation—Freedom, Peace, and Law, so intertwined that, if any one were removed, the other two would fall apart. Under them was the Patrol's own sign, a star blazing in the night.

Tex was one of the last to show up. He was greeting Matt, breathlessly, when a cadet, speaking from the rostrum, called out, "Attention!

"Gather on the left side of the hall," he went on. The candidates milled and shuffled into a compact group. "Remain where you are until muster. When your name is called, answer 'Here!', then walk across to the other side. You will find white guide lines on the deck there. Toe the lines to form ranks."

Another cadet came down from the rostrum and moved toward the mass of boys. He stopped, picked a slip of paper from four such slips he held, and fixed Tex with his eye. "You, mister," he said. "Take this."

Jarman took it, but looked puzzled. "What for?"

"As well as answering to your own name, when you hear this name, speak up. Step out in front and sing out, 'I answer for him!'"

Tex looked at the slip. Matt saw that it read: "John Martin."

"But why?" demanded Tex.

The cadet looked at him. "You really don't know?"

"Nary a notion."

"Hmmph! Well, since the name doesn't ring a bell, just take it that he is a classmate of yours who can't be here to-night, in person. So you answer for him to make the muster complete. Get it?"

"Yes, sir. Can do."

The cadet moved on down the line. Tex turned to Matt. "What gives, d'you s'pose?"

"It beats me."

"Me, too. Well, we'll probably find out."

The cadet on the rostrum moved to stage left. "Silence!" he commanded. "The Commandant!"

From the rear entered two men dressed in the midnight black. The younger of them walked so that his sleeve brushed the elbow of his senior. They moved to the center of the platform; the younger man stopped. The elder halted immediately, whereupon the aide withdrew. The Commandant of the Academy stood facing the new class.

Or, rather, facing down the center of the hall. He stood still for a long moment; someone coughed and shuffled, at which he turned toward the group and faced them thereafter. "Good evening, gentlemen."

Seeing him, Matt was reminded strongly of Cadet Sabbatello's protest: "Not *blind*, Mr. Dodson!" Commodore Arkwright's eyes looked strange—the sockets were deep set and the eyelids drooped like a man in thought. Yet, as that sightless gaze rested on him, it seemed to Matt that the Commandant could not only see him but could peer inside his head.

"I welcome you to our fellowship. You come from many lands, some from other planets. You are of various colors and creeds. Yet you must and shall become a band of brothers.

"Some of you are homesick. You need not be. From this day on every part of this family of planets is your home, each place equally. Each living, thinking creature in this system is your neighbor—and your responsibility.

"You are about to take an oath, by your own choice, as a member of the Patrol of this our System. In time, you expect to become an officer of that Patrol. It is necessary that you understand the burden you assume. You expect to spend long hours studying your new profession, acquiring the skills of the spaceman and the arts of the professional soldier. These skills and arts you must have, but they will not make you an officer of the Patrol."

He paused, then went on, "An officer in command of a ship of the Patrol, away from base, is the last of the absolute monarchs, for there is none but himself to restrain him. Many places where he must go no other authority reaches. He himself must embody law, and the rule of reason, justice and mercy.

"More than that, to the members of the Patrol singly and together is entrusted such awful force as may compel or destroy, all other force we know of—and with this trust is laid on them the charge to keep the peace of the System and to protect the liberties of its peoples. They are soldiers of freedom.

"It is not enough that you be skillful, clever, brave— The trustees of this awful power must each possess a meticulous sense of honor, self-discipline beyond all ambition, conceit, or avarice, respect for the liberties and dignity of all creatures, and an unyielding will to do justice and give mercy. He must be a true and gentle knight."

He stopped and there was no sound at all in the huge room. Then he said, "Let those who are prepared to take the oath be mustered."

The cadet who had been acting as adjutant stepped forward briskly. "Adams!"

"Uh—here, sir!" A candidate trotted across the room. "Akbar."

"Here!"

"Alvarado—"

"Anderson, Peter—"

"Anderson, John—"

"Angelico—"

Then, presently, it was, "Dana—Delacroix—DeWitt—Diaz—Dobbs," and "Dodson!"

"Here!" shouted Matt. His voice squeaked but no one

laughed. He hurried over to the other side, found a place and waited, panting. The muster went on:

"Eddy—Eisenhower—Ericsson—" Boys trickled across the room until few were left. "Sforza, Stanley, Suliman," and then, finally: "Zahm!" The last candidate joined his fellows.

But the cadet did not stop. "Dahlquist!" he called out.

There was no answer.

"Dahlquist!" he repeated. "Ezra Dahlquist!"

Matt felt cold prickles around his scalp. He recognized the name now—but Dahlquist would not be here, not Ezra Dahlquist. Matt was sure of that, for he remembered an alcove in the rotunda, a young man in a picture, and the hot, bright sand of the Moon.

There was a stir in the rank behind him. A candidate pushed his way through and stepped forward. "I answer for Ezra Dahlquist!"

"Martin!"

This time there was no hesitation. He heard Tex's voice, his tone shrill: "I answer for him."

"Rivera."

A strong baritone: "Answering for Rivera!"

"Wheeler!"

"I answer for Wheeler."

The cadet turned toward the Commandant and saluted: "All present, sir. Class of 2075, First Muster complete."

The man in black returned the salute. "Very well, sir. We will proceed with the oath." He stepped forward to the very edge of the platform, the cadet at his elbow. "Raise your right hands."

The Commandant raised his own hand. "Repeat after me: Of my own free will, without reservation—"

" 'Of my own free will, without reservation—' "

"I swear to uphold the peace of the Solar System—"

In chorus they followed him.

"—to protect the lawful liberties of its inhabitants—

"—to defend the constitution of the Solar Federation—

"—to carry out the duties of the position to which I am now appointed—

"—and to obey the lawful orders of my superior officers.

"To these ends I subordinate all other loyalties and renounce utterly any that may conflict with them.

"This I solemnly affirm in the Name I hold most sacred."

"So help me, God," concluded the Commandant. Matt repeated his words, but the response around him took a dozen different forms, in nearly as many languages.

The Commandant turned his head to the cadet by his side. "Dismiss them, sir."

"Aye aye, sir." The cadet raised his voice. "On being dismissed, face to the right and file out. Maintain your formation until clear of the door. Dismissed!"

At the cue of his command, music swelled out and filled the hall; the newly created cadets marched away to the strains of the Patrol's own air, *The Long Watch*. It persisted until the last of them were gone, then faded out.

The Commandant waited until the youngster cadets had left, then faced around. His aide joined him at once, whereupon the acting cadet adjutant moved quickly from his side. Commodore Arkwright turned toward the departing cadet. "Mr. Barnes."

"Yes, sir?"

"Are you ready to be commissioned?"

"Er— I don't think so, sir. Not quite."

"So? Well, come see me soon."

"Yes, sir. Thank you."

The Commodore turned away and headed rapidly for the stage exit, with his aide's sleeve brushing his. "Well, John," asked the senior, "What did you think of them?"

"A fine bunch of boys, sir."

"That was my impression. All youth and eagerness and young expectation. But how many of them will we have to eliminate? It's a sorry thing, John, to take a boy and change him so that he is no longer a civilian, then kick him out. It's the cruelest duty we have to perform."

"I don't see a way to avoid it."

"There is no way. If we had some magic touchstone— Tell the field that I want to raise ship in thirty minutes."

"Aye aye, sir."

V

INTO SPACE

The PATROL ACADEMY may lack ivy-covered buildings and tree-shaded walks; it does not lack room. There are cadets in every reach of the Federation, from ships circling Venus, or mapping the scorched earth of Mercury, to ships patrolling the Jovian moons.

Even on years-long exploration flights to the frozen fringes of the Solar System cadets go along—and are brevetted as officers when their captains think them ready, without waiting to return.

The public thinks of the Academy as the school ship P.R.S. *James Randolph,* but every cadet mess in every ship of the Patrol is part of the Academy. A youngster cadet is ordered to the *Randolph* as soon as he is sworn in and he remains attached to that ship until he is ready to go to a regular Patrol vessel as a passed cadet. His schooling continues; in time he is ordered back to where he started, Hayworth Hall, to receive his final polish.

An oldster, attached to Hayworth Hall, will not necessarily be there. He may be at the radiation laboratories of Oxford University, or studying interplanetary law at the Sorbonne, or he may even be as far away as Venus, at the Institute for System Studies. Whatever his route—and no two cadets pursue exactly the same course of training—the Academy is still in charge of him, until, and *if*, he is commissioned.

How long it takes depends on the cadet. Brilliant young Hartstone, who died on the first expedition to Pluto, was brevetted less than a year after he reported to Hayworth Hall as a groundhog candidate. But it is not unusual to find oldsters at Terra Base who have been cadets for five years or more.

Cadet Matthew Dodson admired himself in the mirror of the 'fresher. The oyster-white uniform he had found waiting when he returned from First Muster the evening before, and with it a small book of regulations embossed with his name and clipped to a new assignment schedule. The schedule had started out: "1. Your first duty as a cadet is to read the regulation book herewith, at once. Hereafter you are responsible for the contents."

He had read it before taps, until his mind was a jumble of undigested rules: "A cadet is an officer in a limited sense—" "—behave with decorum and sobriety appropriate to the occasion—" "—in accordance with local custom rather than Patrol custom unless in conflict with an invariant law of the Federation or regulation of the Patrol." "—but the responsibility of determining the legality of the order rests on the person ordered as well as on the person giving the order." "—circumstances not covered by law or regulation must be decided by the individual in the light of the living tradition of the Patrol." "Cadets will at all times be smooth-shaven and will not wear their hair longer than two inches."

He felt that he understood the last mentioned.

He got up before reveille the next morning and dived into the 'fresher, shaved hastily and rather unnecessarily and got into uniform.

It fit him well enough, but to his eye the fit was perfect, the styling superb. As a matter of fact, the uniform lacked style, decoration, trim, insignia, or flattering cut.

But Matt thought he looked wonderful.

Burke pounded on the 'fresher door. "Have you died in there?" He stuck his head in. "Oh—all right, so you look sweet. Now how about getting out?"

"Coming." Matt stalled around the room for a few minutes, then overcome by impatience, tucked his regulation book in his tunic (regulation #383), and went to the refectory. He walked in feeling self-conscious, proud, and about seven feet tall. He sat down at his table, one of the first to arrive. Cadets trickled in; Cadet Sabbatello was one of the last.

The oldster looked grimly down the table. "Attention," he snapped. "All of you—stand up."

Matt jumped to his feet with the rest. Sabbatello sat down. "From now on, gentlemen, make it a rule to wait until your seniors are seated. Be seated." The oldster studied the studs in front of him, punched his order, and looked up. The youngsters had resumed eating. He rapped the table sharply. "Quiet, please. Gentlemen, you have many readjustments to make. The sooner you make them, the happier you will be. Mr. Dodson—stop dunking your toast; you are dripping it on your uniform. Which brings me," he went on, "to the subject of table manners—"

Matt returned to his quarters considerably subdued.

He stopped by Tex's room and found him thumbing through the book of regulations. "Hello, Matt. Say, tell me something—is there anything in this bible that says Mr. Dynkowski has the right to tell me not to blow on my coffee?"

"I see you've had it, too. What happened?"

Jarman's friendly face wrinkled. "Well, I'd begun to think of Ski as an all-right guy, helpful and considerate. But this morning at breakfast he starts out by asking me how I manage to carry around all that penalty-weight." Tex glanced at his waist line; Matt noted with surprise that Tex looked quite chubby in cadet uniform.

"All us Jarmans are portly," Tex went on defensively. "He should see my Uncle Bodie. Then he—"

"Skip it," said Matt. "I know the rest of it—now."

"Well, I guess I shouldn't have lost my temper."

"Probably not." Matt looked through the book. "Maybe this will help. It says here that, in case of doubt, you may insist that the officer giving the order put it in writing and stamp his thumb print, or use other means to provide a permanent record."

"Does it, really?" Tex grabbed the book. "That's for me!— 'cause I sure am in doubt. Boy! Just wait and see his face when I pull this one."

"I'd like to," agreed Matt. "Which way do you take the

51

lift, Tex?" The Patrol Rocket Ship *Simon Bolivar*, transport, was at Santa Barbara Field, having discharged a battalion of Space Marines, but P.R.S. *Bolivar* could take but about half the new class. The rest were to take the public shuttle rocket from Pike's Peak launching catapult to Terra Space Station, there to be transferred to the *Randolph*.

"Transport," Tex answered. "How about you?"

"Me, too. I'd like to see Terra Station, but I'm glad we're going in a Patrol ship. What are you taking with you?"

Tex hauled out his luggage and hefted it. "It's a problem. I've got about fifty pounds here. Do you suppose if I rolled it up real small I could get it down to twenty pounds?"

"An interesting theory," Matt said. "Let's have a look at it—you've got to eliminate thirty pounds of penalty-weight."

Jarman spread his stuff out on the floor. "Well," Matt said at once, "you don't need all those photographs." He pointed to a dozen large stereos, each weighing a pound or more.

Tex looked horrified. "Leave my harem behind?" He picked up one. "There is the sweetest redhead in the entire Rio Grande Valley." He picked up another. "And Smitty—I couldn't get along without Smitty. She thinks I'm wonderful."

"Wouldn't she still think so if you left her pic behind?"

"Oh, of course. But it wouldn't be gallant." He considered. "I'll compromise—I'll leave behind my club."

"Your club?" Matt asked, failing to see anything of that description.

"The one I use to beat off the little darlings when they get too persistent."

"Oh. Maybe someday you'll teach me your secret. Yes, leave your club behind; there aren't any girls in the *Randolph*."

"Is that good?" demanded Tex.

"I refuse to commit myself." Matt studied the pile. "You know what I'd suggest? Keep that harmonica—I like harmonica music. Have those photos copied in micro. Feed the rest to the cat."

"That's easy for you to say."

"I've got the same problem." He went to his room. The

class had the day free, for the purpose of getting ready to leave Earth. Matt spread his possessions out to look them over. His civilian clothes he would ship home, of course, and his telephone as well, since it was limited by its short range to the neighborhood of an earth-side relay office.

He made a note to telephone home before he packed the instrument. Might as well make one other call, too, he decided; even though he was resolved not to waste time on girls in his new life, it would be polite to phone and say good-by. He did so.

He put the instrument down a few minutes later, baffled to find that he had apparently promised to write regularly.

He called home, spoke with his parents and kid brother, and then put the telephone with things to be shipped. He was scratching his head over what remained when Burke came in. He grinned. "Trying to swallow your penalty-weight?"

"I'll figure it out."

"You don't have to leave that junk behind, you know."

"Huh?"

"Ship it up to Terra Station, rent a locker, and store it. Then, when you go on liberty to the Station, you can bring back what you want. Sneak it aboard, if it's that sort of thing." Matt made no comment; Burke went on, "What's the matter, Galahad? Shocked at the notion of running contraband?"

"No. But I don't have a locker at Terra Station."

"Well, if you're too cheap to rent one, you can ship the stuff to mine. You scratch me and I'll scratch you."

"No, thanks." He thought about expressing some things to the Terra Station post office, then discarded the idea—the rates were too high. He went on sorting. He would keep his camera, but his micro kit would have to go, and his chessmen. Presently he had cut the list to what he hoped was twenty pounds; he took the stuff away to weigh it.

Reveille and breakfast were an hour early the next day. Shortly after breakfast the call-to-muster ran through Hayworth Hall, to be followed by heart-quickening strains of "Raise Ship!" Matt slung his jump bag over his shoulder and hurried down to the lower corridors. He pushed his way through a throng of excited youngster cadets and found his assigned area.

Muster was by squads and Matt was a temporary squad leader, as his name came first, alphabetically, in his squad. He had been given a list; he reached into his pouch and had an agonizing moment of thinking he had left it up in his room before his fingers closed on it. "Dodsworth!"

"Here."

"Dunstan."

"Here."

He was still working through Frankel, Freund, and Funston when the oldster mustering the entire corridor shouted for him to report. He hurried to a conclusion, faced around, and saluted. "Squad nineteen—all present!"

Someone tittered and Matt realized suddenly that he had used the scout salute, rather than the relaxed, open-palmed gesture of the Patrol. His cheeks burned.

A brassy amplified voice called out, "All deck parties report." In turn, the oldster in Matt's corridor called out, "Third deck party, all present." When all reports were in there was a momentary silence, long enough for Matt to have a spine-tingling anticipation of what was to come. Would they? But they were doing so; the voice over the speaker called out: "Dahlquist?"

Another voice—heard only through the speaker—replied, "I answer for him."

It went on, until the Four were mustered, whereupon the first voice stated, "All present, sir."

"Man the ship."

They mounted a slidewalk, to step off in a large underground room, far out under Santa Barbara Field. There were eight large elevators arranged in a wide circle around the room. Matt and his squad were crowded into one of them and mounted to the surface. Up it went, much higher than had been necessary to enter the test-flight rocket, up and up, close by the huge bulk of the *Bolivar*.

It stopped and they trotted across the drawbridge into the ship. Inside the airlock stood a space-marines sergeant, gaudy and splendid who kept repeating, "Seventh deck! Down the hatch to your own deck—step lively!" He pointed to the hatch, down which disappeared a narrow, vertical steel ladder.

Matt hitched his jump bag out of his way and lowered himself into the hatch, moving fast to avoid getting his fingers stepped on by the cadet who followed him. He lost track of the decks, but there was a sergeant master-at-arms on each. He got off when he heard, "Third deck!"

He was in a wide, low cylindrical compartment, the deck of which was covered with plastic-foam padding. It was marked off in sections, each about seven feet by three and fitted with safety belts.

Matt found an unoccupied section, sat down, and waited. Presently cadets stopped dribbling in, the room was crowded. The master-at-arms called out, "Down, everybody—one to a section." He then counted them by noting that all sections were filled.

A loudspeaker warned, "All hands, prepare for acceleration!" The sergeant told them to strap down and remained standing until all had done so. He then lay down, grasped two handholds, and reported the third deck ready.

"All hands, stand by to raise!" called out the speaker.

There was a long and breathless wait.

"Up ship!" shouted the speaker.

Matt felt himself pressed into the padding.

Terra Space Station and the school ship *Randolph* lie in a circular orbit 22,300 miles above the surface of the Earth, where they circle the Earth in exactly twenty-four hours, the natural period of a body at that distance.

Since the Earth's rotation exactly matches their period, they face always one side of the Earth—the ninetieth western meridian, to be exact. Their orbit lies in the ecliptic, the plane of the Earth's orbit around the Sun, rather than in the plane of the Earth's equator. This results in them swinging north and south each day as seen from the earth. When it is noon in the Middle West, Terra Station and the *Ran-*

dolph lie over the Gulf of Mexico; at midnight they lie over the South Pacific.

The state of Colorado moves eastward about 830 miles per hour. Terra Station and the *Randolph* also move eastward nearly 7000 miles per hour—1.93 miles per second, to be finicky. The pilot of the *Bolivar* had to arrive at the *Randolph* precisely matched in course and speed. To do this he must break his ship away from our heavy planet, throw her into an elliptical orbit just tangent to the circular orbit of the *Randolph* and with that tangency so exactly placed that, when he matched speeds, the two ships would lie relatively motionless although plunging ahead at two miles per second. This last maneuver was no easy matter like jockeying a copter over a landing platform, as the two speeds, unadjusted, would differ by 3000 miles an hour.

Getting the *Bolivar* from Colorado to the *Randolph*, and all other problems of journeying between the planets, are subject to precise and elegant mathematical solution under four laws formulated by the saintly, absent-minded Sir Isaac Newton nearly four centuries earlier than this flight of the *Bolivar*—the three Laws of Motion and the Law of Gravitation. These laws are simple; their application in space to get from where you are to where you want to be, at the correct time with the correct course and speed, is a nightmare of complicated, fussy computation.

The "weight" pressing Matt into the padding was four gravities—Matt weighed nearly six hundred pounds. He lay there, breathing with difficulty, while the ship punched its way through the thick soup of air and out into free space. The heavy weight bound down the cadets while the *Bolivar* attained a speed of some six miles per second and climbed to an altitude of 900 miles.

At the end of five minutes and a few odd seconds the drive stopped.

Matt raised his head, while the sudden silence rang in his ears. The master-at-arms detected Matt's movement and others. He shouted, "Stay where you are—don't move."

Matt relaxed. They were in free fall, weightless, even

though the *Bolivar* was speeding away from the Earth at more than 20,000 miles an hour. Each body—ship, planet, meteor, atom—in space falls continually. It moves also with whatever other motion it has inherited from its past experience.

Matt was acutely aware of his weightlessness, for his stomach told him about it, complainingly. To be on the safe side, he removed a sick kit from his jump bag, but he did not put it on. He was feeling queasy; it was not as bad as it had been on his test flight, not half as bad as the "bumps." He hoped to get by without losing his breakfast.

The loudspeaker sang out, "End of acceleration. Four hours of free fall." The master-at-arms sat up. "You can unstrap now," he said.

In a matter of seconds the compartment took on the look of a particularly crowded aquarium. One hundred boys were floating, swimming, squirming in every attitude and position between the deck and the overhead. These two barriers no longer seemed like floor and ceiling since up-and-down was gone; they were simply walls which rotated slowly and erratically for each observer as his own body turned past them.

"Hey, you guys!" yelled the sergeant. "Grab on to something and listen to me." Matt looked around, found himself near the overhead, spotted a handhold, and grasped it. "It's time you kids learned some traffic rules for free flight. You got to learn to zig when the other guy zags. If you happen to meet the Captain and you zig when you should 'a' zagged and bump him, he ain't going to like it. See?"

He stuck out a scarred thumb. "Rule one: all groundhogs—that's you and don't try to tell me anything different—are required to hold on with at least one hand at all times. That applies until you pass your free-fall acrobatics test. Rule two: give way to officers and don't make them have to shout 'Gangway!' Besides that, give way to anybody on duty, or busy, or with his hands full.

"If you're moving aft, pass inboard of the man you meet, and contrariwise if you're moving forward. If you're moving clockwise, figuring 'clockwise' from the bow end of the ship, you pass the man you meet outboard and let him pass inboard—contrariwise for counterclockwise. No matter what direction you're going, if you overtake a man you pass inboard of him. Is that all clear?"

Matt thought it was, though he doubted if he could remember it. But a remaining possibility occurred to him. "Sergeant," he asked innocently, "suppose you're moving directly in or out from the center of the ship—what do you do?"

The sergeant looked disgusted, which gave his face an odd appearance to Matt, as their two faces were upside down with respect to each other. "You get what usually happens to jaywalkers—okay, so you're moving across the traffic: just stay out of everybody's way. It's your lookout. Any more questions?"

No one answered; he went on: "All right, go out and look around the ship—but try to behave yourselves and not bump into anybody so you'll be a credit to deck three."

The third deck had no ports of any sort, but the *Bolivar* was a long-jump transport; she possessed recreation rooms and viewports. Matt started forward, seeking a place from which to get a glimpse of the Earth.

He remembered to pass outboard as he pulled himself along, but apparently some passengers had not been indoctrinated. Each hatchway was a traffic jam of youngsters, each trying to leave his own deck to sight-see in some other deck, any deck.

The sixth deck, he found, was a recreation room. It contained the ship's library—locked—and games equipment, also locked. But it did have six large viewports.

The recreation deck had carried a full load of passengers. Now, in free fall, cadets from all other decks gradually found their way to the recreation deck, just as Matt had, seeking a view of outside; at the same time the original roster of that deck showed no tendency to want to leave their favored billet.

It was crowded.

Crowded as a basket full of kittens—Matt removed someone's space boot from his left eye and tried to worm his way toward one of the ports. Judicious work with his knees and elbows and a total disregard of the rules of the road got him to the second or third layer near one port. He placed a hand on a shoulder in front of him. The cadet twisted around. "Hey! Who do you think you're shoving? Oh—hello, Matt."

"Hi, Tex. How's it going?"

"All right. Say, you should have been here a few minutes ago. We passed one of the television relay stations, close by. Boy, oh, boy, are we traveling!"

"We did, huh? What did it look like?"

"Couldn't see much of it, must have been ten miles away, maybe. But, with the time we're making it was just there she comes and there she goes."

"Can you see the Earth?" Matt squirmed toward the port.

"Natch." Tex gave way and let Matt slide into his place. The frame of the port cut across the eastern Atlantic. Matt could see an arc extending almost from the North Pole to the Equator.

It was high noon over the Atlantic. Beyond it, bright in the afternoon sunlight, he could make out the British Isles, Spain, and the brassy Sahara. The browns and greens of land were in sharp contrast to the deep purple of the ocean. In still greater contrast stood the white dazzle of cloud. As his eye approached the distant, rounded horizon the details softened, giving a strong effect of stereo, of depth, of three-dimensional globularness—the world indeed was round!

Round and green and beautiful! He discovered presently that he had been holding his breath. His nausea was quite gone.

Someone tugged at his leg. "Don't stay there all day. Do you want to hog it?"

Regretfully Matt gave way to another cadet. He turned and shoved himself away from the port and in so doing became disoriented. He could not find Tex in the helter-skelter mass of floating bodies.

He felt a grip on his right ankle. "Let's get out of here, Matt."

"Right." They worked their way to the hatch and moved

to the next deck. Being without ports it was not heavily populated. They propelled themselves toward the center of the room, away from the traffic, and steadied themselves on handholds. "Well," said Matt, "so this is it—space, I mean. How do you like it?"

"Makes me feel like a goldfish. And I'm getting cross-eyed trying to figure out which side is up. How's your gizzard? Been dropsick?"

"No." Matt swallowed cautiously. "Let's not talk about it. Where were you last night, Tex? I looked for you a couple of times, but your rommate said he hadn't seen you since dinner."

"Oh, that—" Tex looked pained. "I was in Mr. Dynkowski's room. Say, Matt, that was a bum steer you gave me."

"Huh? What steer?"

"You know—when you advised me to ask Mr. Dynkowski to put an order in writing if I was in doubt about it. Man, oh man, did you get me in a jam!"

"Wait a minute—I didn't advise you to do that; I just pointed out that the regs let you do it if you wanted to."

"Just the same, you were egging me on."

"The deuce I was! My interest was purely theoretical. You were a free agent."

"Oh, well—skip it. Skip it."

"What happened?"

"Well, last night at dinner I ordered pie for dessert. I picked it up, just like I always have ever since I got too big for Ma to slap my hands for it, and started shoveling it in my face, happy as a pup in a pansy bed. Ski ordered me to cease and desist—told me to use my fork."

"Yeah? Go on."

"I said to put it in writing, please, sir, polite as a preacher."

"It stopped him?"

"Like fun it did! He said, 'Very well, Mr. Jarman,' cool as could be, took out his notebook, wrote it out, stamped his thumb print on it, tore out the page and handed it to me."

"So you used your fork. Or didn't you?"

"I sure did. But that's only the beginning. Immediately he

wrote out another order and handed it to me. He told me to read it aloud. Which I did."

"What did it say?"

"Wait a minute . . . I've got it here somewhere." Tex poked around in his pouch. "Here—read it."

Matt read, " 'Cadet Jarman—immediately after this meal you will report to the officer-of-the-watch, taking with you the first written order I gave you. Explain to him the events leading up to the first order and get an opinion from him as to the legality of orders of this type—S. Dynkowski, psd. cdt.' "

Matt whistled. "Oh, oh. . . . What did you do?"

"I finished my pie, the way he told me to, though I didn't want it very much by then. Ski was nice about it. He grinned at me and said, 'No hard feelings, Mr. Jarman. All according to protocol and all that sort of thing.' Then he wanted to know where in the world I had gotten the idea."

Matt felt his neck grow warm. "You told him it was my idea?"

"Do I look stupid? I just told him somebody had pointed out regulation number nine-oh-seven to me."

Matt relaxed. "Thanks, Tex. I'll remember that."

"Forget it. But he sent you a message."

"Me?"

"It was just one word: 'Don't.' "

"Don't what?"

"Just 'Don't.' He added that amateur space lawyers frequently talked themselves out of the Patrol."

"Oh." Matt tucked this away and started trying to digest it. "What happened afterwards? When you saw the duty officer?"

"I reported to the duty office and the cadet on watch sent me on in. I saluted and announced my name, like a good little boy, and showed him the two orders." Tex paused and stared into the distance.

"Yes? Go on, man—don't stop like that."

"Then he most scientifcially ate my ears off. My Uncle Bodie couldn't have done a better job." Tex paused again, as if the memory were too painfully sharp. "Then he quieted down a little bit and explained to me in words of one syllable that reg nine-oh-seven was for emergencies only and that youngster cadets were under the orders of oldster cadets at all times and in all matters, unless the regulations specifically say otherwise."

"He did? Say, that covers an awful lot of ground. Why, that means a senior cadet can order us to do almost anything. You mean it's covered by law that an oldster can tell me how to part my hair?"

"Just precisely that—you happened to pick the very words Lieutenant von Ritter used. An oldster can't tell you to violate a regulation—he can't tell you to take a poke at the captain and he can't order you to hold still while he takes a poke at you. But that's about all that limits him. Mr. von Ritter says that it's left up to the good judgment and discretion of the senior, and table manners were very definitely Mr. Dynowski's business and not to forget it! Then he told me to report back to Ski."

"Did he crow over you?"

"Not a bit." Tex's brow wrinkled. "That's the funny part about it. Ski treated the whole affair just as if he had been giving me a lesson in geometry. He said that now that I was assured that his orders were according to regulation he wanted me to know why he had told me how to eat my pie. He even said he could see that I would regard it as improper interference with my private life. I said I guessed I didn't have any private life any more. He said no, I had one all right, but it would feel pretty microscopic for a while.

"Then he explained the matter. A patrol officer is supposed to be able to move in all society—if your hostess eats with her knife, then you eat with your knife."

"Everybody knows that."

"Okay. He pointed out that candidates come from everywhere. Some of them even come from families and societies where it's good manners for everybody to eat out of one dish, with their fingers . . . some of the Moslem boys. But there is an over-all way to behave that is acceptable anywhere among the top crust."

"Nuts," said Matt. "I've seen the Governor of Iowa with a hot dog in one hand and a piece of pie in the other."

"I'll bet it wasn't at a state dinner," Tex countered. "No, Matt, it made sense the way he told it. He said pie wasn't important, but it was part of a larger pattern—for instance that you must never mention death on Mars or to a Martian."

"Is that a fact?"

"I guess so. He said that in time I would learn how to 'eat pie with a fork' as he put it, under any possible circumstances on any planet. He let it go at that."

"I should think he would. I take it he lectured you all evening?"

"Oh, my, no. Ten minutes, maybe."

"Then where were you? You still hadn't come back to your room, just before taps."

"Oh, I was still in Ski's room, but I was busy."

"Doing what? Stroking his brow?"

"No." Tex looked mildly embarrassed. "I was writing—'I will always eat my pie with my fork,' two thousand times."

Tex and Matt attempted to explore the ship and did in fact visit every deck that was open to them. But the power-room door was locked and a space-marine guard kept them from entering the passageway leading to the pilot room. They tried to get another view from the ports in the recreation room but found that a degree of order had been instituted; the master-at-arms of that deck was requiring each cadet that entered to state that he had not yet had a chance to look out before the cadet was allowed to tarry.

As for the other passenger decks, they found that when they had seen one, they had seen all. Shipboard refreshers interested them for a while, as the curious and clever modifications necessary to make a refresher function properly in space were new to both of them. But four hours is too long to spend inspecting showers and fixtures; after a while they found another fairly quiet spot to loaf and experienced for the first time the outstanding characteristic of all space travel—its monotony.

Much later the ship's speaker blared, "Prepare for acceleration. Ten minute warning."

Strapped down again, each in his place, the boys felt short blasts of power at rather long intervals, then a very considerable wait, after which there was the softest and gentlest of bumps. "That's the drag line," remarked the sergeant in Matt's compartment. "They'll warp us in. It won't be long now."

Ten minutes later the speaker announced, "By decks, in succession—discharge passengers."

"Unstrap," said the sergeant. He left his midships position and posted himself at the hatch ladder. Transferring passengers was a lengthy process, as the two ships were linked by only one air lock each. Matt's party waited while four decks forward of them were emptied, then they pulled themselves along the ladder to the seventh deck. There a passenger port was open but beyond it, instead of empty space, was the inside of a corrugated tube, six feet in diameter. A line ran down the center of it and was made fast to a padeye in the ship. Along this line swarmed a steady stream of cadets, monkey fashion.

In his turn, Matt grabbed the line and pulled himself along. Fifty feet beyond the air lock, the tube suddenly opened out into another compartment, and Matt found himself inside his new home, the P.R.S. *Randolph*.

VI

"READING, AND 'RITING,

AND 'RITHMETIC—"

THE P.R.S. *Randolph* had been a powerful and modern cruiser of her day. Her length was 900 feet, her diameter 200, making her of moderate size, but her mass, as a school ship, was only 60,000 tons, more or less.

She was kept ten miles astern of Terra Station in their common orbit. Left to the influence of their mutual gravitations, she would have pursued a most leisurely orbit around the ten-times-more-massive Terra Station, but, for the safety of traffic at Terra Station, it was better to keep in a fixed position.

This was easy to accomplish. The mass of Earth is six billion trillion tons; the mass of Terra Station is one hundred-million-billionth of that, a mere 600,000 tons. At ten miles the "weight" of the *Randolph* with respect to Terra Station was roughly one thirtieth of an ounce, about the weight on Earth of enough butter for one half slice of bread.

On entering the *Randolph* Matt found himself in a large, well-lighted compartment of odd shape, somewhat like a wedge of cake. Clumps of youngster cadets were being herded out exits by other cadets who wore black armbands. One such cadet headed toward him, moving through the air with the easy grace of a pollywog. "Squad nineteen—where's the squad leader of squad nineteen?"

Matt held out his arm. "Here, sir! I'm squad leader of nineteen."

The upperclassman checked himself with one hand on the guide line to which Matt still clung. "I relieve you, sir. But stick close to me and help me round up these yahoos. I suppose you know them by sight?"

"Uh, I think so, sir."

"You should—you've had time." Matt was chagrined to find, in the next few moments that the new squad leader—Cadet Lopez—knew the squad muster roll by heart, whereas Matt had to refer to his copy to assist him in locating the members. He was not really aware of the implications of order and efficient preparation; it did impress him as "style." With Matt to spot and Lopez to dive, hawklike, all the way across the compartment if necessary, to round up stragglers, squad nineteen was soon assembled near one exit, where they clung like a colony of bats.

"Follow me," Lopez told them, "and hang on. No free maneuvers. Dodson—bring up the rear."

"Aye aye, sir."

They snaked their way through endless passages, by guide line across compartment after compartment, through hatches, around corners. Matt was quite lost. Presently the man just head of him stopped. Matt closed in and found the squad gathered just inside another compartment. "Soup's on," announced Lopez. "This is your messroom. Lunch in a few minutes."

Behind Lopez, secured firmly to the far wall, were mess tables and benches. The table tops faced Matt—under him, over him, or across from him—what you will. It seemed an impractical arrangement. "I'm not very hungry," one youngster said faintly.

"You ought to be," Lopez answered reasonably. "It's been five hours or more since you had breakfast. We're on the same time schedule here as Hayworth Hall, zone plus eight, Terra. Why aren't you hungry?"

"Uh, I don't know, sir. I'm just not."

Lopez grinned and suddenly looked as young as his charges. "I was just pulling your leg, kiddo. The chief engineer will have some spin on us in no time, as soon as we break loose from the *Bolivar.* Then you can sit down on your soft, round fanny and console your tender stomach in peace. You'll have an appetite. In the meantime, take it easy."

Two more squads filtered in. While they waited Matt said to Lopez, "How fast will the ship spin, sir?"

"We'll build up to one gravity at the outer skin. Takes about two hours to do it, but we'll eat as soon as we're heavy enough for you groundhogs to swallow your soup without choking."

"But how fast is that, sir?"

"Can you do simple arithmetic?"

"Why, yes, sir."

"Then do it. The *Randolph* is two hundred feet through and we spin on her main axis. The square of the rim speed divided by her radius—what's the rpm?"

Matt got a faraway look on his face. Lopez said, "Come, now, Mr. Dodson—pretend you're heading for the surface and about to crash. *What's the answer?*"

"Uh—I'm afraid I can't do it in my head, sir."

Lopez looked around. "All right—who's got the answer?" No one spoke up. Lopez shook his head mournfully. "And you laddies expect to learn to astrogate! Better by far you should have gone to cow colleges. Never mind—it works out to about five and four-tenths revolutions per minute. That gives one full gravity for the benefit of the women and children. Then it's cut down day by day, until a month from now we're in free fall again. That gives you time to get used to it—or else."

Someone said, "Gee, it must take a lot of power."

Lopez answered, "Are you kidding? It's done by electric-braking the main axis flywheels. The shaft has field coils wound on it; you cut it in as a generator and let the reaction between the wheel and the ship put a spin on the ship. You store the juice. Then when you want to take the spin off, you use the juice to drive it as a motor and you are back where you started, free for nothing, except for minor losses. Savvy?"

"Er, I guess so, sir."

"Look it up in the ship's library, sketch the hook-up, and show it to me after supper." The junior cadet said nothing; Lopez snapped. "What's the matter, Mister? Didn't you hear me?"

"Yes, sir—aye aye, sir."

"That's better."

Very slowly they drifted against a side wall, bumped against it, and started sliding slowly toward the outboard wall, the one to which the mess tables were fastened. By the time they reached it there was enough spin on the ship to enable them to stand up and the mess tables now assumed their proper relationship, upright on the floor, while the hatch through which they had lately floated was a hole in the ceiling above.

Matt found that there was no sensation of dizziness; the effect was purely one of increasing weight. He still felt light, but he weighed enough to sit down at a mess table and stay in contact with his seat; minute by minute, imperceptibly, he grew heavier.

He looked over his place at the table, seeking controls that would permit him to order his meal. There were clips and locking holes which he guessed were intended for use in free flight, but nothing else. He looked up as Lopez banged on the table.

"And now, gentlemen, this is not a resort hotel. Count off, around the table." He waited until the youngsters had done so, then said, "Remember your order. Numbers one and two will rustle up the calories today, and all of you in rotation thereafter."

"Where, sir?"

"Use your eyes. Over there."

"Over there" was a door which concealed a delivery conveyor. Cadets from other tables were gathering around it. The two cadets designated as waiters went over and returned shortly with a large metal rack containing twenty rations, each packed in its service platter and still steaming hot. Clipped to each were knife, fork, and spoons—and sipping tubes.

Matt found that the solid foods were covered by lids that snapped back over the food unless clipped up out of the way, while the liquids were in covered containers fitted with valves through which sipping tubes might be slipped. He had never before seen table utensils adapted for free-fall conditions in space. They delighted him, even though Earth-side equipment would have served as long as the ship was under spin.

Lunch was hot roast beef sandwiches with potatoes, green salad, lime sherbert, and tea. Lopez kept up a steady fire of questions throughout the meal, but Matt did not come into his range. Twenty minutes later the metal tray in front of Matt was polished almost as well as the sterilizer would achieve. He sat back, feeling that the Patrol was a good outfit and the *Randolph* a fine place to be.

Before turning his charges loose Lopez gave them each their schedule of assignments. Matt's room number was A-5197. All living quarters were on A-deck which was the insulated outer skin of the ship. Lopez gave them a brief, condescending lecture on the system of numbering the spaces in the ship and dismissed them. His manner gave no hint that he himself had been lost for one full day shortly after his own arrival a year earlier.

Matt got lost, of course.

He attempted to take a short cut straight through the ship on the advice of a passing marine and got completely twisted when he found himself at the no-weight center of the *Randolph*. When he had worked his way back down levels of increasing weight until he found himself at one gravity and could go no further he stopped the first cadet with a black arm band whom he could find and threw himself on his mercy. A few minutes later he was led to corridor five and found his own room.

Tex was already there. "Hello, Matt," he greeted him. "What do you think of our little cabin in the sky?"

Matt put down his jump bag. "Looks all right, but the first time I have to leave it I'm going to unroll a ball of string. Is there a viewport?"

"Not likely! What did you expect? A balcony?"

"I don't know. I sort of hoped that we'd be able to look out and see Earth." He started poking around, opening doors. "Where's the 'fresher?"

"Better start unrolling your ball of string. It's way down the passage."

"Oh. Kind of primitive. Well, I guess we can stand it." He went on exploring. There was a common room about fifteen feet square. It had doors, two on each side, leading into smaller cubicles. "Say, Tex," he announced when he had opened them all, "this place is fitted up for four people."

"Go to the head of the class."

"I wonder who we'll draw."

"So do I." Tex took out his assignment sheet. "It says here that we can reshuffle roommates until supper time tomorrow. Got any ideas, Matt?"

"No, I can't say I really know anybody but you. It doesn't matter as long as they don't snore—and as long as it isn't Burke."

They were interrupted by a rap on the door. Tex called out, "Come in!" and Oscar Jensen stuck his blond head inside. "Busy?"

"Not at all."

"I've got a problem. Pete and I found ourselves assigned to one of these four-way rooms and the two roommates we landed with want us to make room for two other fellows. Are you guys tied down as yet?"

Tex looked at Matt, who nodded. Tex turned back to Oscar. "You can kiss me, Oscar—we're practically married."

An hour later the four had settled down to domesticity. Pete was in high spirits. "The *Randolph* is just what the doctor ordered," he announced. "I'm going to like it here. Any time my legs start to ache all I have to do is go up to G-deck and it's just like being back home—I weigh my proper weight again."

"Yep," agreed Tex, "if the joint were co-educational it would be perfect."

Oscar shook his head. "Not for me. I'm a woman-hater."

Tex clucked sorrowfully. "You poor, poor boy. Now take my Uncle Bodie—he thought he was a woman-hater, too. . . ."

Matt never found out how Uncle Bodie got over his disability. An announcer, mounted in the common room, summoned him to report to compartment B-121. He got there, after a few wrong turns, and found another youngster cadet just coming out. "What's it for?" he asked.

"Go on in," the other told him. "Orientation."

Matt went in and found an officer seated at a desk. "Cadet Dodson, sir, reporting as ordered."

The officer looked up and smiled. "Sit down, Dodson. Lieutenant Wong is my name. I'm your coach."

"My coach, sir?"

"Your tutor, your supervisor, anything you care to call it. It's my business to see that you and a dozen more like you study what you need to study. Think of me as standing behind you with a black snake whip." He grinned.

Matt grinned back. He began to like Mr. Wong.

Wong picked up a sheaf of papers. "I've got your record here—let's lay out a course of study. I see you type, use a slide rule and differential calculator, and can take shorthand—those are all good. Do you know any outer languages? By the way, don't bother to talk Basic; I speak North

American English fairly well. How long have you spoken Basic?"

"Er, I don't know any outer languages, sir. I had Basic in high school, but I don't really *think* in it. I have to watch what I'm saying."

"I'll put you down for Venerian, Martian, and Venus trade talk. Your voicewriter—you've looked over the equipment in your room?"

"Just glanced at it, sir. I saw there was a study desk and a projector."

"You'll find a spool of instructions in the upper righthand drawer of the desk. Play them over when you go back. The voicewriter built into your desk is a good model. It can hear and transcribe not only the Basic vocabulary, but the Patrol's special vocabulary of technical words. If you will stick to its vocabulary, you can even write love letters on it—" Dodson glanced sharply at Lieutenant Wong, but Wong's face was impassive; Matt decided not to laugh.

"—so it's worth your while to perfect your knowledge of Basic even for social purposes. However, if you speak a word the machine can't find on its list, it will just 'beep' complainingly until you come to its rescue. Now about math—I see you have a condition in tensor calculus."

"Yes, sir," Matt admitted. "My high school didn't offer it."

Wong shook his head sadly. "I sometimes think that modern education is deliberately designed to handicap a boy. If cadets arrived here having already been taught the sort of things the young human animal can learn, and *should* learn, there would be fewer casualties in the Patrol. Never mind—we'll start you on tensors at once. You can't study nuclear engineering until you've learned the language of it. Your school was the usual sort, Dodson? Classroom recitations, daily assignments, and so forth?"

"More or less. We were split into three groups."

"Which group were you in?"

"I was in the fast one, sir, in most subjects."

"That's some help, but not much. You're in for a shock, son. We don't have classrooms and fixed courses. Except for laboratory work and group drills, you study alone. It's

71

pleasant to sit in a class daydreaming while the teacher questions somebody else, but we haven't got time for that. There is too much ground to cover. Take the outer languages alone—have you ever studied under hypnosis?"

"Why, no, sir."

"We'll start you on it at once. When you leave here, go to the Psycho Instruction Department and ask for a first hypno in Beginning Venerian. What's the matter?"

"Well. . . . Sir, is it absolutely necessary to study under hypnosis?"

"Definitely. Everything that can possibly be studied under hypno you will have to learn that way in order to leave time for the really important subjects."

Matt nodded. "I see. Like astrogation."

"No, no, no! Not astrogation. A ten-year-old child could learn to pilot a spaceship if he had the talent for mathematics. That is kindergarten stuff, Dodson. The arts of space and warfare are the least part of your education. I know, from your tests, that you can soak up the math and physical sciences and technologies. Much more important is the world around you, the planets and their inhabitants—extraterrestrial biology, history, cultures, psychology, law and institutions, treaties and conventions, planetary ecologies, system ecology, interplanetary economics, applications of extraterritorialism, comparative religious customs, law of space, to mention a few."

Matt was looking bug-eyed. "My gosh! How long does it take to learn all those things?"

"You'll still be studying the day you retire. But even those subjects are not your education; they are simply raw materials. Your real job is to learn how to think—and that means you must study several other subjects: epistemology, scientific methodology, semantics, structures of languages, patterns of ethics and morals, varieties of logics, motivational psychology, and so on. This school is based on the idea that a man who can think correctly will automatically behave morally—or what we call 'morally.' What is moral behavior for a Patrolman, Matt? You are called Matt, aren't you? By your friends?"

"Yes, sir. Moral behavior for a Patrolman . . ."

"Yes, yes. Go on."

"Well, I guess it means to do your duty, live up to your oath, that sort of thing."

"Why should you?"

Matt kept quiet and looked stubborn.

"Why should you, when it may get you some messy way of dying? Never mind. Our prime purpose here is to see to it that you learn how your own mind works. If the result is a man who fits into the purposes of the Patrol because his own mind, when he knows how to use it, works that way—then fine! He is commissioned. If not, then we have to let him go."

Matt remained silent until Wong finally said, "What's eating on you, kid? Spill it."

"Well—look here, sir. I'm perfectly willing to work hard to get my commission. But you make it sound like something beyond my control. First I have to study a lot of things I've never heard of. Then, when it's all over, somebody decides my mind doesn't work right. It seems to me that what this job calls for is a superman."

"Like me." Wong chuckled and flexed his arms. "Maybe so, Matt, but there aren't any supermen, so we'll have to do the best we can with young squirts like you. Come, now, let's make up the list of spools you'll need."

It was a long list. Matt was surprised and pleased to find that some story spools had been included. He pointed to an item that puzzled him—*An Introduction to Lunar Archeology.* "I don't see why I should study that—the Patrol doesn't deal with Selenites; they've been dead for millions of years."

"Keeps your mind loosened up. I might just as well have stuck in modern French music. A Patrol officer shouldn't limit his horizons to just the things he is sure to need. I'm marking the items I want you to study first, then you beat it around to the library and draw out those spools, then over to Psycho for your first hypno. In about a week, when you've absorbed this first group, come back and see me."

"You mean you expect me to study all the spools I'm taking out today in *one week?*" Matt looked at the list in amazement.

"That's right. In your off hours, that is—you'll be busy with drills and lab a lot. Come back next week and we'll boost the dose. Now get going."

"But— Aye aye, sir!"

Matt located the Psycho Instruction Department and was presently ushered into a small room by a bored hypno technician wearing the uniform of the staff services of the Space Marines. "Stretch out in that chair," he was told. "Rest your head back. This is your first treatment?" Matt admitted that it was.

"You'll like it. Some guys come in here just for the rest— they already know more than they ought to. What course was it you said you wanted?"

"Beginning Venerian."

The technician spoke briefly to a pick-up located on his desk. "Funny thing—about a month ago an oldster was in here for a brush up in electronics. The library thought I said 'colonics' and now he's loaded up with a lot of medical knowledge he'll never use. Lemme have your left arm." The technician irradiated a patch on his forearm and injected the drug. "Now just lay back and follow the bouncing light. Take it easy . . . relax . . . relax . . . and . . . close . . . your . . . eyes . . . and . . . relax . . . you're . . . getting—"

Someone was standing in front of him, holding a hypodermic pressure injector "That's all. You've had the antidote."

"Huh?" said Matt. "Wazzat?"

"Sit still a couple of minutes and then you can go."

"Didn't it take?"

"Didn't what take? I don't know what you were being exposed to; I just came on duty."

Matt went back to his room feeling rather depressed. He had been a little afraid of hypnosis, but to find that he apparently did not react to the method was worse yet. He wondered whether or not he could ever keep up with his studies if he were forced to study everything, outer languages as well, by conventional methods.

Nothing to do but to go back and see Lieutenant Wong about it—tomorrow, he decided.

Oscar was alone in the suite and was busy trying to place a hook in the wall of a common room. A framed picture was leaning against the chair on which he stood. "Hello, Oscar."

"Howdy, Matt." Oscar turned his head as he spoke; the drill he was using slipped and he skinned a knuckle. He started to curse in strange, lisping speech. *"May maledictions pursue this nameless thing to the uttermost depths of world slime!"*

Matt clucked disapprovingly. *"Curb thy voice, thou impious fish."*

Oscar looked up in amazement. "Matt—I didn't know you knew any Venerian."

Matt's mouth sagged open. He closed it, then opened it to speak. "Well, I'll be a— Neither did I!"

VII

TO MAKE A SPACEMAN

THE SERGEANT CROUCHED in the air, his feet drawn up. "At the count of one," he was saying, "take the ready position, with your feet about six inches from the steel. At the count of two, place your feet firmly against the steel and push off." He shoved against the steel wall and shot into the air, still talking, "Hold the count of four, turn on the count of five—" His body drew up into a ball and turned over a half turn. "—check your rotation—" His body extended again. "—and make contact on the count of seven—" His toes touched the far wall. "—letting your legs collapse softly so that your momentum will be soaked up without rebound." He collapsed loosely, like an empty sack, and remained floating near the spot where he had landed.

The room was a cylinder fifty feet in diameter in the center of the ship. The entire room was mounted in rollers and was turned steadily in the direction opposite to the spin of the ship and with the same angular speed: thus it had no net spin. It could be entered only from the end, at the center of rotation.

It was a little island of "free fall"—the free-fall gymnasium. A dozen youngster cadets clung to a grab line running fore-and-aft along the wall of the gym and watched the sergeant. Matt was one of the group.

"And now, gentlemen, let's try it again. By the numbers— One! Two! Three!" by the count of five, at which time they all should have turned in the air, neatly and together, all semblance of order was gone. There were collisions, one cadet had even failed to get away from the grab line, and two cadets, refugees from a midair skirmish, were floating aimlessly toward the far end of the room. Their faces had the bewildered look of a dog trying to get traction on smooth ice as they threshed their arms and legs in an effort to stay their progress.

"No! No! No!" said the sergeant and covered his face with his hands. "I can't bear to look. Gentlemen—*please!* A little coordination. Don't throw yourself at the far wall like an Airedale heading into a fight. A steady, firm shove— like this."

He took off sideways, using the traction given him by his space boots, and intercepted the two deserters, gathering one in each arm and letting his momentum carry the three bodies slowly toward the far end of the grab line. "Grab on," he told them, "and back to your places. Now, gentlemen—once more. Places! By the numbers—normal push off, with arrested contact—one!"

A few moments later he was assuring them that he would much rather teach a cat to swim.

Matt did not mind. He had managed to reach the far wall and stay there. Without grace, proper timing, nor at the spot he had aimed for, but he had managed it, after a dozen failures. For the moment he classed himself as a spaceman.

When the class was dismissed he hurried to his room and into his own cubicle, selected a spool on Martian history, inserted it in his projector, and began to study. He had been tempted to remain in the free-fall gymnasium to practice; he wanted very badly to pass the "space legs" test—free-fall acrobatics—as those who had passed it and qualified in the use of basic space suits as well were allowed one liberty a month at Terra Station.

But he had had an extra interview with Lieutenant Wong a few days before. It had been brief, biting, and had been concerned with the efficient use of his time.

Matt did not want another such—nor the five demerits that went with it. He settled his head in the neck rest of his study chair and concentrated on the recorded words of the lecturer while scenes in color-stereo passed in front of him, portraying in chill beauty the rich past of the ancient planet.

The projector was much like the study box he had used at home, except that it was more gadgeted, could project in three dimensions, and was hooked in with the voicewriter. Matt found this a great time-saver. He could stop the lecture, dictate a summary, then cause the projector to throw his printed notes on the screen.

Stereo-projection was a time-saver for manual subjects as well. "You are now entering the control room of a type A-6 utility rocket," the unseen lecturer would say, "and will practice an airless landing on Luna"—while the camera moved through the door of the rocket's pilot room and panned down to a position corresponding to the pilot's head. From there on a pictured flight could be made very realistic.

Or it might be a spool on space suits. "This is a four-hour suit," the voice would say, "type M, and may be worn anywhere outside the orbit of Venus. It has a low-capacity rocket unit capable of producing a total change of speed in a 300-lb. mass of fifty foot-seconds. The built-in radio has a suit-to-suit range of fifty miles. Internal heating and cooling is—" By the time Matt's turn came for space-suit drill he knew as much about it as could be learned without practice.

His turn came when he passed the basic free-fall test. He was not finished with free-fall drill—there remained group precision drill, hand-to-hand combat, use of personal weapons, and other refinements—but he was judged able to handle himself well enough. He was free, too, to go out for free-fall sports, wrestling, bank tennis, jai alai, and several others —up to now he had been eligible only for the chess club. He picked space polo, a game combining water polo and assault with intent to maim, and joined the local league, in the lowest or "bloodynose" group.

He missed his first chance at space-suit drill because a battered nose had turned him into a mouth breather—the respirator for a type-M suit calls for inhaling through the nose and exhaling through the mouth. But he was ready and anxious the following week. The instructor ordered his group to "Suit up!" without preliminary, as it was assumed that they had studied the instruction spool.

The last of the ship's spin had been removed some days before. Matt curled himself into a ball, floating free, and spread open the front of his suit. It was an unhandy process; he found shortly that he was trying to get both legs down one leg of the suit. He backed out and tried again. This time the big fishbowl flopped forward into the opening.

Most of the section were already in their suits. The instructor swam over to Matt and looked at him sharply. "You've passed your free-fall basic?"

"Yes," Matt answered miserably.

"It's hard to believe. You handle yourself like a turtle on its back. Here." The instructor helped Matt to tuck in, much as if he were dressing a baby in a snow suit. Matt blushed.

The instructor ran through the check-off list—tank pressure, suit pressure, rocket fuel charge, suit oxygen, blood oxygen (measured by a photoelectric gadget clipped to the earlobe) and finally each suit's walky-talky unit. Then he herded them into the airlock.

Matt felt his suit swell up as the pressure died away in the lock. It was becoming slightly harder to move his arms and legs. "Hook up your static lines," called out the instructor. Matt uncoiled his from his belt and waited. Reports came in: "Number one hooked." "Number two hooked."

"Number three hooked," Matt sang out into the mike in

his helmet as he snapped his line to the belt of cadet number four. When they were all linked like mountain climbers the instructor hooked himself to the chain and opened the outer door of the lock. They looked out into the star-flecked void.

"Click on," directed the instructor, and placed his boots gently against the side of the lock. Matt did likewise and felt the magnetic soles of his boots click against the steel. "Follow me and stay closed up." Their teacher walked along the wall to the open door and performed an awkward little squatting spread-eagle step. One boot was still inside the door, flat to the wall, with the toe pointing inboard; with the other he reached around the corner, bent his knees, and felt for the outer surface of the ship. He withdrew the foot still in the lock and straightened his body—with which he almost disappeared, for he now stuck straight out from the ship, his feet flat to her side.

Following in order, Matt went out through the door. The ninety degree turn to get outside the lock and "standing" on the outer skin of the ship he found to be tricky; he was forced to use his hands to steady himself on the door frame. But he got outside and "standing up." There was no true up-and-down; they were still weightless, but the steel side was a floor "under" them; they stuck to it as a fly sticks to a ceiling.

Matt took a couple of trial steps. It was like walking in mud; his feet would cling stickily to the ship, then pull away suddenly. It took getting used to.

They had gone out on the dark side of the ship. Sun, Moon and Earth lay behind its bulk, underfoot. Not even Terra Station could be seen.

"We'll take a walk," announced the instructor, his voice hollow in their helmets. "Stick together." He started around the curving side of the ship. A cadet near the end of the chain tried to break both magnetized boots free from the ship at the same time. He accomplished it, by jumping—and then had no way to get back. He moved out until his static line tugged at the two boys on each side of him.

One of them, caught with one foot free of the ship in

walking, was broken loose also, though he reached wildly for the steel and missed. The cadet next to him, last in line, came loose in turn.

No more separated, as the successive tugs on the line had used up the energy of the first cadet's not-so-violent jump. But three cadets now dangled on the line, floating and twisting grotesquely.

The instructor caught the movement out of the corner of his eye, and squatted down. He found what he sought, a steel ring recessed in the ship's side, and snapped his static line to it. When he was certain that the entire party was not going to be dragged loose, he ordered, "Number nine—haul them in, gently—very gently. Don't pull yourself loose doing it."

A few moments later the vagrants were back and sticking to the ship. "Now," said the instructor, "who was responsible for that piece of groundhog stupidity?"

No one answered. "Speak up," he said sharply. "It wasn't an accident; it's impossible to get both feet off unless you hop. Speak up, confound it, or I'll haul every last one of you up in front of the Commandant."

At the mention of that awful word a small, meek voice answered, "I did it, sergeant."

"Hold out your hand, so I'll know who's talking. I'm not a mind reader."

"Vargas—number ten." The cadet held out his arm.

"Okay. Back to the airlock, everybody. Stick together." When they were there, the instructor said, "Inside, Mr. Vargas. Unhook your line, snap to the lock and wait for us. You'll take this drill over—about a month from now."

"But sergeant—"

"Don't give me any lip, or swelp me, I'll report you for AWOL—jumping ship."

Silently the cadet did as ordered. The instructor leaned inside to see that Vargas actually anchored himself, then straightened out. "Come, gentlemen—we'll start again—and no monkey-shines. This is a drill, not a tea party."

Presently Matt said, "Sergeant Hanako—"

"Yes? Who is it?"

80

"Dodson. Number three. Suppose we had all pulled loose?"

"We'd 'ave had to work our way back on our rocket units."

Matt thought about it. "Suppose we didn't have reaction units?"

"Nothing much—under these circumstances. The officer of the watch knows we're outside; the radio watch is guarding our frequency. They would just have tracked us by radar until they could man a scooter and come get us. Just the same—listen, all of you—just because they've got you wrapped in cotton batting is no reason to behave like a bunch of school girls. I don't know of any nastier, or lonelier, way to die than all by yourself in a space suit, with your oxygen running out." He paused. "I saw one once, after they found him and fetched him back."

They were rounding the side of the ship, and the bulging sphere of the Earth had been rising over their metal horizon.

Suddenly the Sun burst into view.

"Mind the glare!" Sergeant Hanako called out. Hastily Matt set his visor for maximum interference and adjusted it to shade his face and eyes. He did not attempt to look at the Sun; he had dazzled his eyes often enough from the viewports of the ship's recreation rooms, trying to blank out the disc of the Sun exactly, with a coin, so that he might see the prominences and the ghostly aurora. It was an unsatisfactory business; the usual result was a headache and spots before his eyes.

But he never grew tired of looking at Earth.

She hung before him, great and fat and beautiful, and seeming more real than when seen through a port. She swelled across Aquarius, so huge that had she been in Orion she would have concealed the giant hunter from Betelgeuse to Rigel.

Facing them was the Gulf of Mexico. Above it sprawled North America wearing the polar cap like a chef's hat. The pole was still bright under the failing light of late northern summer. The sunrise line had cleared North America except for the tip of Alaska; only the central Pacific was dark.

Someone said, "What's that bright dot in the Pacific, over near the edge? Honolulu?"

Honolulu did not interest Matt; he searched, as usual, for Des Moines—but the Mississippi Valley was cloudy; he could not find it. Sometimes he could pick it out with his naked eyes, when the day was clear in Iowa. When it was night in North America he could always tell which jewel of light was home—or thought he could.

They were facing Earth so that the north pole seemed "up" to them. Far off to the right, almost a ship's width from the Earth, nearly occulting Regulus in Leo, was the Sun, and about half way between the Sun and Earth, in Virgo, was a crescent Moon. Like the Sun, the Moon appeared no larger than she did from Earth surface. The gleaming metal sides of Terra Station, in the sky between Sun and Moon and ninety degrees from Earth, outshone the Moon. The Station, a mere ten miles away, appeared half a dozen times as wide as the Moon.

"That's enough rubbernecking," announced Hanako. "Let's move around." They walked forward, looking the ship over and getting the feel of her size, until the sergeant stopped them. "Any further and we'd be slapping our feet over the Commandant's head. He might be asleep." They sauntered aft and Hanako let them work around the edge of the stern until they looked across the openings of her mighty tubes. He called them back promptly. "Even though she ain't blasted in years, this area is a little bit hot—and you're not shielded from the pile abaft frame ninety-three anyhow. Forward, now!"

By hot he did not mean warm to the touch, but radioactive.

He led them amidships, unhooked himself from the cadet next to him and hooked the lad's line to the ship. "Number twelve—hook to steel," he added.

"The trick to jetting yourself in space," he went on, "lies in balancing your body on the jet—the thrust has to pass through your center of gravity. If you miss and don't correct it quickly, you start to spin, waste your fuel, and have the devil's own time stopping your spin.

"It's no harder than balancing a walking stick on your finger—but the first time you try it, it seems hard.

"Rig out your sight." He touched a stud at his belt; a light metal gadget snapped up in front of his helmet so that a small metal ring was about a yard in front of his face. "Pick out a bright star, or a target of any sort, lined up in the direction you want to go. Then take the ready position— no, no! Not yet—I'll take it."

He squatted down, lifted himself on his hands, and very cautiously broke his boots loose from the side, then steadied himself on a cadet within reach. He turned and stretched out, so that he floated with his back to the ship, arms and legs extended. His rocket jet stuck straight back at the ship from the small of his back; his sight stuck out from his helmet in the opposite direction.

He went on, "Have the firing switch ready in your right hand. Now, have you fellows ever seen a pair of adagio dancers? You know what I mean—a man wears a piece of leopard skin and a girl wearing less than that and they go leaping around the stage, with him catching her?"

Several voices answered yes. Hanako continued, "Then you know what I'm talking about. There's one stunt they always do—the girl jumps and the man pushes her up and balances her overhead on one hand. He has his hand at the small of her back and she lays there, artistic-like.

"That's exactly the way you got to ride a jet. The push comes at the small of your back and you balance on it. Only *you* have to do the balancing—if the push doesn't pass exactly through your center of gravity, you'll start to turn. You can see yourself starting to turn by watching through your sight.

"You have to correct it before it. gets away from you. You do this by shifting your center of gravity. Drag in the arm or leg on the side toward which you've started to turn. The trick is—"

"Just a second, Sarge," someone cut in, "you said that just backwards. You mean; haul in the arm or leg on the *other* side, don't you?"

"Who's talking?"

"Lathrop, number six. Sorry."

"I meant what I said, Mr. Lathrop."

"But—"

"Go ahead, do it your way. The rest of the class will do it my way. Let's not waste time. Any questions? Okay, stand clear of my jet."

The half circle backed away until stopped by the anchored static lines. A bright orange flame burst from the sergeant's back and he moved straight out or "up," slowly at first, then with increasing speed. His microphone was open; Matt could hear, by radio only, the muted rush of his jet—and could hear the sergeant counting seconds: "And . . . *one!* . . . and . . . *two!* . . . and . . . *three!*" With the count of ten, the jet and the counting stopped.

Their instructor was fifty feet "above" them and moving away, back toward them. He continued to lecture. "No matter how perfectly you've balanced you'll end up with a small amount of spin. When you want to change direction, double up in a ball—" He did so. "—to spin faster—and snap out of it when you've turned as far as you want." He suddenly flattened out and was facing them. "Cut in your jet and balance on it to straighten out on your new course—before you drift past the direction you want."

He did not cut in his jet, but continued to talk, while moving away from them and slowly turning. "There is always some way to squirm around on your axis of rotation so that you can face the way you need to face for a split second at least. For example, if I wanted to head toward the Station—" Terra Station was almost a right angle away from his course; he went through contortions appropriate to a monkey dying in convulsions and again snapped out in starfish spread, facing the Station—but turning slow cartwheels now, his axis of rotation unchanged.

"But I don't want to go to the Station; I want to come back to the ship." The monkey died again; when the convulsions ceased, the sergeant was facing them. He cut in his jet and again counted ten seconds. He hung in space, motionless with respect to the ship and his class and about a quarter mile away. "I'm coming in on a jet landing, to save time." The jet blasted for twenty seconds and died; he moved toward them rapidly.

When he was still a couple of hundred feet away, he flipped over and blasted *away* from the ship for ten seconds. The sum of his maneuvers was to leave him fifty feet away and approaching at ten feet per second. He curled up in a ball again and came out of it feet toward the ship.

Five seconds later his boots clicked to steel and he let himself collapse without rebound. "But that is not the way you'll do it," he went on. "My tanks hold more juice than yours do—you've got fifty seconds of power, with each second good for a change of speed on one foot-second—that's for three hundred pounds of mass; some of you skinny guys will go a little faster.

"Here's your flight plan: ten seconds out, counted. Turn as quick as you can and blast fifteen seconds back. That means you'll click on with five foot-seconds. Even your crippled grandmother ought to be able to do that without bouncing off. Lathrop! Unhook—you're first."

As the cadet came up, Hanako anchored himself to the ship with two short lines and took from his belt a very long line. He snapped one end to a hook in the front of the cadet's belt and the other to his own suit. The student looked at it with distaste. "Is the sky hook necessary?"

Sergeant Hanako stared at him. "Sorry, Commodore—regulations. And shut up. Take the ready position."

Silently the cadet crouched, then he was moving away, a fiery brush growing out of his back. He moved fairly straight at first, then started to turn.

He pulled in a leg—and turned completely over.

"Lathrop—cut off your jet!" snapped Hanako. The flame died out, but the figure in the suit continued to turn and to recede. Hanako paid out his safety line. "Got a big fish here, boys," he said cheerfully. "What do you think he'll weigh?" He tugged on the line, which caused Lathrop to spin the other way, as the line had wound itself around him. When the line was free he hauled the cadet in.

Lathrop clicked on. "You were right, sergeant. I want to try it again—your way."

"Sorry. The book says a hundred per cent reserve fuel for this drill; you'd have to recharge." Hanako hesitated. "Sign up for tomorrow morning—I'll take you as an extra."

"Oh—thanks, Sarge!"

"Don't mention it. Number one!"

The next cadet moved out smoothly, but returned on an angle and had to be snubbed with the safety line before he could click on. The next cadet had trouble orienting himself at all. He receded, his back to the ship, and seemed to be about to continue in the direction of Draco till the end of time. Hanako tugged gently on the safety line while letting it run through his gloves and turned him around toward the ship. "Ten seconds on the jet, while I keep a strain on the line," he ordered. The safety line kept the cadet straightened out until he got back. "Number three!" called out Hanako.

Matt stepped forward with a feeling of tight excitement. The instructor hooked the safety line and said, "Any questions? Go ahead when ready."

"Okay." Matt crouched, broke his boots free, and stretched out. He steadied himself against the sergeant's knee. In front of him lay the northern constellations. He picked out the Pole Star as a target, then loosened the safety catch of the firing switch in his glove.

"And . . . one!" He felt a soft, steady pressure across his saddle, a shove of not quite ten pounds. Polaris seemed to vibrate to the blasting of the tiny jet. Then the star swung to the left, beyond the ring of the sight.

He pulled in his right arm and right leg. The star swung faster, checked and started back. Cautiously he extended his right-side limbs again—and almost forgot to cut the jet on the count of ten.

He could not see the ship. Earth swam in the velvety darkness off to the right. The silence and aloneness were more intense, more complete, than he had ever experienced.

"Time to turn," said Hanako in his ear.

"Oh—" said Matt, and grabbed his knees.

The heavens wheeled around him. He saw the ship swinging into sight, too late. He checked by starfishing, but it had moved on past. "Take it easy," advised the sergeant. "Don't curl up quite so tight, and catch it on the next time around. There's no hurry."

He drew himself in again, but not so much. The ship came around again, though twice as far away as it had been before. This time he checked before it swung past. The figures crawling on her side were about three hundred feet away and still backing away from him. He got someone's helmet centered in his sight, pressed the switch and began to count.

For a few worried seconds he thought that something had gone wrong. The figures on the ship did not seem to be getting nearer and now they were swinging slowly past him. He was tempted to blast again—but Hanako's orders had been specific; he decided not to.

The ship swung out of sight; he doubled up in a ball to bring it around more quickly. When it showed up it was distinctly nearer and he felt relieved. Actually the two bodies, ship and man, had been closing at five feet per second—but five feet per second is a slow walk.

A little more than a minute after cutting his jet, he jack-knifed to bring his boots in front of him and clicked on, about ten feet from the instructor.

Hanako came over and placed his helmet against Matt's so he could speak to him privately, with the radio shut off. "A good job, kid, the way you kept your nerve when you swung past. Okay—I'll post you for advanced training."

Matt remembered to cut out his walky-talky. "Gee, thanks!"

"You did it, not me." Hanako cut back in the voice circuit. "Okay, there—number four."

Matt wanted to chase back to his room, find Tex, and do some boasting. But there were seven more to go. Some did well, some had to be fished out of difficulty.

- The last-man outdid himself. He failed to cut off his power in spite of Hanako's shouts for him to do so. He moved away from the ship in a wide curve and commenced to spin, while the sergeant whipped at the safety line to try to stop the spin and head him back. At the end of a long fifty seconds his power gave out; he was nearly a thousand feet away and still receding rapidly.

The sergeant played him like a fisherman fighting a barracuda, then brought him in very, very slowly, for there was no way to check whatever speed the tension on the line placed on him.

When at last he was in, clicked down, and anchored by static line, Hanako sighed. "Whew!" he said. "I thought I was going to have to go get him." He went to the cadet and touched helmets, radio off.

The cadet did not shut off his instrument. "I don't know," they heard him reply. "The switch didn't go bad—I just couldn't seem to move a muscle. I could hear you shouting but I couldn't move."

Matt went back to the airlock with the group, feeling considerably sobered. He suspected that there would be a vacant place at supper. It was the Commandant's policy to get a cadet who was to be dropped away from the ship without delay. Matt did not question the practice, but it jarred him when he saw it happening—it brought the cold breath of disaster on his own neck.

But he cheered up as soon as he was dismissed. Once he was out of his suit and had inspected it and stowed it as the rules required, he zipped to his room, bouncing his turns in a fashion not approved for in-ship progress.

He banged on the door of Tex's cubicle. "Hey, Tex! Wake up! I've got news for you."

No answer—he opened the door, but Tex was not there. Nor, as it happened, were Pete nor Oscar. Disconsolately he went into his own sanctum and picked out a study spool.

Nearly two hours later Tex came bouncing in as Matt was getting ready for lunch and shouted, "Hey! Matt! Mitt me, big boy—shake hands with a spaceman!"

"Huh?"

"I just passed 'basic space suit'—sergeant said it was the best first test he had ever seen."

"He did? Oh—"

"He sure did. Oh boy—Terra Station, here I come!"

VIII

TERRA STATION

"LIBERTY PARTY—man the scooter!"

Matt zipped up the front of his space suit and hurriedly ran through the routine check. Oscar and Tex urged him along, as the liberty party was already filing through the door of the lock. The cadet officer-of-the-watch checked Matt in and sealed the door of the lock behind him.

The lock was a long corridor, sealed at each end, leading to a hangar pocket in the side of the *Randolph* in which the scooter rockets were stowed. The pressure died away and the far end of the lock opened; Matt pulled himself along, last in line, and found the scooter loaded. He could not find a place; the passenger racks were filled with space-suited cadets, busy strapping down.

The cadet pilot beckoned to him. Matt picked his way forward and touched helmets. "Mister," said the oldster, "can you read instruments?"

Guessing that he referred only to the simple instrument panel of a scooter, Matt answered, "Yes, sir."

"Then get in the co-pilot's chair. What's your mass?"

"Two eighty-seven, sir," Matt answered, giving the combined mass, in pounds, of himself and his suit with all its equipment. Matt strapped down, then looked around, trying to locate Tex and Oscar. He was feeling very important, even though a scooter requires a co-pilot about as much as a hog needs a spare tail.

The oldster entered Matt's mass on his center-of-gravity and moment-of-inertia chart, stared at it thoughtfully and said to Matt, "Tell Gee-three to swap places with Bee-two."

Matt switched on his walky-talky and gave the order. There was a scramble while a heavy-set youngster changed seats with a smaller cadet. The pilot gave a high sign to the cadet manning the hangar pocket; the scooter and its launching cradle swung out of the pocket, pushed by power-driven lazy tongs.

A scooter is a passenger rocket reduced to its simplest terms and has been described as a hat rack with an outboard motor. It operates only in empty space and does not have to be streamlined.

The rocket motor is unenclosed. Around it is a tier of light metal supports, the passenger rack. There is no "ship" in the sense of a hull, airtight compartments, etc. The passengers just belt themselves to the rack and let the rocket motor scoot them along.

When the scooter was clear of the ship the cadet in the hangar pocket turned the launching cradle, by power, until the scooter pointed at Terra Station. The pilot slapped the keys in front of him; the scooter took off.

The cadet pilot watched his radarscope. When the distance to the Station was closing at eighty-eight feet per second he cut his jet. "Latch on to the Station," he told Matt.

Matt plugged in and called the station. "Scooter number three, *Randolph*—scheduled trip. Arriving nine minutes, plus or minus," Matt sent, and congratulated himself on having studied the spool on small-craft procedures.

"Roger," a feminine voice answered, then added, "Use out-orbit contact platform Bee-for-Busy."

"Bee-for-Busy," acknowledged Matt. "Traffic?"

"None out-orbit. *Winged Victory* in-orbit, warping in."

Matt reported to his pilot. "No traffic," repeated the oldster. "Mister, I'm going to catch forty winks. Wake me when we've closed to a mile and a half."

"Aye aye, sir."

"Think you could bring her in?"

Matt gulped. "I'll try, sir."

"Figure it out while I'm asleep." The cadet promptly closed his eyes, floating as comfortably in free fall as if he had been in his own cubicle. Matt concentrated on the instrument dials.

Seven minutes later he shook the oldster, who opened his eyes and said, "What's your flight plan, Mister?"

"Well, uh—if we keep going as is, we'll just slide past on the out-orbit side. I don't think I'd change it at all. When we close to four thousand feet I'd blast until our relative speed is down to about ten foot-seconds, then forget the radar and brake by eye as we pass along the side."

"You've been studying too hard."

"Is that wrong?" Matt asked anxiously.

"Nope. Go ahead. Do it." The oldster bent over the tracking 'scope to assure himself that the scooter would miss the Station. Matt watched the closing range, while excitement built up inside him. Once he glanced ahead at the shining cylindrical bulk of the Station, but looked back quickly. A few seconds later he punched his firing key and a plume of flame shot out in front of them.

A scooter has jets at both ends, served by the same interconnected tanks, fuel pumps and piping. Scooters are conned "by the seat of your pants" rather than by complex mathematics. As such they are invaluable in letting student pilots get the feel of rocket ships.

As the distance decreased Matt felt for the first time the old nightmare of rocket pilots: is the calculated maneuver enough to avoid a crash? He felt this, even though he knew his course would slide him past the corner of the mammoth structure. It was a relief to release the firing key.

The oldster said, "Can you spot Bee-for-Busy when you see it?"

Matt shook his head. "No, sir. This is my first trip to Terra Station."

"It is? And I let you pilot! Well, there it is, ahead—third platform down. Better start braking."

"Aye aye, sir." The scooter was passing along the side of the Station and about a hundred yards out, at the speed of a brisk walk. Matt let Bee-for-Busy approach for a few moments more, then gave a short, experimental blast. It did not seem to slow them much; he gave a somewhat longer blast.

A few minutes later he had the scooter almost dead in space and practically abreast their contact point. He looked inquiringly at the pilot. "I've seen worse," the oldster grunted. "Tell them to bring us in."

"*Randolph* number three—ready for contact," Matt reported, via radio.

"We see you," the girl's voice answered. "Stand by for a line."

A line, shot by a gun, came sailing out in perfectly flat trajectory and passed through a metal loop sticking out from the scooter. "I relieve you, sir," the pilot told Matt. "Shinny out there and make that line fast."

A few minutes later the scooter was secured to platform Bee-for-Busy and the cadets were filing into the platform's airlock. Matt located Oscar and Tex in the suiting room and they undressed together. "What did you think of that contact?" Matt said to them, with studied casualness.

"All right, I guess," answered Tex. "What about it?"

"*I* made it."

Oscar raised his eyebrows. "You did? Nice going, kid."

Tex looked amazed. "The pilot let you jockey it? On your first trip?"

"Well, why not? You think I'm kidding?"

"No, I'm just impressed. May I touch you? How about an autograph?"

"Oh, come off it!"

They were, of course, in the free-fall part of the Station. As soon as they had stowed their suits, they hurried to the centrifuged belt frequented by the traveling public. Oscar knew his way around somewhat, having changed ships at the Station when he was a candidate, and led them to the door at the axis of rotation—the only possible place to pass from the free-fall zone to the weight zone.

From the axis they went down several levels, past offices and private quarters to the first of the public levels. It was, in effect, a wide, brightly lighted street, with a high ceiling and with slideways down the middle. Shops and restaurants lined it. The slideways curved up and away in the distance, for the corridor curved completely around the Station. "This," Oscar told them, "is Paradise Walk."

"I see why," agreed Tex, and gave a low whistle. The others followed his gaze. A tall, willowy blonde, dressed in some blue wisps of nothing much, was looking in the display window of a jewelry shop.

"Take it easy, Tex," advised Oscar. "She's taller than you are."

"I like them tall," Tex answered. "Watch me."

He sauntered over to the young woman. Matt and Oscar could not hear his opening remark, but it did not offend her, for she laughed. Then she looked him up and down with cool amusement and spoke. Her voice carried quite clearly. "I am married and at least ten years older than you are. I never pick up cadets."

Tex appeared to tuck his tail between his legs and slunk back toward his friends. He started to say, fiercely, "Well, you can't rule a guy out for try—," when the woman called out:

"Wait a moment! All three of you." She came up to them and looked from Matt to Oscar, "You are youngsters, aren't you?"

"Younster cadets, yes, ma'am," answered Oscar.

She fumbled in her jewelled pouch. "If you want to have some fun and meet some younger girls, you might try this address." She handed Oscar a card.

He looked startled and said, "Thank you, ma'am."

"Not at all." She moved away and managed to lose herself in the crowd at once.

"What does it say?" demanded Matt.

Oscar looked at it, then held it out. "Read it."

Terra Station First Baptist Church
Ralph Smiley, D.D., Pastor

SOCIAL HALL

#2437, Level "C"

Tex grinned. "Well, you can't say I scored a clean miss."

There ensued an argument. Matt and Tex wanted to go at once to the social hall; Oscar insisted that he was hungry and wanted some civilized food. The longer they argued the more reasonable seemed Oscar's case. Finally Tex switched sides and Matt gave in to the majority.

He regretted it a few minutes later, when he saw the prices on the menu. The restaurant they selected was a tourist trap, a fancy dining room with an adjoining bar. It had human waiters instead of automatic tables and items were priced accordingly.

Tex saw the expression on his face. "Relax, Matt," he told him. "This is on me—Pop sent me a check."

"Oh, I wouldn't want to do that."

"Want to fight?"

Matt grinned. "Okay, thanks."

Oscar said, "How hard shall we punish you, Tex? Tea and toast?"

"Anything you want. Let's really celebrate. Which reminds me—I think we ought to have a drink."

"Huh?" said Oscar. "And have an M.P. catch us? No, thank you."

Matt started to protest but Tex stood up. "Just leave this to Father Jarman. It's high time you two poor, underprivileged outlanders tasted a real old Southern mint julep." He started for the bar. Oscar shrugged.

Tex scouted out the bar before entering. There were no cadets, of course; more important there were no officers and no marine M.P.'s. The hour was early and the bar almost deserted. He went up to the bartender. "Can you make a mint julep?" he asked.

The bartender looked up and answered, "Beat it. I'm not supposed to serve you liquor. This is off limits to cadets."

"I didn't ask you if this was off limits—I asked you if you could make a mint julep." Tex slid a bill across the counter. "Three mint juleps, in fact."

The barman eyed the bill. Finally he caused it to disappear. "Go on back into the dining room."

"Right!" said Tex.

A few minutes later a waiter placed a complete tea service in front of them, but the teapot did not contain tea. Tex poured out the drink, splitting it carefully three ways, in tea cups. "Here's to you, chums—drink up."

Matt took a sip. "It tastes like medicine," he announced.

"Like medicine?" Tex protested. "This noble potion? I'll meet you at dawn, suh—coffee and pistols for two."

"I still say it tastes like medicine. What do you think of it, Oscar?"

"It's not bad."

Matt pushed his aside. "Aren't you going to drink it?" asked Tex.

"No. Thanks, Tex, really—but I think it would make me sick. I guess I'm a sissy."

"Well, we won't waste it." He picked up Matt's cup and poured some into his own. "Split it with me, Oscar?"

"No. You go ahead."

"Okay, if you say so." He poured the rest into his cup. When the food they ordered was served, Tex was no longer interested. While Matt and Oscar were busily chewing he kept urging them to sing. "Come on, Oscar! You can learn it."

"I can't sing."

"Sure you can. I've heard you sing, with the Hog Alley band. I'll sing the verse, we'll all clap, then hit the chorus together: 'Deep in . . . the heart of . . . Texas!' Like that."

"Shut up," said Oscar, "or you'll be deep in the heart of trouble."

"Kill-joy! Come on, Matt."

"I can't sing with my mouth full."

"Look," said Oscar to Matt, in a tense, low voice. "Do you see what I see?"

Matt looked and saw Lieutenant Wong entering the far end of the dining room. He went to a table, sat down, looked around, spotted the table of cadets, nodded, and started studying a menu. "Oh, mother!" Matt breathed softly.

"Then we'll sing 'Ioway,' " announced Tex. "I'm broad-minded."

"We won't sing anything. For the love of Mike, Tex—shut up! An officer just came into the joint."

"Where?" demanded Tex. "Invite him over. I don't hold any grudges. They're good boys, all of 'em, the stinkers." Matt shot a quick glance at Lieutenant Wong and was dismayed to see the officer crooking a finger at him, beckoning. He got up and walked stiffly toward the officer.

"Dodson—"

"Yes, sir."

"Go back and tell Jarman to quiet down before I have to come over there and ask him what his name is."

"Uh—aye aye, sir!"

When he got back to the table, Tex was already quiet and appeared sobered but very much puzzled. Oscar's usually pleasant face was dark with anger. "What's the verdict?"

Matt reported. "I see. Wong's all right. Well, we got to get him out of here." Oscar flagged the waiter, then opened Tex's pouch and paid the bill.

He stood up. "Let's go. Pull yourself together, Tex, or I'll break your neck."

"Where to?" asked Matt.

"Into the 'fresher."

Fortunately it turned out that they had that room to themselves. Oscar marched Tex to a washbasin and told him to stick his finger down his throat. "Why?" objected Tex.

"Because if you don't, I'll do it for you. Look, Matt—can you take care of him? I'll be back in a few minutes."

It was nearly twenty minutes before Oscar returned, bearing a carton of hot, black coffee and a tube of pills. He forced the coffee and half a dozen of the pills on the patient. "What are the pills?" Matt wanted to know.

"Thiamin chloride."

"You seem to know your way around?"

"Well . . ." Oscar wrinkled his brow. "Venus isn't like Earth, you know. Still sort of wild and woolly. You see a lot of things go on. Drink the rest of the coffee, Tex."

"Yessir."

"The front of his uniform is all messed up," said Matt.

"So I see. I guess we should have undressed him."

"What'll we do? If he goes back like that, there will be questions asked—bad ones."

"Let me think." Presently he said to Tex, "Go in there—" Oscar indicated one of a row of 'fresher booths. "—and take off your uniform. Hand it out and lock yourself in. We'll be back after a while." Tex seemed to feel that he was being consigned to the salt mines, but there was no real opposition left in him. He went. Shortly thereafter Matt and Oscar left, Oscar with a tightly rolled bundle of a cadet uniform under one arm.

They took the slideway half around the Station, through crowds of gorgeously dressed and hurrying people, past rich and beckoning shops. Matt enjoyed it thoroughly.

"They say," said Oscar, "that this is what the big cities used to be like, back before the Disorders."

"It certainly doesn't look like Des Moines."

"Nor like Venus." Oscar found what he was looking for, an automatic laundry service, in a passageway off the waiting room of the emigrant zone. After a considerable wait the uniform came back to them, clean, pressed, and neatly packaged. It being Terra Station, the cost was sky high. Matt looked at what remained of his funds.

"Might as well be broke," he said and invested the remainder in a pound of chocolate-coated cherries. They hurried back. Tex looked so woe-begone and so glad to see them that Matt had a sudden burst of generosity and handed the box to Tex. "Present to you, you poor, miserable, worthless critter."

Tex seemed touched by the gesture—it was no more than a gesture, since candy and such are, by ancient right, community property among roommates.

"Hurry up and get dressed, Tex. The scooter shoves off in just thirty-two minutes." Twenty-five minutes later, suited up, they were filing into the airlock, Tex with the chocolates under his arm.

The trip back was without incident, except for one thing: Matt had not thought to specify a pressure container for the candy. Before Tex could strap down the box had bulged.

By the time they reached the *Randolph* the front and left side of his space suit was covered with a bubbly, sticky mess compounded of cherry juice, sugar syrup, and brown stains of chocolate as the semi-liquid confection boiled and expanded in the vacuum. He would have thrown the package away had not the oldster, strapped next to him in the rack, reminded him of the severe penalties for jettisoning anything in a traffic lane.

The cadet in charge of the hangar pocket in the *Randolph* looked Tex over in disgust. "Why didn't you pack it inside your suit?"

"Uh, I just didn't think of it, sir."

"Hummph! Next time you will, no doubt. Go on inside and place yourself on the report for 'gross untidiness in uniform.' And clean up that suit."

"Aye aye, sir."

Pete was in their suite when they got back. He came out of his cubicle. "Have fun? Gee, I wish I hadn't had the duty."

"You didn't miss much," said Oscar.

Tex looked from one to the other. "Gee, fellows, I'm sorry I ruined your liberty."

"Forget it," said Oscar. "Terra Station will still be there next month."

"That's right," agreed Matt, "but see here, Tex—tell us the truth. That was the first drink you ever had—wasn't it?"

Tex looked shame-faced. "Yes . . . my folks are all temperance—except my Uncle Bodie."

"Never mind your Uncle Bodie. If I catch you taking another, I'll beat you to death with the bottle."

"Aw, shucks, Matt!"

Oscar looked at Matt quizzically. "Easy on that holier-than-thou stuff, kid. Maybe it could happen to you."

"Maybe it could. Maybe some day I'll get you to chaperone me and find out what happens. But not in public."

"It's a date."

"Say," demanded Pete, "what goes on here? What's it all about?"

IX

LONG HAUL

LIFE IN THE *Randolph* had a curious aspect of timelessness —or, rather, datelessness. There was no weather, there were no seasons. The very divisions into "night" and "day" were arbitrary and were continually being upset by night watches and by laboratory periods at any hour, in order to make maximum use of limited facilities. Meals were served every six hours around the clock and the meal at one in the "morning" was almost as well attended as breakfast at seven hundred.

Matt got used to sleeping when he could find time—and the "days" tumbled past. It seemed to him that there was never time enough for all that he was expected to do. Mathematics and the mathematical subjects, astrogation and atomic physics in particular, began to be a bugaboo; he was finding himself being rushed into practical applications of mathematics before he was solidly grounded.

He had fancied himself, before becoming a cadet, as rather bright in mathematics, and so he was—by ordinary standards. He had not anticipated what it would be like to be part of a group of which every member was unusually talented in the language of science. He signed up for personal coaching in mathematics and studied harder than ever. The additional effort kept him from failing, but that was all.

It is not possible to work all the time without cracking up, but the environment would have kept Matt from overworking even if he had been so disposed. Corridor number five of "A" deck, where Matt and his roommates lived, was known as "Hog Alley" and had acquired a ripe reputation for carefree conduct even before Tex Jarman added his talents.

The current "Mayor of Hog Alley" was an oldster named Bill Arensa. He was a brilliant scholar and seemed able to absorb the most difficult study spool in a single playing, but he had been in the *Randolph* an unusually long time—a matter of accumulated demerits.

One evening after supper, soon after arrival, Matt and Tex were attempting to produce a little harmony. Matt was armed with a comb and a piece of tissue paper; Tex had his harmonica. A bellow from across the hallway stopped them. "Open up in there! You youngsters—come busting out!"

Tex and Matt appeared as ordered. The Mayor looked them over. "No blood," he remarked. "I'd swear I heard someone being killed. Go back and get your noisemakers."

Arensa ushered them into his own room, which was crowded. He waved a hand around at the occupants. "Meet the Hog Alley People's Forum—Senator Mushmouth, Senator Filibuster, Senator Hidebound, Doctor Dogoodly, and the Marquis de Sade. Gentlemen, meet Commissioner Wretched and Professor Farflung." The oldster went into his study cubicle.

"What's your name, Mister?" said one of the cadets, addressing Tex.

"Jarman, sir."

"And yours?"

"We've got no time for those details," announced Arensa, returning bearing a guitar. "That number you gentlemen were working on—let's try it again. Brace yourself for the down beat . . . and a one, and a two!"

Thus was born the Hog Alley band. It grew to seven pieces and started working on a repertoire to be presented at a ship's entertainment. Matt dropped out when he became eligible for the space polo league, as he could not spare time for both—his meager talent was no loss to the band.

Nevertheless he remained in the orbit of the oldster. Arensa adopted all four of them, required them to report to his room from time to time, and supervised their lives. However, he never placed them on the report. By comparing notes with other youngster cadets on this point, Matt discovered that he and his friends were well off. They attended numerous sessions of the "Forum," first by direction, later from choice. The staple recreation in the *Randolph,* as it is in all boarding schools, was the bull session. The talk ranged through every possible subject and was kept spiced by Arensa's original and usually radical ideas.

However, no matter what was discussed, the subject usually worked around to girls and then broke up with the unstartling conclusion: "There's no sense in talking about it—there aren't any girls in the *Randolph.* Let's turn in."

Almost as entertaining was the required seminar in "Doubt." The course had been instituted by the present commandant and resulted from his own observation that every military organization—with the Patrol no exception—suffered from an inherent vice. A military hierarchy automatically places a premium on conservative behavior and dull conformance with precedent; it tends to penalize original and imaginative thinking. Commodore Arkwright realized that these tendencies are inherent and inescapable; he hoped to offset them a bit by setting up a course that could not be passed without original thinking.

The method was the discussion group, made up of youngsters, oldsters, and officers. The seminar leader would chuck out some proposition that attacked a value usually regarded as axiomatic. From there on anything could be said.

It took Matt a while to get the hang of it. At his first session the leader offered: "Resolved: that the Patrol is a detriment and should be abolished." Matt could hardly believe his ears.

In rapid succession he heard it suggested that the past hundred years of Patrol-enforced peace had damaged the race, that the storm of mutations that followed atomic warfare were necessarily of net benefit under the inexorable laws of evolution, that neither the human race nor any of the other races of the system could expect to survive permanently in the universe if they deliberately forsook war, and that, in any case, the Patrol was made up of a bunch of self-righteous fatheads who mistook their own trained-in prejudices for the laws of nature.

Matt contributed nothing to the first discussion he attended.

The following week he heard both mother love and love of mother questioned. He wanted to reply, but, for the life of him, could think of no other answer than "Because!" Thereafter came attacks on monotheism as a desirable religious form, the usefulness of the scientific method, and the rule of the majority, in reaching decisions. He discovered that it was permissible to express opinions that were orthodox as well as ones that were unorthodox and began to join the debate by defending some of his own pet ideas.

At once he found his own unconscious assumptions that lay behind his opinions subjected to savage attack and found himself again reduced to a stubborn and unvoiced "Because!"

He began to catch on to the method and found that he could ask an innocent question that would undermine someone else's line of argument. From then on he had a good time.

He particularly enjoyed it after Girard Burke was assigned to his seminar. Matt would lie in wait until Girard would express some definite opinion, then jump him—always with a question; never with a statement. For some reason not clear to Matt, Burke's opinions were always orthodox; to attack them Matt was forced to do some original thinking.

But he asked Burke about it after class one day. "See here, Burke—I thought you were the bird with a new slant on everything?"

"Well, maybe I am. What about it?"

"You don't sound like it in 'Doubt.' "

Burke looked wise. "You don't catch me sticking my neck out."

"What do you mean?"

"Do you think our dear superiors are really interested in your bright ideas? Won't you ever learn to recognize a booby trap, son?"

Matt thought about it. "I think you're crazy." Nevertheless he chewed it over.

The days rolled past. The pace was so hard that there

was little time to be bored. Matt shared the herd *credo* of all cadets that the *Randolph* was a madhouse, unfit for human habitation, sky junk, etc., etc.—but in fact he had no opinion of his own about the school ship; he was too busy. At first he had had some acute twinges of homesickness; thereafter it seemed to recede. There was nothing but the treadmill of study, drill, more study, laboratory, sleep, eat, and study again.

He was returning from the communications office, coming off watch late one night, when he heard sounds from Pete's cubicle. At first he thought Pete must be running his projector, studying late. He was about to bang on his door and suggest going up to the galley to wheedle a cup of cocoa when he became convinced that the sound was not a projector.

Cautiously he opened the door a crack. The sound was sobbing. He closed the door noiselessly and knocked on it. After a short silence Pete said, "Come in."

Matt went in. "Got anything to eat?"

"Some cookies in my desk."

Matt got them out. "You look sick, Pete. Anything wrong?"

"No. Nothing."

"Don't give me the space drift. Out with it."

Pete hesitated. "It's nothing. Nothing anybody can do anything about."

"Maybe so, maybe not. Tell me."

"There's nothing you can do. I'm *homesick*, that's all!"

"Oh—" Matt had a sudden vision of the rolling hills and broad farms of Iowa. He suppressed it. "That's bad, kid. I know how you feel."

"No, you don't. Why, you're practically *at* home—you can just step to a port and *see* it."

"That's no help."

"And it hasn't been so terribly long since you've been home. Me—it took me two years just to make the trip to Terra; there's no way of telling when I'll ever see home again." Pete's eyes got a faraway look; his voice became almost lyrical. "You don't know what it's like, Matt. You've never *seen* it. You know what they say: 'Every civilized man has two planets, his own and Ganymede.'"

"Huh?"

Pete did not even hear him. "Jupiter hanging overhead, filling half the sky—" He stopped. "It's beautiful, Matt. There's no place like it."

Matt found himself thinking about Des Moines in a late summer evening . . . with fireflies winking and the cicadas singing in the trees, and the air so thick and heavy you could cup it in your hand. Suddenly he hated the steel shell around him, with its eternal free-fall and its filtered air and its artifical lights. "Why did we ever sign up, Pete?"

"I don't know. I don't know!"

"Are you going to resign?"

"I can't. My father had to put up a bond to cover my passage both ways—if I leave voluntarily he's stuck for it."

Tex came in, yawning and scratching. "What's the matter with you guys? Can't you sleep? Don't you want anybody else to sleep?"

"Sorry, Tex."

Jarman looked them over. "You both look like your pet dog had died. What's the trouble?"

Matt bit his lip. "Nothing much. I'm homesick, that's all."

Pete spoke up at once. "That's not quite straight. I was the one that was pulling the baby act—Matt was trying to cheer me up."

Tex looked puzzled. "I don't get it. What difference does it make where you are so long as you aren't in Texas?"

"Oh, Tex, for heaven's sake!" Matt exploded.

"What's the matter? Did I say something wrong?" Tex looked from Matt to Pete. "Pete, you certainly are a mighty far piece away from your folks, I've got to admit. Tell you what—comes time we get some leave, you come home with me. I'll let you count the legs on a horse."

Pete grinned feebly. "And meet your Uncle Bodie?"

"Sho', sho'! Uncle Bodie'll tell you about the time he rode the twister, bareback. Is it a deal?"

"If you'll come to visit at my home someday. You, too, Matt."

"It's a deal." They shook hands all around.

The effects of the nostalgic binge with Pete might have worn off if another incident had not happened soon after. Matt went across the passage to Arensa's room, intending to ask the oldster for some help in a tricky problem in astrogation. He found the oldster packing. "Come in, Senator," said Arensa. "Don't clutter up the doorway. What's on your mind, son?"

"Uh, nothing, I guess. You got your ship, sir?" Arensa had been passed for outer duty the month before; he was now technically a "passed cadet" as well as an "oldster."

"No." He picked up a sheaf of papers, glanced at them, and tore them across. "But I'm leaving."

"Oh."

"No need to be delicate about it—I wasn't fired. I've resigned."

"Oh."

"Don't stare at me and say 'oh'! What's so odd about resigning?"

"Nothing. Nothing at all."

"You were wondering why, weren't you? Well, I'll tell you. I've had it, that's why. I've had it and I'm sick of it. Because, sonny, I have no wish to be a superman. My halo is too tight and I'm chucking it. Can you understand that?"

"Oh, I wasn't criticizing!"

"No, but you were thinking it. You stick with it, Senator. You're just the sort of serious-minded young squirt they want and need. But not for me—I'm not going to be an archangel, charging around the sky and brandishing a flaming sword. Did you ever stop to think what it would feel like to atom-bomb a city? Have you ever really *thought about it?*"

"Why, I don't know. It hasn't been necessary for the Patrol actually to *use* a bomb since they got it rolling right. I don't suppose it ever will be."

"But that's what you signed up for, just the same. It's your reason for being, my boy." He stopped and picked up his guitar. "Forget it. Now what can I do with this? I'll sell it to you cheap, Earth-side price."

"I couldn't even pay Earth-side prices right now."

"Take it as a gift." Arensa chucked it at him. "The Hog Alley band ought to have a gitter and I can get another. In thirty minutes I shall be in Terra Station, Senator, and six hours later I shall be back with the ground crawlers, the little people who don't know how to play God—and wouldn't want to!"

Matt couldn't think of anything to say.

It seemed odd thereafter not to have Arensa's bellowing voice across the passageway, but Matt did not have time to think about it. Matt's drill section in piloting was ordered to the Moon for airless-landing.

The section had progressed from scooters to drill in an A-6 utility rocket rigged for instruction. The cargo space of this ship—P.R.S. *Shakysides* to the cadets; drill craft #106 on the rolls of the *Randolph*—had been fitted as a dozen duplicate control rooms, similar in every visible detail to the real control rooms, to the last switch, dial, scope and key. The instruments in the duplicate rooms showed the same data as their twins in the master room but when a cadet touched a control in one of the instruction rooms, it had no effect on the ship; instead the operation was recorded on tape.

The pilot's operations were recorded, too, so that each student pilot could compare what he did with what he should have done, after having practiced under conditions identical with those experienced by the actual pilot.

The section had completed all it could learn from practice contacts at the *Randolph* and at Terra Station. They needed the hazard of a planet. The two-day trip to Moon Base was made in the *Shakysides* herself, under conditions only a little worse than those encountered by an emigrant.

Matt and his companions saw nothing of the Lunar colonies. There was no liberty; they lived for two weeks in pressurized underground barracks at the Base and went up to the field each day for landing drill, first in the dummy control rooms of the *Shakysides*, then in dual-controlled A-6 rockets for actual piloting.

Matt soloed at the end of the first week. He had the "feel" for piloting; given a pre-calculated flight plan he could make his craft respond. It was as natural to him as mathematical astrogation was difficult.

Soloing left him with time on his hands. He explored the Base and took a space-suited walk on the burned and airless Lunar plain. The student pilots were quartered in a corner of the marine barracks. Matt killed time by watching the space marines and chinning with the non-coms.

He liked the spit-and-polish style with which the space marines did things, the strutting self-confidence with which they handled themselves. There is no more resplendent sight in the solar system than an old space-marine sergeant in full dress, covered with stripes, hash marks, and ribbons, the silver at his temples matching the blazing sunburst on his chest. Matt began to feel dowdy in the one plain, insignialess uniform he had brought in his jump bag.

He enjoyed their frequent ceremonials. At first it startled him to hear a unit mustered without the ghostly repetition of the names of the Four—"Dahlquist! Martin! Rivera! Wheeler!"—but the marines had traditional rites of their own and more of them.

Faithful to his intention of swotting astrogation as hard as possible, Matt had brought some typical problems along. Reluctantly he tackled them one day. "Given: Departure from the orbit of Deimos, Mars, not earlier than 1200 Greenwich, 15 May 2087; chemical fuel, exhaust velocity 10,000 meters per second; destination, suprastratospheric orbit around Venus. Required: Most economical orbit to destination and quickest orbit, mass-ratios and times of departure and arrival for each. Prepare flight plan and designate check points, with pre-calculation for each point, using stars of 2nd magnitude or brighter. Questions: Is it possible to save time or fuel by tacking on the Terra-Luna pair? What known meteor drifts will be encountered and what evasive plans, if any, should be made? All answers must conform to space regulations as well as to ballistic principles."

The problem could not be solved in any reasonable length of time without machine calculation. However, Matt could set it up and then, with luck, sweet-talk the officer in charge of the Base's computation room into letting him use a ballistic integrator. He got to work.

The sweet voice of a bugle reached him, first call for changing the guard. He ignored it.

He was sweating over his preliminary standard approximation when the bugle again interrupted him with call-to-muster. It completely disrupted his chain of reasoning. Confounded problem!—why would they assign such a silly problem anyhow? The Patrol didn't fiddle around with chemical fuels and most economical orbits—that was merchant service stuff.

Two minutes later he was watching guard mount, down in the main hall under the barracks. When the band sounded off with *"Till the Suns are cold and the heavens dark—"* Matt found himself choking up.

He stopped by the guard office, reluctant to get back to the fussy complexities of mathematics. The new sergeant of the guard was an acquaintance, Master Sergeant Macleod. "Come in, young fellow, and rest yourself. Did you see the guard mount?"

"Thanks. Yes, I did. It's pretty wonderful to see."

"Know what you mean. Been doing it twenty years and I get more of a bang out of it than I did when I was a recruit. How's tricks? They keeping you busy?"

Matt grinned sheepishly. "I'm playing hooky. I should be studying astrogation, but I get so darned sick of it."

"Don't blame you a bit. Figures make my head ache."

Matt found himself telling the older man his troubles. Sergeant Macleod eyed him with sympathetic interest. "See here, Mr. Dodson—you don't like that long-haired stuff. Why don't you chuck it?"

"Huh?"

"You like the space marines, don't you?"

"Why, yes."

"Why not switch over and join a man's outfit? You're a likely lad and educated—in a year I'd be saluting you. Ever thought about it?"

"Why, no, I can't say that I have."

"Then do so. You don't belong with the Professors—you

didn't know that was what we call the Patrol, did you?—the 'Professors.' "

"I'd heard it."

"You had? Well, we work for the Professors, but we aren't of them. We're . . . well, you've seen. Think it over."

Matt did think it over, so much so that he took the Mars-to-Venus problem back with him, still unsolved.

It was no easier to solve for the delay, nor were other and more complicated problems made any simpler by virtue of the idea, buzzing in the back of his mind, that he need not belabor himself with higher mathematics in order to be a spaceman. He began to see himself decked out in the gaudy, cock-pheasant colors of the space marines.

At last he took it up with Lieutenant Wong. "You want to transfer to the marines?"

"Yes. I think so."

"Why?"

Matt explained his increasing feeling of frustration in dealing with both atomic physics and astrogation.

Wong nodded. "I thought so. But we knew that you would have tough sledding since you came here insufficently prepared. I don't like the sloppy work you've been doing since you came back from Luna."

"I've done the best I could, sir."

"No, you haven't. But you *can* master these two subjects and I will see to it that you do."

Matt explained, almost inaudibly, that he was not sure he wanted to. Wong, for the first time, looked vexed.

"Still on that? If you turn in a request for transfer, I won't okay it and I can tell you ahead of time that the Commandant will turn it down."

Matt's jaw muscles twitched. "That's your privilege, sir."

"Damn it, Dodson, it's not my privilege; it's my duty. You would never make a marine and I say so because I know you, your record, and your capabilities. You have a good chance of making a Patrol officer."

Matt looked startled. "Why couldn't I become a marine?"

"Because it's too easy for you—so easy that you would fail."

"Huh?"

"Don't say 'huh.' The spread in I.Q. between leader and follower should not be more than thirty points. You are considerably more than thirty points ahead of those old sergeants—don't get me wrong; they are fine men. But your mind doesn't work like theirs." Wong went on, "Have you ever wondered why the Patrol consists of nothing but officers—and student officers, cadets?"

"Mmm, no, sir."

"Naturally you wouldn't. We never wonder at what we grow up with. Strictly speaking, the Patrol is not a military organization at all."

"Sir?"

"I know, I know—you are trained to use weapons, you are under orders, you wear a uniform. But your purpose is not to fight, but to prevent fighting, by every possible means. The Patrol is not a fighting organization; it is the repository of weapons too dangerous to entrust to military men.

"With the development last century of mass-destruction weapons, warfare became all offense and no defense, speaking broadly. A nation could launch a horrific attack but it could not even protect its own rocket bases. Then space travel came along.

"The spaceship is the perfect answer in a military sense to the atom bomb, and to germ warfare and weather warfare. It can deliver an attack that can't be stopped—and it is utterly impossible to attack that spaceship from the surface of a planet."

Matt nodded. "The gravity gauge."

"Yes, the gravity gauge. Men on the surface of a planet are as helpless against men in spaceships as a man would be trying to conduct a rock-throwing fight from the bottom of a well. The man at the top of the well has gravity working for him.

"We might have ended up with the tightest, most nearly unbreakable tyranny the world has ever seen. But the human race got a couple of lucky breaks and it didn't work out that way. It's the business of the Patrol to see that it stays lucky.

"But the Patrol can't drop an atom bomb simply because

some pipsqueak Hitler has made a power grab and might some day, when he has time enough, build spaceships and mass-destruction weapons. The power is too great, too awkward—it's like trying to keep order in a nursery with a loaded gun instead of a switch.

"The space marines are the Patrol's switch. They are the finest—"

"Excuse me, sir—"

"Yes?"

"I know how the marines work. They do the active policing in the System—but that's why I want to transfer. They're a more active outfit. They are—"

"—more daring, more adventurous, more colorful, more glamorous—and they don't have to study things that Matthew Dodson is tired of studying. Now shut up and listen; there is a lot you don't know about the set-up, or you wouldn't be trying to transfer."

Matt shut up.

"People tend to fall into three psychological types, all differently motivated. There is the type, motivated by economic factors, money . . . and there is the type motivated by 'face,' or pride. This type is a spender, fighter, boaster, lover, sportsman, gambler; he has a will to power and an itch for glory. And there is the professional type, which claims to follow a code of ethics rather than simply seeking money or glory—priests and ministers, teachers, scientists, medical men, some artists and writers. The idea is that such a man believes that he is devoting his life to some purpose more important than his individual self. You follow me?"

"I . . . think so."

"Mind you this is terrifically over-simplified. And don't try to apply these rules to non-terrestrials; they won't fit. The Martian is another sort of a cat, and so is the Venerian."

Wong continued, "Now we get to the point: The Patrol is meant to be made up exclusively of the professional type. In the space marines, every single man jack, from the generals to the privates, is or should be the sort who lives by pride and glory."

"Oh . . ."

Wong waited for it to sink in. "You can see it in the very uniforms; the Patrol wears the plainest of uniforms, the marines wear the gaudiest possible. In the Patrol all the emphasis is on the oath, the responsibility to humanity. In the space marines the emphasis is on pride in their corps and its glorious history, loyalty to comrades, the ancient virtues of the soldier. I am not disparaging the marine when I say that he does not care a tinker's damn for the political institutions of the Solar System; he cares only for his organization.

"But it's not your style, Matt. I know more about you than you do yourself, because I have studied the results of your psychological tests. You will never make a marine."

Wong paused so long that Matt said diffidently, "Is that all, sir?"

"Almost. You've got to learn astrogation. If deep-sea diving were the key to the Patrol's responsibility, it would be that that you would have to learn. But the key happens to be space travel. So—I'll lay out a course of sprouts for you. For a few weeks you'll do nothing but astrogate. Does that appeal to you?"

"No, sir."

"I didn't think it would. But when I get through with you, you'll be able to find your way around the System blindfolded. Now let me see—"

The next few weeks were deadly monotony but Matt made progress. He had plenty of time to think—when he was not bending over a calculator. Oscar and Tex went to the Moon together; Pete was on night shift in the power room. Matt kept sullenly and stubbornly at work—and brooded. He promised himself to stick it out until Wong let up on him. After that—well, he would have a leave coming up one of these days. If he decided to chuck it, why, lots of cadets never came back from their first leave.

In the meantime his work began to get the grudging approval of Lietuenant Wong.

At last Wong let up on him and he went back to a normal routine. He was settling into it when he found himself posted for an extra duty. Pursuant thereto, he reported one morning to the officer of the watch, received a briefing, memorized a list of names, and was issued a black armband. Then he went to the main airlock and waited.

Presently a group of scared and greenish boys began erupting from the lock. When his turn came, he moved forward and called out, "Squad seven! Where is the squad leader of squad seven?"

He got his charges rounded up at last and told the acting squad leader to follow along in the rear, then led them slowly and carefully down to "A" deck. He was glad to find when he got there that none of them had gotten lost. "This is your messroom," he told them. "We'll have lunch before long."

Something about the expression of one of them amused him. "What's the matter, Mister?" he asked the boy. "Aren't you hungry?"

"Uh, no, sir."

"Well, cheer up—you will be."

X

QUIS CUSTODIET IPSOS CUSTODES?

INTERPLANETARY PATROL Cadet Matthew Dodson sat in the waiting room of Pikes Peak Catapult Station and watched the clock. He had an hour to wait before boarding the *New Moon* for Terra Station; meanwhile he was expecting his roommates.

It had been a good leave, he supposed; he had done everything he had planned to do—except joining the others at the Jarman ranch at the end; his mother had kicked up such a fuss at the idea.

Still, it had been a good leave. His space-burned face,

lean and beginning to be lined, looked slightly puzzled. He had confided to no one his tentative intention of resigning while on leave. Now he was trying to remember just when and why it had ceased to be his intention.

He had been sent on temporary duty to the P.R.S *Nobel*, as assistant to the astrogator during a routine patrol of circum-Terra bomb-rockets. Matt had joined his ship at Moon Base and, at the conclusion of the patrol when the *Nobel* had grounded at Terra Base for overhaul, was detached with permission to take leave before reporting back to the *Randolph*. He had gone straight home.

The entire family met him at the station and copted him home. His mother had cried a little and his father had shaken hands very vigorously. It seemed to Matt that his kid brother had grown almost incredibly. It was good to see them, good to be back in the old family bus. Matt would have piloted the copter himself had not Billie, his brother, gone straight to the controls.

The house had been redecorated throughout. His mother obviously expected favorable comment and Matt had given it—but he hadn't really liked the change. It had not been what he had pictured. Besides that, the rooms seemed smaller. He decided that it must be the effect of redecorating; the house couldn't have shrunk!

His own room was filled with Bill's things, although Bill had been temporarily evicted to his old room, now turned into a hobby room for his mother. The new arrangements were sensible, reasonable—and annoying.

In thinking it over Matt knew that the changes at home had had nothing to do with his decision. Certainly not! Nor his father's remarks about posture, even though they had stuck in his craw—

He and his father had been alone in the living room, just before dinner, and Matt had been pacing up and down, giving an animated and, he believed, interesting account of the first time he had soloed. His father had taken advantage of a pause to say, "Stand up, son."

Matt stopped. "Sir?"

"You are all crouched over and seem to be limping. Does your leg still bother you?"

"No, my leg is fine."

"Then straighten up and square your shoulders. Look proud. Don't they pay any attention to your posture at school?"

"What's wrong with the way I was walking?"

Bill had appeared in the door just as the subject had come up. "I'll show you, Mattie," he had interrupted, and proceeded to slouch across the room in a grotesque exaggeration of a spaceman's relaxed and boneless glide. The boy made it look like the amble of a chimpanzee. "You walk like that."

"The devil I do!"

"The devil you don't."

"Bill!" said his father. "Go wash up and get ready for dinner. And don't talk that way. Go on, now!" When the younger son had left his father turned again to Matt and said, "I thought I was speaking privately, Matt. Honestly, it's not as bad as Bill makes out; it's only about half that bad."

"But— Look, Dad, I walk just like everybody else—among spacemen, I mean. It comes of getting used to free-fall. You carry yourself sort of pulled in, for days on end, ready to bounce a foot off a bulkhead, or grab with your hands. When you're back under weight, after days and weeks of that, you walk the way I do. 'Cat feet' we call it."

"I suppose it would have that effect," his father had answered reasonably, "but wouldn't it be a good idea to practice walking a little every day, just to keep in form?"

"In free-fall? But—" Matt had stopped, suddenly aware that there was no way to bridge the gap.

"Never mind. Let's go in to dinner."

There had been the usual round of family dinners with aunts and uncles. Everyone asked him to tell about school, about what it felt like to go out into space. But, somehow, they had not actually seemed very interested. Take Aunt Dora.

Great-aunt Dora was the current family matriarch. She

had been a very active woman, busy with church and social work. Now she was bedfast and had been for three years. Matt called on her because his family obviously expected it. "She often complains to me that you don't write to her, Matt, and—"

"But, Mother, I don't have time to write to everyone!"

"Yes, yes. But she's proud of you, Matt. She'll want to ask you a thousand questions about everything. Be sure to wear your uniform—she'll expect it."

Aunt Dora had not asked a thousand questions; she had asked just one—why had he waited so long to come to see her? Thereafter Matt found himself being informed, in detail, on the shortcomings of the new pastor, the marriage chances of several female relatives and connections, and the states of health of several older women, many of them unknown to him, including details of operations and post-operative developments.

He was a bit dizzy when he escaped, pleading a previous date.

Yes, maybe that was it—it might have been the visit to Aunt Dora that convinced him that he was not ready to resign and remain in Des Moines. It could not have been Marianne.

Marianne was the girl who had made him promise to write regularly—and, in fact, he had, more regularly than had she. But he had let her know that he was coming home and she had organized a picnic to welcome him back. It had been jolly. Matt had renewed old acquaintances and had enjoyed a certain amount of hero worship from the girls present. There had been a young man there, three or four years older than Matt, who seemed unattached. Gradually it dawned on Matt that Marianne treated the newcomer as her property.

It had not worried him. Marianne was the sort of girl who never would get clearly fixed in her mind the distinction between a planet and a star. He had not noticed this before, but it and similar matters had come up on the one date he had had alone with her.

And she had referred to his uniform as "cute."

He began to understand, from Marianne, why most Patrol officers do not marry until their mid-thirties, after retirement.

The clock in Pikes Peak Station showed thirty minutes until up-ship. Matt began to worry that Tex's casual way might have caused the other three to miss connections, when he spotted them in the crowd. He grabbed his jump bag and went toward them.

They had their backs toward him and had not seen him as yet. He sneaked up behind Tex and said in a hoarse voice, "Mister—report to the Commandant's office."

Tex jumped into the air and turned completely around. "Matt! You horse-thief, don't scare me like that!"

"Your guilty conscience. Hi, Pete. Hello, Oscar."

"How's the boy, Matt? Good leave?"

"Swell."

"Here, too." They shook hands all around.

"Let's-get aboard."

"Suits." They weighed in, had their passes stamped, and were allowed to proceed on up to where the *New Moon* stood upright and ready in the catapult cradle, her mighty wings outstretched. A stewardess showed them to their seats.

At the ten-minute warning Matt announced, "I'm going up for some makee-learnee. Anybody with me?"

"I'm going to sleep," denied Tex.

"Me, too," added Pete. "Nobody ever sleeps in Texas. I'm dead."

Oscar decided to come along. They climbed up to the control room and spoke to the captain. "Cadets Dodson and Jensen, sir—request permission to observe."

"I suppose so," the captain grunted. "Strap down." The pilot room of any licensed ship was open to all members of the Patrol, but the skippers on the Terra-to-Station run were understandably bored with the practice.

Oscar took the inspector's chair; Matt had to use deck pads and straps. His position gave him an excellent view of the co-pilot and mate, waiting at the airplane-type controls. If the rocket motor failed to fire, after catapulting, it would be the mate's business to fight the ship into level flight and bring her down to a deadstick landing on the Colorado prairie.

The captain manned the rocket-type controls. He spoke to the catapult control room, then sounded the siren. Shortly thereafter the ship mounted up the face of the mountain, at a bone-clamping six gravities. The acceleration lasted only ten seconds; then the ship was flung straight up at the sky, leaving the catapult at 1300 miles per hour.

They were in free-fall and climbing. The captain appeared to be taking his time about cutting in the jet; for a moment Matt held to the excited hope that an emergency landing was going to be necessary. But the jet roared on time.

When they had settled in their orbit and the jet was again silent, Matt and Oscar thanked the captain and went back to their proper seats. Tex and Pete were both asleep; Oscar followed suit at once. Matt decided that he must have missed quite a bit in letting himself be talked out of finishing his leave in Texas.

His thoughts went back to the problem he had been considering. Certainly he had not decided to stick simply because his own leave had been fairly quiet; he had never thought of home as being a night club, or a fair ground.

One night at dinner his father had asked him to describe just what it was that the *Nobel* did in circum-Terra patrol. He had tried to oblige. "After we lift from Moon Base we head for Terra on an elliptical orbit. As we approach the Earth we brake gradually and throw her into a tight circular orbit from pole to pole—"

"Why pole to pole? Why not around the equator?"

"Because, you see, the atom-bomb rockets are in pole-to-pole orbits. That's the only way they can cover the whole globe. If they were circling around the equator—"

"I understand that," his father had interrupted, "but your purpose, as I understand it, is to inspect the bomb rockets. If you—your ship—circled around the equator, you could just wait for the bomb rockets to come past."

"*You* may understand it," his mother had said to his father, "but *I* don't."

Matt looked from one to the other, wondering which one to answer—and how. "One at a time . . . please," he protested. "Dad, we can't just intercept the bombs; we have to sneak up on them, match orbits until you are right alongside it and making exactly the same course and speed. Then you bring the bomb inside and ship and inspect it."

"And of what does that inspection consist?"

"Just a sec, Dad. Mother, look here for a moment." Matt took an orange from the table's centerpiece. "The rocket bombs go round and round, like this, from pole-to-pole, every two hours. In the meantime the Earth is turning on its axis, once every twenty-four hours." Matt turned the orange slowly in his left hand while moving a finger of his right hand rapidly around it from top to bottom to simulate a pole-to-pole bomb. "That means that if a bomb passes over Des Moines on this trip, it will just about pass over the Pacific Coast on its next trip. In twenty-four hours it covers the globe."

"Goodness! Matthew, I wish you wouldn't talk about an atom bomb being over Des Moines, even in fun."

"In fun?" Matt had been puzzled. "As a matter of fact . . . let me think; we're about forty-two north and ninety-four west—" He glanced at his watch finger and studied for a few moments. "Jay-three ought to be along in about seven minutes—yes, it will be almost exactly overhead by the time you finish your coffee." Long weeks in the *Nobel*, plotting, calculating, and staring in radarscopes had gotten Matt so that he knew the orbits of circum-Terra prowler rockets a bit better than a farmer's wife knows her own chickens; Jay-three was an individual to him, one with fixed habits.

His mother was looking horrified. She spoke directly to her husband as if she expected him to do something about it. "John. . . . I don't like this. I don't like it, do you hear me? What if it should fall?"

"Nonsense, Catherine—it can't fall."

Matt's younger brother chortled. "Mom doesn't even know what holds the Moon up!"

Matt turned to his brother. "Who pushed your button squirt? Do *you* know what holds the Moon up?"

"Sure—gravity."

"Not exactly. Suppose you give me a quick tell, with diagrams."

The boy tried; his effort was hardly successful. Matt shut him off. "You know somewhat less about astronomy than the ancient Egyptians. Don't make fun of your elders. Now, look, Mother—don't get upset. Jay-three *can't* fall on us. It's in a free orbit that does not intersect the Earth—like smarty-pants here says, it can't fall down any more than the Moon can fall. Anyhow, if the Patrol was to bomb Des Moines tonight, at this time, it wouldn't use Jay-three for the very reason that it *is* overhead. To bomb a city you start with a rocket heading for your target and a couple of thousand miles away, because you have to signal its robot to start the jet and seek the target. You have to slow it down and bend it down. So it wouldn't be Jay-three; it would be—" He thought again. "—Eye-two, or maybe Ache-one." He smiled wryly. "I got bawled out over Eye-two."

"Why?" demanded his brother.

"Matt, I don't think you have picked the right tack to quiet your mother's fears," his father said dryly. "I suggest we not talk about bombing cities."

"But I didn't— Sorry, Father."

"Catherine, there really is nothing to get worked up over —you might just as well be afraid of the local policeman. Matt, you were going to tell me about inspection. Why do the rockets have to be inspected?"

"I want to know why Mattie got bawled out!"

Matt cocked an eyebrow at his brother. "I might as well start by telling him, Dad—it has to do with inspection. Okay, Bill—I made a poor dive when we started to pick it up and had to come back on my suit jet and try again."

"What do you mean, Matthew?"

"He means—"

"Pipe down, Billie. Dad, you send a man out in a suit to insert the trigger guard and attach a line to the rocket so you can bring her inboard of the ship and work on her. I was the man. I made a bad push-off and missed the rocket entirely. She was about a hundred yards away and I guess I misjudged the distance. I turned over and found I was floating on past her. I had to jet back and try again."

His mother still seemed confused, but did not like what she heard. "Matthew! That sounds dangerous to me."

"Safe as houses, Mother. You *can't* fall, any more than the rocket can, or the ship. But it's embarrassing. Anyhow, I finally got a line on her and rode her back into the ship."

"You mean you were *riding* an atom bomb?"

"Shucks, Mother, it's safe—the tamper around the fission material stops most of the radioactivity. Anyhow, the exposure is short."

"But suppose it went off?"

"It can't go off. To go off it has to either crash into the ground with a speed great enough to slap the sub-critical masses together as fast as its trigger-gun could do it, or you have to fire the trigger-gun by radio. Besides that, I had inserted the trigger guard—that's nothing more nor less than a little crowbar, but when it's in place not even a miracle could set it off, because you can't bring the sub-critical masses together."

"Maybe we had better drop this subject, Matt. It seems to make your mother nervous."

"But, Dad, she asked me."

"I know. But you still haven't told me what you inspect for."

"Well, in the first place, you inspect the bomb itself, but there's never anything wrong with the bomb. Anyhow, I haven't had the course for bomb-officer yet—he has to be a nucleonics engineer. You inspect the rocket motor, especially the fuel tanks. Sometimes you have to replace a little that has escaped through relief valves. But mostly you give her a ballistic check and check her control circuits."

"Ballistic check?"

"Of course, theoretically you ought to be able to predict where a prowler bomb would be every instant for the next thousand years. But it doesn't work out that way. Little things, the effect of the tidal bulges and the fact that the Earth is not a perfect uniform sphere and such, cause them to gradually wander a little away from the predicted orbits. After you find one and service it—they're never very far from where they ought to be—you correct the orbit by putting the whole ship in just precisely the proper trajectory and then put the rocket outside the ship again. Then you go after the next one."

"Clear enough. And these corrections have to be made often enough that a ship is kept busy just inspecting them?"

"Well, no, Dad, we inspect oftener than we really have to—but it keeps the ship and the crew busy. Keeps it from getting monotonous. Anyhow, frequent inspections keep you on the safe side."

"Sounds like a waste of taxpayers' money to inspect too often."

"But you don't understand—we're not there to inspect; we're there to *patrol*. The inspection ship is the ship that would deliver an attack in case anybody started acting up. We have to stay on patrol until the next ship relieves us, so we might as well inspect. Granted that you can bomb a city from Moon Base, you can do a better, more accurate job, with less chance of hitting the wrong people, from close by."

His mother was looking very upset. His father raised his eyebrows and said, "We've wandered back to the subject of bombing, Matt."

"I was simply answering your questions, sir."

"I'm afraid I asked the wrong question. Your mother is not able to take the answers impersonally. Catherine, there isn't the slightest chance of the North American Union being bombed. Tell her that, Matt—I think she'll believe you."

Matt had remained silent. His father had insisted, "Go ahead, Matt. Catherine, after all, it's *our* Patrol. For all practical purposes the other nations don't count. A majority of the Patrol officers are from North America. That's true, Matt, isn't it?"

"I've never thought about it. I guess so."

"Very well. Now, Catherine, you can't imagine Matt bombing Des Moines, now can you? And that is what it amounts to. Tell, her, Matt."

"But— Dad, you don't know what you are saying!"

"What? What's that, young man!"

"I—" Matt had looked around him, then had gotten up very suddenly and left the room.

His father came into his room some time later. "Matt?"

"Yes, sir?"

"Look, Matt, I let the conversation get out of hand tonight. I'm sorry and I don't blame you for getting upset. Your mother, you know. I try to protect her. Women get worked up so easily."

"It's all right, Dad. I'm sorry I walked out."

"No matter. Let's forget it. There's just one thing I feel we ought to get straight on. I know that you feel loyal to the Patrol and its ideals and it's good that you should, but—well, you are a little young still to see the political realities involved, but you must know that the Patrol could not bomb the North American Union."

"It would in a show down!"

"But there won't be any show down. Even if there were, you couldn't bomb your own people and neither could your shipmates."

Matt thought about it, fiercely. He remembered Commander Rivera—one of the Four, of the proud Tradition—how Rivera, sent down to reason with the official in his own capital, his very native city, had kept the trust. Suspecting that he might be held as hostage, he had left orders to go ahead with the attack unless he returned in person to cancel the orders. Rivera, whose body was decaying radioactive dust but whose name was mustered whenever a unit of the Patrol called the roll.

His father was still talking. "Of course, the Patrol has to patrol this continent just as it patrols all through the

System. It would look bad, otherwise this is no reason to frighten women with an impossibility."

"I'd rather not talk about it, Dad."

Matt glanced at his watch and figured how long it would be until the *New Moon* reached Terra Station. He wished he could sleep, like the others. He was sure now what it was that had changed his mind about resigning and remaining in Des Moines. It was not a desire to emulate Rivera. No, it was an accumulation of things—all of them adding up to just one idea, that little Mattie didn't live there any more!

For the first few weeks after leave, Matt was too busy to fret. He had to get back into the treadmill, with more studying to do and less time to do it in. He was on the watch list for cadet officer of the watch now, and had more laboratory periods in electronics and nucleonics as well. Besides this he shared with other oldsters the responsibility for bringing up the youngster cadets. Before leave his evenings had usually been free for study, now he coached youngsters in astrogation three nights a week.

He was beginning to think that he would have to give up space polo, when he found himself elected captain of the Hog Alley team. Then he was busier than ever. He hardly thought about abstract problems until his next session with Lieutenant Wong.

"Good afternoon," his coach greeted him. "How's your class in astrogation?"

"Oh, that— It seems funny to be teaching it instead of flunking it."

"That's why you're stuck with it—you still remember what it was that used to stump you and why. How about atomics?"

"Well . . . I suppose I'll get by, but I'll never be an Einstein."

"I'd be amazed if you were. How are you getting along otherwise?" Wong waited.

"All right, I guess. Do you know, Mr. Wong—when I went on leave I didn't intend to come back."

"I rather thought so. That space-marines notion was just your way of dodging around, trying to avoid your real problem."

"Oh. Say, Mr. Wong—tell me straight. Are you a regular Patrol officer, or a psychiatrist?"

Wong almost grinned. "I'm a regular Patrol officer, Matt, but I've had the special training required for this job."

"Uh, I see. What was it I was running away from?"

"I don't know. You tell me."

"I don't know where to start."

"Tell me about your leave, then. We've got all afternoon."

"Yes, sir." Matt meandered along, telling as much as he could remember. "So you see," he concluded, "it was a lot of little things. I was home—but I was a stranger. We didn't talk the same language."

Wong chuckled. "I'm not laughing at you," he apologized. "It isn't funny. We all go through it—the discovery that there's no way to go back. It's part of growing up—but with spacemen it's an especially acute and savage process."

Matt nodded. "I'd already gotten that through my thick head. Whatever happens I won't go back—not to stay. I might go into the merchant service, but I'll stay in space."

"You're not likely to flunk out at this stage, Matt."

"Maybe not, but I don't know yet that the Patrol is the place for me. That's what bothers me."

"Well . . . can you tell me about it?"

Matt tried. He related the conversation with his father and his mother that had gotten them all upset. "It's this: if it comes to a show down, I'm expected to bomb my own home town. I'm not sure it's in me to do it. Maybe I don't belong here."

"Not likely to come up, Matt. Your father was right there."

"That's not the point. If a Patrol officer is loyal to his oath only when it's no skin off his own nose, then the whole system breaks down."

Wong waited before replying. "If the prospect of bomb-

ing your own town, your own family, didn't worry you,
I'd have you out of this ship within the hour—you'd be an
utterly dangerous man. The Patrol doesn't expect a man to
have godlike perfection. Since men are imperfect, the Patrol works on the principle of calculated risk. The chance
of a threat to the System coming from your home town
in your lifetime is slight; the chance that you might be
called on to carry out the attack is equally slight—you might
be away on Mars. Taking the two chances together you
have something close to zero.

"But if you did hit the jackpot, your commanding officer would probably lock you up in your room rather than
take a chance on you."

Matt still looked troubled. "Not satisfied?" Wong went
on. "Matt, you are suffering from a disease of youth—you
expect moral problems to have nice, neat, black-and-white
answers. Suppose you relax and let *me* worry about whether or not you have what it takes. Oh, some day you'll be
caught in a squeeze and no one around to tell you the
right answer. But *I* have to decide whether or not *you*
can get the right answer when the problem comes along—
and I don't even know what your problem will be! How
would you like to be in my boots?"

Matt grinned sheepishly. "I wouldn't like it."

XI

P.R.S. *AES TRIPLEX*

OSCAR, MATT, AND TEX were gathered in their common
room just before lunch when Pete bounced in. Literally
so—he caromed off the door frame and zipped into the
room, shouting, "Hey, fellows!"

Oscar grabbed his arms as he rebounded from the inner wall. "Cut your jet and ground—what's the excitement?"

Peter turned in the air and faced them. "The new 'Passed' list is posted!"

"Who's on it?"

"Don't know—just heard about it. Come on!"

They streamed after him. Tex came abreast of Matt and said, "I don't know why I should be getting in a sweat—*I* won't be on it."

"Pessimist!" They turned out of Hog Alley, went inboard three decks, and forward. There was a clot of cadets gathered around the bulletin board outside the watch office. They crowded in.

Pete spotted his own name at once. "Look!" The paragraph read: "Armand, Pierre—temporary duty P.R.S. *Charles' Wain,* rpt. Terr.St., dtch. Leda, Gnymd, d.&a.o."

"Look!" he repeated. *"I'm going home—*'delay and await orders.' "

Oscar patted his shoulder. "Congratulations, Pete—that's swell. Now if you will kindly get your carcass out of the way—"

Matt spoke up. "I'm on it!"

"What ship?" asked Tex.

"The *Aes Triplex.*"

Oscar turned at this. *"What* ship?"

"Aes Triplex."

"Matt—that's *my* ship. We're shipmates, boy!"

Tex turned disconsolately away. "Just as I said—no 'Jarman.' I'll be here five years, ten years, fifteen years—old and grizzled. Promise to write on my birthday."

"Gee, Tex, I'm sorry!" Matt tried to swallow his own elation.

"Tex, did you look on the other half of the list?" Pete wanted to know.

"What other half? Huh?"

Pete pointed. Tex dove back into the swarm; presently he reappeared. "What do you know? They passed me!"

"Probably didn't want to expose another class of youngsters to you. What ship?"

"P.R.S. *Oak Ridge*. Say, you and Oscar got the same ship?"

"Yep—the *Aes Triplex*."

"Rank discrimination, that's what it is. Well, come on, we'll be late to lunch."

They ran into Girard Burke in the passageway. Tex stopped him. "No use bothering to look, Stinky. Your name's not on the list."

"What list? Oh, you mean the 'Passed' list. Don't bother me, children—you're talking to a free man."

"So they finally bounced you?"

"Like fun! Resignation accepted, effective today. I'm going in business with my father."

"Going to build sky junk, eh? I don't envy you."

"No, we're starting an export line, with our own ships. The next time you see me, just remember to address me as 'Captain.' " He moved away.

"I'll 'captain' him," Tex muttered. "I'll bet he resigned by request."

"Maybe not," conceded Matt. "Girard is a smooth character. Well, we've seen the last of him."

"And a good thing, too."

Tex was missing after lunch. He showed up after nearly two hours. "I worked it. Shake hands with your new shipmate."

"Huh? No fooling!"

"Fact. First I located Dvorak and convinced him that he would rather have a ship in the circum-Terra patrol than the *Aes Triplex*—so he could see his girl oftener. Then I went to see the Commandant and pointed out to him that you guys were used to having the benefit of my advice and would be lost without it. That's all there was to it. The Commandant saw the wisdom of my words and approved the swap with Dvorak."

"Not for that reason, I'll bet," Matt answered. "Probably he wanted me to continue to look out for you."

Tex took on an odd look. "Do you know, Matt, you aren't so far wrong."

"Really? I was just kidding."

"What he did say was that he thought Cadet Jensen would be a good influence on me. What do you think of that, Oscar?"

Oscar snorted. "If I've reached the place where I'm a good influence on anybody, it's time I cultivated some new vices."

"I'd be glad to help."

"I don't want you, I want your Uncle Bodie—there's a man of the world."

Three weeks later, at Moon Base, Oscar and Matt were settling into their stateroom in the *Aes Triplex*. Matt was not feeling his best; the previous evening at Tycho Colony had been late and noisy. They had taken the last possible shuttle to Moon Base.

The ship's phone in their room sounded; Matt answered it to get the squeal out of his ears. "Yes? Cadet Dodson speaking—"

"Officer of the watch. Is Jensen there too?"

"Yes, sir."

"Both of you report to the Captain."

"Aye aye, sir." Matt turned a troubled face to Oscar. "What'll I do, Oz? The rest of my uniforms are over at the base tailor shop—and this one I've got on looks as if I had slept in it."

"You did. Wear one of mine."

"Thanks, but it would fit me like socks on a rooster. Do you suppose I have time to run over and pick up my clean ones?"

"Hardly!"

Matt rubbed the stubble on his chin. "I ought to shave, anyhow."

"Look," said Oscar, "if I'm any judge of skippers, you'll do better to show up naked as an oyster and with a beard down to here, than to keep him waiting. Let's get going."

The door opened and Tex stuck his head in. "Say—did you guys get a call to report to the Old Man?"

"Yes—Tex, can you lend me a clean uniform?"

Tex could. Matt crossed the passageway to Tex's tiny

room and changed. He belted in tightly at the waist, distributed the wrinkles in back, and hoped for the best. The three headed for the cabin.

"I'm glad I don't have to report by myself," Tex announced. "I'm nervous."

"Relax," Oscar advised. "Captain McAndrews is supposed to be a very human sort of a guy."

"Hadn't you heard? McAndrews is detached—busted his ankle. At the last minute the Department ordered Captain Yancey to command the expedition."

"Yancey!" Oscar let out a low whistle. "Oh, my sore feet!"

"What's the matter, Oscar?" Matt demanded. "You know him?"

"My father knew him. Father had the fresh-foods contract for the port at New Auckland when Yancey—Lieutenant Yancey, then—was portmaster." They stopped outside the commanding officer's cabin.

"That ought to give you an inside track."

"Not likely! They didn't get along."

"I wonder if I did right," Tex mused darkly, "when I wangled the swap from the *Oak Ridge?*"

"Too late to fret. Well, I guess we might—" Oscar stopped speaking, for the door in front of them suddenly opened and they found themselves facing the commanding officer. He was tall, wide-shouldered, and flat-hipped, and so handsome that he looked like a television star playing a Patrol officer.

"Well?" he snapped. "Don't stand chatting outside my door. Come in!"

They filed in silently. Captain Yancey sat down, facing them, and looked them over, one after the other. "What's the trouble, gentlemen?" he said presently. "Are you all struck dumb?"

Tex found his voice. "Cadet Jarman, sir, reporting to the Captain." Yancey's eyes flicked over to Matt.

Matt wet his lips. "Cadet Dodson, sir."

"Cadet Jensen, sir, reporting as ordered." The officer looked at Oscar sharply, then spoke to him in Venerian.

"Do these ears detect some echo of the speech of the Fair Planet?"

"It is true, thou old and wise one."

"Never could stand that silly talk," Yancey commented, relapsing into Basic. "I won't ask you where you are from, but—is your father in the provisions racket?"

"My father is a food wholesaler, sir."

"I thought so." The Captain continued to look at him for a moment, then turned to Matt. "Now, Mister, what is the idea of the masquerade? You look like a refugee from an emigrant ship."

Matt tried to explain; Yancey cut him short. "I'm not interested in excuses. I keep a taut ship. Remember that."

"Aye aye, sir."

The Captain settled back and struck a cigarette. "Now, gentlemen, you are no doubt wondering as to why I sent for you. I must admit to a slight curiosity as to the sort of product the old school is turning out. In my day, it was a real course of sprouts and no nonsense about it. But now I understand that the psychologists have taken over and the old rules are all changed."

He leaned forward and fixed Matt with his eyes. "They aren't changed here, gentlemen. In my ship, the old rules still obtain."

No one answered. Yancey waited, then went on, "The regulations state that you shall pay a social call on your commanding officer within twenty-four hours after reporting to a new ship or station. Please consider that the social call has commenced. Sit down, gentlemen. Mr. Dodson, you will find coffee over there on your left. Will you please favor me by pouring it?"

Forty minutes later they left, feeling quite confused. Yancey had demonstrated that he could put them most charmingly at their ease and had displayed a dry, warm wit and a gift for telling anecdotes. Matt decided that he liked him.

But just as they left Yancey glanced at his clock and said, "I'll see you later, Mr. Dodson—in fifteen minutes."

Once they were outside Tex demanded, "What's he want to see you for, Matt?"

"Can't you guess?" answered Oscar. "Look, Matt, I'll tear over to the tailor shop for you—you can't do that and shave, too, not in fifteen minutes."

"You're a lifesaver, Oz!"

P.R.S. *Aes Triplex* blasted from Moon Base thirteen hours later in a trajectory intended to produce an elliptical orbit with its far end in the asteroid belt. Her orders were to search for the missing P.R.S. *Pathfinder*. The *Pathfinder* had been engaged in radar-charting a sector of the asteroid belt for the Uranographic Office of the Patrol. Her mission had taken her beyond the range of ship-type radio; nevertheless she should have reported in by radio nearly six months earlier, at which time she should have been approaching conjunction with Mars. But Deimos Station, around Mars, had been unable to raise the *Pathfinder;* she was presumed lost.

The possible locations of the *Pathfinder* were a moving zone in space, defined by using geometry, ballistics, the characteristics of the ship, her mission, and her last reported location, course, and speed. This zone was divided into four sectors and the *Aes Triplex* was to search one sector while three other Patrol vessels covered the other sectors. The joint task was designated "Operation Samaritan" but each ship was independent as they necessarily would be too far apart to be commanded as a task force.

While searching, the rescue vessels would continue the *Pathfinder's* mission of charting the space drift that clutters the asteroid belt.

In addition to the commanding officer and the three cadets, the company of the *Aes Triplex* included Commander Hartley Miller, executive officer and astrogator, Lieutenant Novak, Chief Engineer, Lieutenant Thurlow, Bomb Officer, Lieutenant Brunn, Communications Officer, Sublieutenants Peters, Gomez, and Cleary, assistant engineer and communications watch officers respectively, and

Dr. Pickering, ship's surgeon, along to care for survivors—if any were found.

The ship contained no marines, unless one chooses to count Dr. Pickering, who was technically a staff corps member of the marines rather than a member of the Patrol. Every task in the ship would be performed by the officers or cadets. Time was when the lowliest subaltern in an infantry regiment had his personal servant, but servants are too expensive a luxury in terms of fuel and space and food to lift through millions of miles of space. Besides that, some few manual tasks are a welcome relief from boredom in the endless monotony of space; even the undesirable chore of cleaning the refresher was taken in turn by the entire ship's company, in accordance with custom, except for the Captain, the Executive Officer, and the Surgeon.

Captain Yancey assigned Lieutenant Thurlow as training officer who in turn set up the jobs of assistant astrogator, junior communication watch officer, junior assistant engineer, and assistant bomb officer and arranged a schedule of rotation among these—quite unnecessary—positions. It was also Mr. Thurlow's job to see to it that Matt, Oscar, and Tex made intensive use of the one study projector available to the cadets.

The Executive Officer assigned other tasks not directly concerned with formal training. Matt was appointed the ship's "farmer." As the hydroponics tanks supply both fresh air and green vegetables to a ship he was responsible for the ship's air-conditioning and shared with Lieutenant Brunn the tasks of the ship's mess.

Theoretically every ration taken aboard a Patrol vessel is pre-cooked and ready for eating as soon as it is taken out of freeze and subjected to the number of seconds, plainly marked on the package, of high-frequency heating required. Actually many Patrol officers fancy themselves as chefs. Mr. Brunn was one and his results justified his conceit—the *Aes Triplex* set a good table.

Matt found that Mr. Brunn expected more of the "farm" than that the green plants should scavenge carbon dioxide from the air and replace it with oxygen; the mess officer wanted tiny green scallions, fragrant fresh mint, cherry tomatoes, Brussels sprouts, new potatoes. Matt began to wonder whether it wouldn't have been simpler to have stayed in Iowa and grown tall corn.

When he started in as air-conditioning officer Matt was not even sure how to take a carbon-dioxide count, but shortly he was testing his growing solutions and adding capsules of salts with the confidence and speed of a veteran, thanks to Brunn and to spool #62A8134 from the ship's files—"Simplified Hydroponics for Spaceships, with Growth Charts and Additives Formulae." He began to enjoy tending his "farm."

Until human beings give up the habit of eating, spaceships on long cruises must carry about seven hundred pounds of food per man per year. The green plants grown in a ship's air-conditioner enable the stores officer to get around this limitation to some extent, as the growing plants will cycle the same raw materials—air, carbon dioxide, and water—over and over again with only the addition of quite small quantities of such salts as potassium nitrate, iron sulphate, and calcium phosphate.

The balanced economy of a spaceship is much like that of a planet; energy is used to make the cycles work but the same raw materials are used over and over again. Since beefsteak and many other foods can't be grown conveniently aboard ship some foods have to be carried and the ship tends to collect garbage, waste paper, and other trash. Theoretically this could be processed back into the cycles of balanced biological economy, but in practice this is too complicated.

However, *all* mass in an atomic powered ship can be used, if desired, as reaction mass, mass for the rocket jet. The radioactive materials in the power pile of an atom-powered ship are not themselves used up to any great extent; instead they heat other materials to extreme temperatures and expel them out the rocket tube at very high speeds, as a sort of "steam" jet.

Even though turnip greens and such can be used in the jet, the primary purpose of the "farm" is to take the carbon dioxide out of the air. For this purpose each man in the ship must be balanced by about ten square feet of green plant leaf. Lieutenant Brunn, with his steady demands for variety in fresh foods, usually caused Matt to have too much growing at one time; the air in the ship would get too fresh and the plants would start to fail for lack of carbon dioxide to feed on. Matt had to watch his CO_2 count and sometimes build it up by burning waste paper or plant cuttings.

Brunn kept a file of seeds in his room; Matt went there one "day" (ship's time) to draw out Persian melon seeds and set a crop. Brun told him to help himself. Matt rummaged away, then said, "For the love of Pete! Look at this, Mr. Brunn."

"Huh?" The officer looked at the package Matt held. The outside was marked, "Seeds, melon, Persian—jumbo fancy, stock #12-Q4728-a"; the envelope inside read "Seed, pansies, giant variegated."

Brunn shook his head. "Let that be a lesson, Dodson—never trust a stock clerk—or you'll wind up half way to Pluto with a gross of brass spittoons when you ordered blank spacecharts."

"What'll I substitute? Cantaloupe?"

"Let's grow some watermelon—the Old Man likes watermelon."

Matt left with watermelon seed but he took along the truant pansy seeds.

Eight weeks later he devised a vase of sorts by covering a bowl from the galley with the same sponge-cellulose sheet which was used to restrain the solutions used in his farming, thereby to keep said solutions from floating around the "farm" compartment during free fall. He filled his vase with water, arranged his latest crop therein, and clipped the whole to the mess table as a centerpiece.

Captain Yancey smiled broadly when he appeared for dinner and saw the gay display of pansies. "Well, gentlemen," he applauded, "this is most delightful. All the comforts of home!" He looked along the table at Matt. "I suppose we have you to thank for this, Mr. Dodson?"

"Yes, sir." Matt's ears turned pink.

"A lovely idea. Gentlemen, I move that we divest Mr. Dodson of the plebeian title of 'farmer' and designate him 'horticulturalist extraordinary.' Do I hear a second?" There were nine "ayes" and a loud "no" from Commander Miller. A second ballot, proposed by the Chief Engineer, required the Executive Officer to finish his meal in the galley.

Lieutenant Brunn explained the mishap that resulted in the flower garden. Captain Yancey frowned. "You've checked the rest of your supply of seeds, of course, Mr. Brunn?"

"Uh, no, sir."

"Then do so." Lieutenant Brunn immediately started to leave the table. "—after dinner," added the Captain. Brunn resumed his place.

"That puts me in mind of something that happened to me when I was 'farmer' in the old *Percival Lowell*—the one before the present one," Yancey went on. "We had touched at Venus South Pole and had managed somehow to get a virus infection, a sort of rust, into the 'farm'—don't look so superior, Mr. Jensen; someday you'll come a cropper with a planet that is new to you!"

"Me, sir? I wasn't looking superior."

"No? Smiling at the pansies, no doubt?"

"Yes, sir."

"Hmmph! As I was saying, we got this rust infection and about ten days out I didn't have any more farm than an Eskimo. I cleaned the place out, sterilized, and reseeded. Same story. The infection was all through the ship and I couldn't chase it down. We finished that trip on preserved foods and short rations and I wasn't allowed to eat at the table the rest of the trip." He smiled to himself, then shouted at the galley door, "How you getting along in there, Red?"

The Executive Officer appeared in the doorway, a spoon in one hand, covered dish in the other. "Fine," he answered in a muffled voice, "I just ate your dessert, Captain."

Lieutenant Brunn shouted, "Hey! Commander! Stop! Don't! Those berries are for breakfast."

136

"Too late." Commander Miller wiped his mouth.

"Captain?"

"Yes, Dodson?"

"What did you do about air-conditioning?"

"Well. Mister, what would you have done?"

Matt studied it. "Well, sir, I would have jury-rigged something to take the Cee-Oh-Two out of the air."

"Precisely. I exhausted the air from an empty compartment, suited up, and drilled a couple of holes to the outside. Then I did a piping job to carry foul air out of the dark side of the ship in a fractional still arrangement—freeze out the water first, then freeze out the carbon dioxide. Pesky thing was always freezing up solid and forcing me to tinker with it. But it worked well enough to get us home." Yancey backed away from the table. "Hartley, if you're through making a pig of yourself, let's run over that meteor-layout. I've got an idea."

The ship was approaching the orbit of Mars and soon would be in the comparatively hazardous zone of the asteroids and their company of space drift. Matt was rotated, in turn, to assistant astrogator, but continued as ship's farmer. Tex looked him up one day in the hydroponics compartment. "Hey! Hayseed—"

"Hey yourself, Tex."

"Got the south forty plowed yet? Looks like rain." Tex pretended to study the blinking lights used to stimulate plant growth, then looked away. "Never mind—I'm here on business. The Old Man wants to see you."

"Well, for heaven's sake, why didn't you say so, instead of banging your choppers?" Matt stopped what he was doing and hurriedly started climbing into his uniform. Because of the heat and the humidity in the "farm" Matt habitually worked there bare naked, both for comfort and to save his clothes.

"Well, I did tell you, didn't I?"

The Captain was in his cabin. "Cadet Dodson, sir."

"So I see." Yancey held up a sheet of paper. "Dodson, I've just written a letter to the Department, to be transmitted as soon as we are in radio contact, recommending that fresh flowers be grown in all ships, as a means of stimulating morale. You are credited therein as the originator of the idea."

"Er . . . thank you, sir."

"Not at all. Anything that relieves the tedium, the boredom, the barrenness of life in deep space is in the interest of the Patrol. We have enough people going space-happy as it is. Flowers are considered good for psychotics on Earth; perhaps they will help to keep spacemen from going wacky. Enough of that—I've a question to ask you."

"Yes, sir?"

"I want to know why in the devil you were spending your time growing pansies when you are behind in your study schedule?"

Matt did not have anything to say.

"I've been looking over the reports Mr. Thurlow sends me and I find that both Mr. Jensen and Mr. Jarman are covering more ground than you are. In the past few weeks they have pulled 'way ahead of you. It's a fine thing to have hobbies but your duty is to study."

"Yes, sir."

"I've marked your performance unsatisfactory for this quarter; you have the next quarter in which to make up the deficiency. By the way, have you made up your mind about your next move?"

Matt did a double-take, then realized that the Captain had changed the subject to chess; he and Matt were fighting it out for first place in the ship's tournament. "Uh, yes, sir—I've decided to take your pawn."

"I thought so." Yancey reached behind him; Matt heard the pieces click into their sockets as the Captain made the move on his own board. "Wait till you see what's going to happen to your queen!"

The speeds of the asteroids, flying boulders, rocks, sand, and space drift that infest the area between Mars and Jupiter vary from about fifteen miles per second near Mars to about eight miles per second near Jupiter. The orbits of this flying junkyard are erratically inclined to the plane of the ecliptic an average of about nine degrees and some of the orbits are quite eccentric as well.

All this means that a ship on a circular orbit, headed "east," or with the traffic, may expect the possibility of side-swiping collisions at relative speeds averaging two miles per second, with crashes remotely possible at double that speed.

Two miles per second is only about twice the muzzle velocity of a good sporting rifle. With respect to small stuff, sand and gravel, the *Aes Triplex* was built to take it. Before the ship reached the danger zone, an all-hands chore in space suits took place; armor-plate segments, as thick as the skin of the ship, were bolted over the ship's quartz ports, leaving only the eyes of the astrogational instruments and the radar antennae exposed.

To guard against larger stuff Captain Yancey set up a meteor-watch much tighter than is usual in most parts of space. Eight radars scanned all space through a global 360°. The only condition necessary for collision is that the other object hold a steady bearing—no fancy calculation is involved. The only action necessary then to avoid collision is to change your own speed, any direction, any amount. This is perhaps the only case where theory of piloting is simple.

Commander Miller put the cadets and the sublieutenants on a continuous heel-and-toe watch, scanning the meteor-guard 'scopes. Even if the human being failed to note a steady bearing the radars would "see" it, for they were so rigged that, if a "blip" burned in at one spot on the screen, thereby showing a steady bearing, an alarm would sound—and the watch officer would cut in the jet, fast!

However, even the asteroid belt is very empty space indeed; the chances were strongly against collision with anything larger than a grain of sand. The only difference in the *Aes Triplex,* aside from the increased work for the junior officers, was a ship's order directing all hands to strap down when sleeping, instead of floating loosely and comfortably about, so that the sleeper would not break his neck in case of sudden acceleration.

P.R.S. *Aes Triplex* was equipped with two jeeps, nestled in hangar pockets—quite ordinary short-range, chemically-powered rockets except that they were equipped with search radar as powerful as the ship's. When they reached their search area a pilot and co-pilot were assigned to each jeep—and a second crew also, as each rocket was to remain away from the ship a week at a time, then swap crews and go out again.

Lieutenants Brunn, Thurlow, and Novak, and Sublieutenant Peters were designated pilots. A cadet was assigned to each senior lieutenant and Sublieutenant Gomez was teamed with Sublieutenant Peters. Matt drew Lieutenant Thurlow.

Dr. Pickering took over the mess. That left Sublieutenant Cleary as "George," the man who does everything—an impossibility, since meteor-guard and search watches would have to be kept up. Consequently the two jeep crews not actually in space had to help out even during their week of rest.

Each Monday the ship placed the jeep rockets on station so that the three vessels would sweep the largest possible volume of space, with their search fields barely overlapping. The placement was made by the mother ship, so that the jeep would be left with full tanks in the unhappy event that she was not picked up—and thereby have enough fuel to shape an orbit toward the inner planets, if need be.

XII

P.R.S. *PATHFINDER*

MATT TOOK ALONG a supply of study spools on his first week of search intending to play them on the jeep's tiny, earphones-type viewer. He did not get much chance; four hours out of eight he had to keep his eyes glued to the search scopes. During the four hours off watch he had to sleep, eat, attend to chores, and study, if possible.

Besides that, Lieutenant Thurlow liked to talk.

The bomb officer was expecting Earth-side duty in post-graduate study at the end of the cruise. "And then I'll have to make up my mind, Matt. Do I stay in and make physics a part-time specialty, or resign and go in for research?"

"It depends on what you want to do."

"Trite but true. I think I want to be a scientist, full time—but after a few years the Patrol becomes a father and a mother to you. I don't know. That pile of rock is creeping up on us—I can see it through the port now."

"It is, eh?" Matt moved forward until he, too, could see the undersized boulder that Thurlow had been watching by radar. It was of irregular shape, a pattern of sunlight and sharp, dark shadow.

"Mister Thurlow," said Matt, "look—about the middle. Doesn't that look like striation to you?"

"Could be. Some specimens have been picked up that were definitely sedimentary rock. That was the first proof that the asteroids used to be a planet, you know."

"I thought that Goodman's integrations were the first proof?"

"Nope, you're switched around. Goodman wasn't able to run his checks until the big ballistic computer at Terra Station was built."

"I knew that—I just had it backwards, I guess." The theory that the asteroids had once been a planet, between Mars and Jupiter, was denied for many years because their orbits showed no interrelation, i.e., if a planet had blown to bits the orbits should intersect at the point of the explosion. Professor Goodman, using the giant, strain-free computer, had shown that the lack of relationship was caused by the perturbations through the ages of the other planets acting on the asteroids.

He had assigned a date to the disaster, nearly half a billion years ago, and had calculated as well that most of the ruined planet had escaped from the System entirely. The debris around them represented about one per cent of the lost planet.

Lieutenant Thurlow measured the angular width of the fragment, noted its distance by radar, and recorded the result as gross size. The rock, large as it was, was too small to merit investigation of its orbit; it was simply included in the space-drift survey. Smaller objects were merely listed while collisions with minute particles were counted by an electronic circuit hooked to the hull of the jeep.

"The thing that bothers me," went on Thurlow, "about getting out is this— Matt, have you noticed the difference between people in the Patrol and people not in the Patrol?"

"Haven't I, though!"

"What is the difference?"

"The difference? Uh, why, we're spacemen and they're not. I guess it's a matter of how big your world is."

"Partly. But don't get carried away by mere size. A hundred million miles of empty space isn't significant—if it's empty. No, Matt, the split goes deeper. We've given the human race a hundred years of peace, and now there is no one left who remembers war. They've come to accept peace and comfort as the normal way of life. But it isn't. The human animal has millions of years of danger and starving and death behind him; the past century is just a flicker of an eyelash in his history. But only the Patrol seems aware of it."

"Would you abolish the Patrol?"

"Oh, my, no, Matt! But I wish there were some way to make people realize by how thin a barrier the jungle has been shut out. And another thing, too—" Thurlow grinned sheepishly. "—I wish they had some understanding of what we are. The taxpayer's hired man, that's what they think of us."

Matt nodded. "They think we're some sort of traffic cop. There is a man back home who sells used copters—asked me why Patrolmen should be pensioned when they retire. He said that he hadn't been able to sit back and take it easy at thirty-five and he didn't see why he should have to support somebody else who did." Matt looked puzzled. "At the same time he sort of glamorized the Patrol—wants his son to be a cadet. I don't understand it."

"That's it. To them we are a kind of expensive, useless prize pet—their property. They don't understand that we are not for hire. The sort of guardian you can hire is worth about as much as the sort of wife you can buy."

The following week Matt found time to look up what the ship's library afforded on the subject of the exploded planet. There was not much—dry statistics on sizes of asteroids, fragments, and particles, distributional and orbital data, Goodman's calculations summarized. Nothing at all about what he wanted to know—how it happened!—nothing but some fine-spun theories.

He took it up with Thurlow the next time they were out on Patrol. The lieutenant shrugged. "What do you expect, Matt?"

"I don't know, but more than I found."

"Our time scale is all wrong for us to learn much. Suppose you pick out one of the spools you've been studying—here, this one." The officer held out one marked "Social structures of the Martian aborigines." "Now suppose you examine a couple of frames in the middle. Can you reconstruct the thousands and thousands of frames that come before it, just by logic?"

"Naturally not."

"That's the situation. If the race manages to keep from blowing its top for a few million years, maybe we'll begin to find out some things. So far, we don't even know what questions to ask."

Matt was dissatisfied, but had no answer ready. Thurlow knit his brows. "Maybe we aren't built to ask the right questions. You know the Martian 'double-world' idea—"

"Certainly, but I don't understand it."

"Who does? Let's forget the usual assumption that a Martian is talking in religious symbols when he says that we live just on 'one side' while he lives on 'both sides.' Suppose that what he means is as real as butter and eggs, that he really does live in two worlds at the same time and

143

that we are in the one he regards as unimportant. If you accept that, then it accounts for the Martian being unwilling to waste time talking with us, or trying to explain things to us. He isn't being stuffy, he's being reasonable. Would you waste time trying to explain rainbows to an earthworm?"

"The cases aren't parallel."

"Maybe they are to a Martian. An earthworm can't even see, much less have a color sense. If you accept the 'double world' as real, then to a Martian we just don't have the proper senses to be able to ask the right questions. Why bother with us?"

The radio squealed for attention. Thurlow glanced toward it and said, "Someone calling, Matt. See who it is and tell 'em we don't want any."

"Okay." Matt flipped the switch and answered, "Jeep One, *Triplex*—go ahead."

"*Triplex* calling," came Sublieutenant Cleary's familiar voice. "Stand by to be picked up."

"Huh? Cut the comedy—we're only three days out."

"Stand by to be picked up—official. Jeep Two has found the *Pathfinder*."

"The deuce you say! Did you hear that, Mr. Thurlow? Did you hear that?"

It was true; Peters and Gomez, in the other jeep, had discovered the missing ship, almost by accident. The *Pathfinder* was found anchored to a smallish asteroid about a mile in greatest dimension. Since it was a listed body, 1987-CD, the crew of the jeep had paid little attention to it, until its rotation brought the *Pathfinder* into view.

With fine consideration Captain Yancey had elected to pick up Thurlow and Dodson before rendezvousing with the second jeep. Once they were inside, the *Aes Triplex* moved toward 1987-CD and matched orbits. Sublieutenant Peters had elected to expend some of his get-away fuel and had matched orbits also.

Matt fidgeted while the second jeep was brought into the ship. He could see nothing, since the ports were covered, and for the moment had no assigned duties. With maddening deliberation Captain Yancey secured his ship to the *Pathfinder,* sending a line over by Sublieutenant Gomez. The rest of the ship's company was crowded into the control room. Tex and Matt took the opportunity to question Sublieutenant Peters.

"Couldn't tell much," he informed them. "Off hand, she looks undamaged, but the door of the lock was standing open."

"Any chance anyone is alive inside?" asked Tex.

"Possible. Hardly likely."

Captain Yancey looked around. "Pipe down," he ordered. "This is a control room, not a sewing circle." When he had finished he ordered Peters and Gomez to come with him; the three suited up and left the ship.

They were gone about an hour. When they returned the Captain called them all into the mess room. "I am sorry to tell you, gentlemen, that none of our comrades is alive."

He went on heavily, "There is not much doubt as to what happened. The outer armored door of the lock was open and undamaged. The inner door had been punched through by a missile about the size of my fist, producing explosive decompression in the connecting compartments. Apparently they had had the enormous bad luck to have a meteor enter the ship through the door just as it was opened."

"Wait a minute, Skipper," objected Miller. "Was every airtight door in the ship wide open? One rock shouldn't have done the trick."

"We couldn't get into the after part of the ship; it still holds pressure. But we could reconstruct what happened, because we could count the bodies—seven of them, the entire ship's company. They were all near the lock and not in spacesuits, except for one man in the lock—his suit was pierced by a fragment apparently. The others seem to have been gathered at the lock, waiting for him to come in." Yancey looked grave. "Red, I think we are going to have to put in a recommended technical order over this— something to require personnel to spread out while suit operations are going on, so that an accident to the lock won't affect the entire ship's company."

Miller frowned. "I suppose so, Captain. Might be awkward to comply with, sometimes, in a small ship."

"It's awkward to lose your breath, too. Now about the investigation—you'll be the president, Red, and Novak and Brunn will be your other two members. The rest of us will remain in the ship until the board has completed its work. When they have finished and have removed from the *Pathfinder* anything needed as evidence I will allow sufficient time for each of you to satisfy his curiosity."

"How about the surgeon, Captain? I want him for an expert witness."

"Okay, Red. Dr. Pickering, you go with the board."

The cadets crowded into the stateroom shared by Matt and Oscar. "Can you beat it?" said Tex. "Of all the cheap tricks! We have to sit in here, a week or ten days, maybe, while a board measures how big a hole there is in the door."

"Forget it, Tex," advised Oscar. "I figure the Old Man didn't want you carving your initials in things, or maybe snagging the busted door for a souvenir, before they found out what the score was."

"Oh, nuts!"

"Quit crabbing. He promised you that you could snoop around and take pictures and satisfy your ghoulish appetites as soon as the board is finished. In the meantime, enjoy the luxury of eight hours of sleep for a change. No watches, none of any sort."

"Say, that's right!" agreed Matt. "I hadn't thought about it, but there's no point in watching for rocks when you're tied down and can't duck."

"As the crew of the *Pathfinder* know only too well."

Last Muster was held for the *Pathfinder* on the following day. The bodies themselves had been sealed into a compartment of the dead ship; muster took place in the wardroom of the *Aes Triplex*. It was rather lengthy, as it was necessary to read the services of three different

146

faiths before the Captain concluded with the Patrol's own all-inclusive farewell: *"Now we shape our orbit home—"*

It so happened that there were just enough persons present to answer the roll. The *Aes Triplex*'s company was a captain and eleven others. For the *Pathfinder* there were exactly eleven—six patrol officers, one civilian planetologist, and the Four who are present at every muster. Captain Yancey called off the *Pathfinder*'s roll and the others answered, one after the other, from Commander Miller down to Tex—while *The Long Watch,* muted down to a requiem, played softly over the ship's speaker system.

Matt found his throat almost too dry to answer. Tex's chubby cheeks ran with tears and he made no effort to wipe them.

Lieutenant Brunn was a source of information for the first couple of days of the investigation. He described the *Pathfinder* as in good shape, except for the damaged door. On the third day he suddenly shut up. "The Captain doesn't want the board's findings discussed until he has had time to study them."

Matt passed the word on to the others. "What's cooking?" demanded Tex. "What can there possibly be to be secret about?"

"How should I know?"

"I've got a theory," said Oscar.

"Huh? What? Spill it."

"The Captain wants to prove a man can't die of curiosity. He figures that you are a perfect test case."

"Oh, go soak your head."

Captain Yancey called them all together again the following day. "Gentlemen, I appreciate your patience. I have not wanted to discuss what was found in the *Pathfinder* until I had time to decide what should be done about it. It comes to this: the planetologist with the *Pathfinder*, Professor Thorwald, came to the unmistakable conclusion that the disrupted planet was inhabited."

The room started to buzz. "Quiet, please! There are samples of fossil-bearing rock in the *Pathfinder*, but there are other exhibits as well, which Professor Thorwald concluded —Dr. Pickering and Commander Miller and I concur—concluded to be artifacts, items worked by intelligent hands.

"That fact alone would be enough to send a dozen ships scurrying into the asteroid belt," he went on. "It is probably the most important discovery in System-study since they opened the diggings in Luna. But Professor Thorwald formed another conclusion even more startling. With the aid of the ship's bomb officer, using the rate-of-radioactive-decay method, he formed a tentative hypothesis that the planet—he calls it Planet Lucifer—was disrupted by artificial nuclear explosion. In other words, they did it themselves."

The silence was broken only by the soft sighing of the room's ventilators. Then Thurlow exploded, "But Captain, that's impossible!"

Captain Yancey looked at him. "Do you know all the answers, young man? I'm sure I don't."

"I'm sorry, sir."

"In this case I wouldn't even venture to have an opinion. I'm not competent. However, gentlemen, if it be true, as Professor Thorwald certainly thought it was, then I hardly need point out to you that we have more reason than ever to be proud of our Patrol—and our responsibility is even heavier than we had thought.

"Now to business—I am very reluctant to leave the *Pathfinder* where she is. Aside from sentimental reasons she is a ship of the Patrol and she is worth a good many millions. I think we can repair her and take her back."

XIII

LONG WAY HOME

MATT TOOK PART in the rebuilding of the inner door of the *Pathfinder*'s airlock and the checks for airtightness, all under the careful eye of the chief engineer. There was little other damage inside the ship. The rock, or meteor, that had punched the gaping hole in the inner door had expended most of its force in so doing; an inner bulkhead had to be patched and a few dents smoothed. The outer, armored door was quite untouched; it was clear that the invader, by bad chance, had come in while the outer door was standing open.

The plants in the air-conditioner had died for lack of attention and carbon dioxide. Matt took over the job while the others helped in the almost endless chores of checking every circuit, every instrument, every gadget necessary to the ship's functioning. It was a job which should have been done at a repair base and could not have been accomplished if there had actually been much wrong.

Oscar and Matt squeezed an hour out of sleep to explore 1987-CD, a job that mixed mountain climbing with suit-jet work. The asteroid had a gravitational field, of course, but even a mass the size of a small mountain is negligible compared with that of a planet. They simply could not feel it; muscles used to opposing the tenacious pull of robust Terra made nothing of the frail pull of 1987-CD.

At last the *Pathfinder* was cast loose and her drive tested by a scratch crew consisting of Captain Yancey at the controls and Lieutenant Novak in the power room. The *Aes Triplex* lay off a few miles, waited until she blasted her jet for a few seconds, then joined her. The two ships tied together and Captain Yancey and the chief engineer came back into the *Aes Triplex*.

"She's all yours, Hartley," he announced. "Test her yourself, then take over when you are ready."

"If she suits you she suits me. With your permission, sir, I'll transfer my crew now."

"So? Very well, Captain—take command and carry out your orders. Log it, Mister," Captain Yancey added, over his shoulder to the officer of the watch.

Thirty minutes later the split crew passed out through the airlock of the *Aes Triplex* and into the airlock of the other. P.R.S. *Pathfinder* was back in commission.

Remaining with the *Aes Triplex* was Captain Yancey,

Lieutenant Thurlow, now executive officer and astrogator, Sublieutenant Peters, now chief engineer, Cadet Jensen, chief communications officer, and Cadets Jarman and Dodson, watch officers, all departments—and Dr. Pickering, ship's surgeon.

Commander Miller, captain of the *Pathfinder*, had one less officer than Captain Yancey, but all of his officers were experienced; Captain Yancey had elected to burden himself with the cadets. He would have assumed command of the derelict himself and taken his chances with her, except for one point—the law did not permit it. He could place a master aboard her and put her back in commission, but there was no one present with authority to relieve him of his own ship—he was prisoner of his own unique status, commanding officer operating alone.

In her original flight plan it had been intended that the *Pathfinder* should make port at Deimos, Mars, when Mars overtook her and was in a favorable position. The delay caused by the disaster made the planned orbit quite out of the question; Mars would not be at the rendezvous. Furthermore Captain Yancey wanted to get the astounding evidence contained in the *Pathfinder* to Terra Base as quickly as possible; there was little point in sending it to the outpost on Mars' outer satellite.

Accordingly reaction mass was pumped from the *Aes Triplex* to the smaller ship until her tanks were full and a fast, fairly direct, though uneconomical, orbit to Earth was plotted for her. The *Aes Triplex*, using an economical "Hohmann"-type,* much longer orbit, would mosey in past the orbit of Mars, past the orbit of Earth (Earth would not be anywhere close at the time), in still further, swinging around the Sun and out again, catching up with Earth nearly a year later than the *Pathfinder*. She had mass to

---

* Hohmann, Dr. Walter—*The Attainability of the Celestial Bodies*, Munich, 1925. This pioneer work in astrogation, written long before the flight of the *Kilroy Was Here*, remains the foundation work in its field. All subsequent work is refinement of basic principles set forth by Hohmann.

accomplish this, even after replenishing the *Pathfinder,* but she was limited to time-wasting, but fuel-saving, orbits more usual to merchant vessels than to ships of the Patrol.

Matt, in one of his multiple roles as assistant astrogator, noticed a peculiarity of the orbit and called it to Oscar's attention. "Say, Oz, come and look at this—when we get to perihelion point, the other side of the Sun, we almost clip a cloud off your home town. See?"

Oscar looked over the charted positions. "Well, darn if we don't! What's the nearest approach?"

"Less than a hundred thousand miles. We'll tack on her a bit—the Old Man is a heller for efficient orbits, I find. Want to jump ship?"

"We'd be going a trifle fast for that," Oscar commented dryly.

"Oh, where's the old pioneer spirit? You could swipe one of the jeeps and be gone before you're missed."

"Gosh, I'd like to. It would be nice to have some leave." Oscar shook his head sadly and stared at the chart.

"I know what's eating on you—since you've been made the head of a department you've acquired a sense of responsibility. How does it feel to be one of the mighty?"

Tex had come into the chartroom while they were talking. He chipped in with, "Yeah, come on, Oz—tell your public."

Oscar's fair skin turned pink. "Quit riding me, you guys. It's not my fault."

"Okay, you can get up now. Seriously," Matt went on, "this is quite a break for all of us—acting ship's officers on what was supposed to be a training tour. You know what I think?"

"*Do* you think?" inquired Tex.

"Shut up. If we keep our noses clean and get any chance to show some stuff, it might mean brevet commissions for all of us."

"Captain Yancey give me a brevet?" said Tex. "A fat chance!"

"Well, Oscar almost certainly. After all, he *is* chief comm officer."

"I tell you that doesn't mean a thing," protested Oscar. "Sure, I've got the tag—with nobody to communicate with. We're out of range, except for the *Pathfinder*, and she's pulling away fast."

"We won't always be out of range."

"It won't make any difference. Can you see the Old Man letting me—or any of us—do anything without staring down the backs of our necks? Anyhow, I don't want a brevet. Suppose we got back and it wasn't confirmed? Embarrassing!"

"I'd jump at the chance," announced Tex. "It may be the only way I'll ever get one."

"Drop the orphan-child act, Tex. Suppose your Uncle Bodie heard you talking like that."

In fact, the atmosphere in the ship was very different, even though the Captain, or Lieutenant Thurlow, or both, supervised them very carefully. Captain Yancey took to calling them by their first names at mess and dropped the use of "cadet" entirely. He sometimes referred to the "ship's officers," using the term so that it plainly included the three cadets. But there was no suggestion of brevet rank made.

Out of the asteroid belt, out of radio range, and in interminable free fall, the ship's duties were light. The cadets had plenty of time to study, enough time for card games and bull sessions. Matt caught up with his assignments and reached the point where he was digging into the ship's library for advanced work, for the courses outlined for them when they left the *Randolph* had been intended for a short cruise.

The Captain set up a seminar series, partly to pass his own time and partly as a supplement to their education. It was supposed to illustrate various problems faced by a Patrol officer as a spaceman, or in his more serious role as a diplomatic representative. Yancey lectured well; the cadets found, too, that he could be drawn into reminiscence. It was both enjoyable and instructive and helped to pass the weary weeks.

At long, long last they were within radio range of Venus —and there was mail for all of them, messages that had been chasing them half around the Solar System. An official despatch from the Department congratulated the Commanding Officer on the recovery of the *Pathfinder* and commended the ship's company—this was entered, in due course, in the record of each. A private message from Hartley Miller told Captain Yancey that the trip home had been okay and that the long-hairs were tearing same over the contents of the ship. Yancey read this aloud to them.

In addition to letters from home, Matt received a wedding announcement from Marianne. He wondered if she had married the young man he had met at the picnic, but he could not be sure of the name—the whole thing seemed very remote. There was a letter, too, to all three cadets datemarked "Leda, Ganymede" from Pete, of the having-a-wonderful-time-wish-you-were-here sort. "Lucky stiff!" said Tex.

" 'Touring the world'—phooey!"

Other messages poured in—ships' movements, technical orders, personnel changes, the accumulated minutiae of a large military organization—and a detailed resumé of the news of four planets from the time they had lost contact to the present.

Oscar found that Captain Yancey did not breathe on his neck in his duties as communications chief—but by then it did not surprise him. Oscar simply was the comm chief and had almost forgotten that he had ever been anything else.

He felt, however, that he was really confirmed in his office the day a message came in top cipher, the first not in "clear." He was forced to ask the Captain for the top-cipher machine, kept in the Captain's safe. It was turned over to him without comment.

Oscar was bug-eyed when he took the translated message to Yancey. It read: TRIPLEX—CAN YOU INVESTIGATE TROUBLE EQUATORIAL REGION VENUS—OPERATIONS.

Yancey glanced at it. "Tell the Executive Officer I want to see him, please. And don't discuss this."

"Aye aye, sir."

Thurlow came in somewhat mystified. "What's up, Captain?"

Yancey handed him the flimsy. The lieutenant read it and whistled.

"Can you see any way to comply?"

"You know how much reaction potential we have, Captain. We could manage a circular orbit. We can't land."

"That's the way I see it. I suppose we'll have to refuse—dammit, I'd rather take a whipping than send in a negate. Why did they pick on us? There must be half a dozen other ships better located."

"I don't think so, Captain. I think we are the only available ship. Have you studied the movements file?"

"Not especially. Why?"

"Well, the *Thomas Paine* should be the ship—but she's grounded at New Aukland for emergency repairs."

"I see. There ought to be a standing circum-Venus patrol —there'll have to be, some day." Yancey scratched his chin and looked unhappy.

"How about this, Captain—"

"Yes?"

"If we change course right now we could do it cheaply. Then we could bring her in for atmospheric braking with no further expenditure. Then ease her down with the jet."

"Hmmm—how much margin?"

Lieutenant Thurlow got a far-away look in his eyes, while he approximated a fourth-order solution in his head. Captain Yancey joined him in the trance, his lips moving soundlessly.

"Practically none, Captain. After you've steadied in circum, you'd have to dive in and accept atmospheric terminal speed, or close to it, before you blasted."

Yancey shook his head. "Into *Venus?* I'd as soon fly a broom on Walpurgis night. No, Mr. Thurlow, we'll just have to call them up and confess."

"Just a minute, Captain—they know we don't have marines."

"Of course."

"Then they don't expect us to deliver police action. What we *can* do is to send a jeep down."

"I've been wondering when you would work around to that. All right, Mr. Thurlow—it's yours. I hand it over reluctantly, but I can't seem to help it. Never had a mission of your own, have you?"

"No, sir."

"You're getting one young. Well, I'll ask Operations for the details while you're preparing the course change."

"Fine, sir! Does the Captain care to designate the cadet to go with me, or shall I pick him?"

"You're not going with just one, Lieutenant—you'll take all three. I want you to leave the jeep manned at all times and I want you to have an armed man at your elbow. The equatorial region of Venus—there is no telling what you'll run into."

"But that leaves you with no one but Peters, sir—not counting the surgeon, of course."

"Mr. Peters and I will make out all right. Peters plays a very good hand of cribbage."

Details from Operations were slight. The M.R.S. *Gary* had radioed for help claiming to be imperiled by a native uprising. She had given her position, then radio contact had been lost.

Yancey elected to use atmospheric braking in any case to save his reaction mass for future use—otherwise the *Aes Triplex* might have circled Venus until she could be succored. The ship's company spent a crowded, tiring fifty-six hours shut up in the control room while the ship dipped into the clouds of Venus and out again, a bit deeper and a bit slower on each round trip. The ship grew painfully hot and the time spent in free space on each lap was hardly enough to let her radiate what she picked up. Most of the ship was intolerably hot, for the control room and the "farm" were refrigerated at the expense of the other spaces. In space, there is no way to get rid of unwanted heat, permanently, except by radiation—and the kinetic energy difference between the original orbit and the circum-Venus orbit the Captain wanted had to be absorbed as heat, a piece at a time, then radiated into space.

But at the end of that time three hot, tired, but very excited, young men, with one a little older, were ready to climb into jeep no. 2.

Matt suddenly remembered something. "Oh, Doctor—Doctor Pickering!" The surgeon had spent a medically uneventful voyage writing a monograph entitled "Some Notes on Comparative Pathologies of the Inhabited Planets" and was now at loose ends. He had relieved Matt as "farmer."

"Yes, Matt?"

"Those new tomato plants—they have to be cross-pollenated three days from now. You'll do it for me? You won't forget?"

"Can do!"

Captain Yancey guffawed. "Get your feet out of the furrows, Dodson. Forget the farm—we'll look out for it. Now, gentlemen—" He looked around and caught their eyes. "Try to stay alive. I doubt very much if this mission warrants expending four Patrol officers."

As they filed in Tex dug Matt in the ribs. "Did you hear that, kid—'four Patrol officers.'"

"Yeah, but look what else he said."

Thurlow tucked his orders in his pouch. They were simple: proceed to latitude north two degrees seven, longitude two hundred twelve degrees zero; locate the *Gary* and investigate reported native uprising. Keep the peace.

The lieutenant settled himself and looked around at his crew. "Hold your hats, boys. Here we go!"

XIV

"THE NATIVES ARE FRIENDLY . . ."

WITH THURLOW at the controls and Matt in the co-pilot's seat the jeep started down. It started with an orbital speed of better than four miles per second, the speed of the *Aes*

Triplex in her tight circular orbit around the equator of Venus. The lieutenant's purpose was to kill this speed exactly over his destination, then balance the jeep down on its tail. A jet landing was necessary, as the jeep had no wings.

He needed to do this precisely, with the least use of fuel. He was helped somewhat by riding "with the current" from west to east; the 940-mile-per-hour rotational speed of Venus at her equator was profit rather than loss. However, exact placement was another matter. A departure time was selected so that the entire descending curve would be on the day side of the planet in order to use the Sun as a reckoning point for placement in longitude; placement in latitude would have to depend on dead reckoning by careful choice of course.

The Sun is the only possible celestial body to use in air navigation at Venus, and even Sol is lost to the naked eye as soon as one is inside the planet-wide blanket of cloud. Matt "shot the Sun" by keeping one eye glued on the eyepiece of an infra-red adapter which had been fitted to the ship's octant, and was enabled thereby to coach his skipper from a prepared flight plan. It had not been considered practical to cut a cam for the automatic robot; too little was known about the atmospheric conditions to be expected.

When Matt informed his pilot that they were about thirty miles up, by radar, and approaching the proper longitude, as given by the infra-red image of the Sun, Thurlow brought the jeep down toward their target, ever lower and slower, and finally braked her with the jet to let her drop in a parabola distorted by air resistance.

They were enveloped in the ever-present Venerian clouds. The pilot's port was utterly useless to them. Matt now started watching the surface under them, using an infra-red-sensitive "cloud piercer."

Thurlow watched his radar altimeter, checking it against the height-time plan for grounding.

"If we are going to dodge around any, it's got to be now," he said quietly to Matt. "What do you see?"

"Looks fairly smooth. Can't tell much."

Thurlow sneaked a look. "It's not water, anyway—and it's not forest. I guess we'll chance it."

Down they dropped, with Matt watching the ghostly infra-red-produced picture narrowly at the end, ready to tell Thurlow to give her full power if it were a meadow.

Thurlow eased off his jet—and cut it. There was a bump as if they had fallen a couple of feet. They were down, landed on Venus.

"Whew!" said the pilot and wiped sweat from his forehead. "I don't want to have to try that every day."

"Nice landing, Skipper!" called out Oscar.

"Yea bo!" agreed Tex.

"Thanks, fellows. Well, let's get the stilts down." He punched a stud on the control board. Like most rockets built for jet landings, the jeep was fitted with three stabilizing jacks which came telescoping out of the craft's sides and slanting downward. Hydraulic pressure forced them down until they touched something solid enough to hold them, whereupon the thrusting force was automatically cut off and they locked in place, propping the rocket on three sides, tripod fashion, and holding it erect.

Thurlow waited until three little green lights appeared under the stud controlling the stilts, then unclutched the jeep's stabilizing gyros. The jeep held steady, he unstrapped. "All right, men. Let's take a look. Matt and Tex, stay inside. Oscar, if you don't mind my mentioning it, since it's your home town, you should do the honors."

"Right!" Oscar unstrapped and hurried to the lock. There was no need to check the air, since Venus is man-inhabited, and all of them, as members of the Patrol, had been immunized to the virulent Venerian fungi.

Thurlow crowded close behind him. Matt unstrapped and came down to sit by Tex in the passenger rest Oscar had left. The space around the lock was too limited in the little craft to make it worthwhile to do anything but wait.

Oscar stared out into the mist. "Well, how does it feel to be home?" asked Thurlow.

"Swell! What a beautiful, beautiful day!"

Thurlow smiled at Oscar's back and said, "Let's get the ladder down and see where we are." The access door was more than fifty feet above the jeep's fins, with no convenient loading elevator.

"Okay." Oscar turned and squeezed past Thurlow. The jeep settled suddenly on the side away from the door, seemed to catch itself, then started to fall over with increasing speed.

"The gyros!" yelled Thurlow. "Matt, clutch the gyros!" He tried to scramble past Oscar; they fouled each other, then the two fell sprawling backwards as the jeep toppled over.

At the pilot's yell Matt tried to comply—but he had been sprawled out, relaxing. He grabbed the sides of the rest, trying to force himself up and back to the control station, but the rest tilted backwards; he found himself "skinning the cat" out of it, and then was resting on the side of the craft, which was now horizontal.

Oscar and Thurlow were the first things he saw as he untangled himself. They were piled up on the inner wall of the ship, with Oscar mostly on top. Oscar started to get up—and stopped. "Eeeyowp!"

"You hurt, Oz?"

"My arm."

"What's the trouble?" This was Tex, who appeared from behind Matt, apparently untouched by the tumble.

Oscar helped himself up with his right arm, then tenderly felt his left forearm. "I don't know. A sprain—or a break, maybe. Eeee—ah! It's a break."

"Are you sure?" Matt stepped forward. "Let me see it."

"What's the matter with the skipper?" asked Tex.

"Huh?" said Matt and Oscar together. Thurlow had not moved. Tex went to him and knelt over him.

"Looks like he's knocked out cold."

"Throw some water over him."

"No, don't do that. Do—" The craft settled again. Oscar looked startled and said, "I think we had better get out of here."

"Huh? We can't," protested Matt. "We've got to bring Mr. Thurlow to."

Oscar did not answer him but started climbing up toward the open lock, now ten feet over their heads, swearing in Venerian as he struggled painfully and awkwardly, using one hand, from strut to brace. " 'S'matter with old Oz?" asked Tex. "Acts like he's blown his top."

"Let him go. We've got to take care of the skipper." They knelt over Thurlow and gave him a quick, gentle examination. He seemed unhurt, but remained unconscious. "Maybe he's just had the breath knocked out of him," suggested Matt. "His heart beat is strong and steady."

"Look at this, Matt." It was a lump on the back of the lieutenant's head. Matt felt it gently.

"Didn't bash in his skull. He's just had a wallop on his noggin. He'll be all right—I think."

"I wish Doc Pickering was here."

"Yeah, and if fish had feet, they'd be mice. Quit worrying, Tex. Stop messing with him and give him a chance to come out of it naturally."

Oscar stuck his head down into the open door. "Hey, you guys! Come up out of there—and fast!"

"What for?" asked Matt. "Anyhow, we can't—we got to stay with the boss, and he's still out cold."

"Then carry him!"

"How? Piggy-back?"

"Any way—but *do it!* The ship is sinking!"

Tex opened his mouth, closed it again, and dived toward a small locker. Matt yelled. "Tex—get a line!"

"What do you think I'm doing? Ice-skating?" Tex reappeared with a coil of thin, strong line used in warping the little craft in to her mother ship. "Easy now—lift him as I slip it under his chest."

"We ought to make a proper sling. We might hurt him."

"No time for that!" urged Oscar from above them. "Hurry!"

Matt swarmed up to the door with the end of the line while Tex was still fastening the loop under the armpits of the unconscious man. A quick look around was enough to confirm Oscar's prediction; the jeep lay on her side with her fins barely touching solid ground. The nose was lower than the tail and sinking in thin, yellow mud. The mud stretched away into the mist, like a flat field, its surface carpeted with a greenish-yellow fungus except for a small space adjacent to the ship where the ship, in falling, had splashed a gap in the surface.

Matt had no time to take the scene in; the mud was almost up to the door. "Ready down there?"

"Ready. I'll be right up."

"Stay where you are and steady him. I think I can handle him." Thurlow weighed one hundred forty pounds, Earth-side; his Venus weight was about one hundred and seventeen. Matt straddled the door and took a strain on the line.

"I can give you one hand, Matt," Oscar said anxiously.

"Just stay out of my way." With Matt pulling and Tex pushing and steadying from below, they got the limp lieutenant over the lip of the door and laid out on the rocket.

The craft lurched again as a tail fin slid off the bank. "Let's get going, troops," Matt urged. "Oz, can you get up on that bank by yourself?"

"Sure."

"Then do so. We'll leave the line on the skipper and chuck the end to you and you can hang onto it with your good hand. That way, if he goes in the mud, we can haul him out."

"Quit talking and get busy." Oscar trotted the length of the craft, taking the end of the line with him. He made it to the bank by stepping from a tail fin.

Matt and Tex had no trouble carrying Thurlow as far as the fins, but the last few feet, from fins to bank, were awkward. They had to work close to the jet tube, still sizzling hot, and balance themselves in a trough formed by a fin and the converging side of the ship. They finally made it by letting Oscar take most of the lieutenant's weight by hauling from the bank with his one good arm.

When they had gotten Thurlow laid out on the turf Matt jumped back aboard the jeep. Oscar shouted at him. "Hey, Matt—where do you think you're going?"

"Back inside."

"Don't do it. Come back here." Matt hesitated, Oscar added, "That's an order, Matt."

Matt answered, "I'll only be a minute. We've got no weapons and no survival kits. I'll duck in and toss them out."

"Don't try it." Matt stood still a moment, balanced between Oscar's unquestioned seniority and the novelty of taking direct orders from his roommate. "Look at the door, Matt," Oscar added. "You'd be trapped."

Matt looked. The far end of the door was already in the mud and a steady stream was slopping into the ship, like molasses. As he looked the jeep rolled about a quarter turn, seeking a new stability. Matt made it to the bank in one flying leap.

He looked back and saw that the door was out of sight; a big bubble formed and *plopped!*—and then another. "Thanks, Oz!"

They stood and watched as the tail slid away from the bank. A cloud of steam came up and joined the mist as the jet tube hit the wetness; then the tail lifted and the jeep was almost vertical, upside down, for a few moments, with only her after end showing above the slime.

She sank slowly. Presently there was nothing but bubbles in the mud and a ragged break in the false lawn to show where it had been.

Matt's chin was trembling. "I should have stayed at the controls. I could have caught her on her gyros."

"Nonsense," said Oscar. "He didn't tell you to stay put."

"I should have known better."

"Quit beating yourself with it. The procedures say it's the pilot's business. If there was any doubt in his mind he should have left her stabilized on gyro until he inspected. Right now we got to take care of him, so cut out the post-mortem."

"Okay." Matt knelt down and tried Thurlow's pulse. It was still steady. "Nothing we can do for him at the moment but let him rest. Let's see your arm."

"Okay, but take it easy. Ouch!"

"Sorry. I'm afraid I'll have to hurt you; I've never actually set a bone before."

"I have," said Tex, "out on the range. Here you go, Oz old boy—lie down on your back. And relax—it's going to hurt."

"Okay. Only I thought that down in Texas you just shot 'em." Oscar managed to smile.

"Just for broken legs. Broken arms we usually save. Matt, you whip up a couple of splints. Got a knife?"

"Yep."

"Good thing—I don't have. Better take your blouse off first, Oscar." With help Jensen complied; Tex placed a foot in Oscar's left armpit, grasped his left hand in both of his, and gave a steady tug.

Oscar yelped. "I think that did it," said Tex. "Matt, hurry up with those splints."

"Coming." Matt had found a clump of grass, twelve to fifteen feet tall and superficially similar to Earth-side bamboo. He cut about a dozen lengths as thick as his little finger and around fifteen inches long, brought them back and gave them to Tex. "Will these do?"

"I guess so. Here goes your blouse, Oscar." Tex attempted to tear strips from the garment, then gave up. "Golly, that stuff is tough. Gimme your knife, Matt."

Ten minutes later Oscar was adequately splinted and bandaged, with what remained of his blouse rigged as a sling. Tex took off his own blouse and sat down on it, for the turf was damp and the day was hot and muggy as only Venus can be. "That's done," he said, "and the skipper hasn't blinked an eye. That leaves you holding the sack, Oz—when do we have lunch?"

"A fine question, that." Oscar wrinkled his brows. "First, let's see what we've got to work with. Turn out your pouches."

Matt had his knife. Oscar's pouch contained nothing of significance. Tex contributed his harmonica. Oscar looked worried. "Fellows, do you suppose I'm justified in looking through Mr. Thurlow's pouch?"

"I think you ought to," said Tex. "I've never seen anybody stay out so long."

"I agree," added Matt. "I think we had better admit he's got a concussion and assume that he's going to be out of the running for a while. Go ahead, Oscar."

Thurlow's pouch contained some personal items that they skipped over quickly, the orders to the expedition, and a second knife—which had set in its handle a small, ornamental, magnetic compass. "Golly, I'm glad to find that item. I've been wondering how we would ever find our way back to this spot without natives to guide us."

"Who wants to?" asked Tex. "It doesn't seem to have any attractions for me."

"The jeep is here."

"And the *Triplex* is somewhere over your head. One is about as close as the other—to a pedestrian, meaning me."

"Look, Tex—somehow we've got to get that firecracker out of the mud and put her back into commission. Otherwise we stay here for life."

"Huh? I'd been depending on you, the old Venerian hand, to lead us back to civilization."

"You don't know what you're saying. Maybe you can walk five or six thousand miles through swamps, and sink holes, and cane brake; I can't. Just remember that there isn't a permanent settlement, not even a plantation, more than five hundred miles from either one of the poles. You know Venus isn't really explored—I know about as much about this neck of the woods as you know about Tibet."

"I wonder what in the world the *Gary* was doing here?" Matt commented.

"Search me."

"Say!" said Tex. "Maybe we can get home in the *Gary*."

"Maybe we can, but we haven't even found the *Gary* yet. Consequently if we find we can't, just as soon as we carry out these orders—" Oscar held up the paper he had taken from Thurlow's pouch. "—we've got to find some way to haul the jeep out of the sinkhole."

"With our own little pink patty-paws?" inquired Tex. "And what's that about our orders? We don't seem to be in very good shape to go around quelling riots, putting down insurrection, and generally throwing our weight about. We haven't even got a bean shooter, much less a bean. Come to think about it, if I had a bean, I'd eat it."

"Oscar's right," agreed Matt. "We're here; we've got a mission to perform; we've got to carry it out. That's what Mr. Thurlow would say. After that comes trying to figure out a way to get back."

Tex stood up. "I should have gone into the cattle business. Okay, Oscar—what next?"

"The first thing is for you and Matt to build a litter to carry the boss. We've got to find open water and I don't want to split up the party."

The same clump of cane grass that furnished splints provided material for a litter frame. Using both knives Matt and Tex cut two seven-foot lengths as thick as their upper arms. The stuff was light and, in that thickness, satisfactorily stiff. They slipped the poles through the sleeves of their blouses, then notched in cross pieces near each end. There was a wide gap in the middle which they wound about with the line salvaged from the jeep.

The result was a sloppy piece of work, but serviceable. Thurlow was still unconscious. His breathing was shallow but his pulse was still steady. They lifted him onto the stretcher and set out, with Oscar in the lead, compass in hand.

For about an hour they tramped through swampy land, splashing through mud, getting welts from the undergrowth, and pursued by clouds of insects. At last Matt called out, "Oz! We've just got to have some rest."

Jensen turned around. "Okay—this is the end of the line, anyhow. Open water."

They crowded forward and joined him. Beyond the cane brake, perfectly flat and calm under the fog, was a pond or lake. Its size was uncertain as the far shore was lost in the mist.

They tramped out a spot to put the litter down, then Oscar bent over the water and slapped it—*Slap!—Slap!—Slap, slap, slap—Slap, slap!*

"What do we do now?"

"We wait—and pray. Thank goodness the natives are usually friendly."

"Do you think they can help us?"

"If they want to help I'll lay you even money that they can snake the jeep out of that muck and polish it clean in three days."

"You really think so? I knew the Venerians were friendly but a job like that—"

"Don't underrate the Little People. They don't look like us but don't let that throw you."

Matt squatted down and started fanning the insects away from the unconscious officer. Presently Oscar slapped the water again, in the same pattern.

"Looks like nobody's home, Oz."

"I hope you're wrong, Tex. Most of Venus is supposed to be inhabited, but this might be a tabu spot."

A triangular head, large as a collie's, broke water about ten feet from them. Tex jumped. The Venerian regarded him with shiny, curious eyes. Oscar stood up. *"Greetings, thou whose mother was my mother's friend."*

The Venerian turned her attention to Oscar. *"May thy mother rest happily."* She surface-dived and disappeared almost without a ripple.

"That's a relief," said Oscar. "Of course they say this planet has only one language but this is the first time I've put it to a test."

"Why did it leave?"

"Gone back to report, probably. And don't say 'it,' Matt; say 'she.'"

"It's a difference that could only matter to another Venerian."

"Well, it's a bad habit, anyway." Oscar squatted down and waited.

After a time made longer by insects, heat, and sultriness the water was broken in a dozen places at once. One of the amphibians climbed gracefully up on the bank and stood up. She came about to Matt's shoulder. Oscar repeated the formal greeting. She looked him over. *"My mother tells me that she knows thee not."*

"Doubtless being busy with important thoughts she has forgotten."

"Perhaps. Let us go to my mother and let her smell thee."

"Thou art gracious. Canst thou carry my sibling?" Oscar pointed to Thurlow. *"Being ill, 'she' cannot close 'her' mouth to the waters."*

The Venerian agreed. She called one of her followers to her side and Oscar joined the consultation, illustrating how Thurlow's mouth must be covered and his nose pinched together *"—lest the waters return 'her' to 'her' mother's mother's mother."* The second native argued but agreed.

Tex was getting more and more round-eyed. "See here, Matt," he said urgently in Basic, "surely you're not figuring on going under water?"

"Unless you want to stay here until the insects eat you up, you've got to. Just take it easy, let them tow you, and try to keep your lungs full. When they dive you may have to stay under several minutes."

"I don't like it either," said Matt.

"Shucks, I visited my first Venerian home when I was nine. They know you can't swim the way they do. At least the ones around the colonies know it," he admitted doubtfully.

"Maybe you had better impress them with it."

"I'll try."

The leader cut him short with assurances. She gave a sharp command and six of her party placed themselves by the cadets, two to each man. Three others took over Thurlow, lifting him and sliding him into the water. One of them was the one who had been instructed.

Oscar called out, "Take it easy, fellows!" Matt felt little hands urging him into the lake. He took a deep breath and stepped off into the water.

The water closed over his head. It was blood warm and fresh. He opened his eyes, saw the surface, then his head broke water again. The little hands grasped his sides and propelled him along, swimming strongly. He told himself to relax and stop fighting it.

After a while it even began to seem pleasant, once he was sure that the little creatures did not intend to pull him under. But he remembered Oscar's advice and tried to watch out for a dive. Luckily, he saw the trio of which Tex was the middle go under; he gulped air just in time.

They went down and down, until his eardrums hurt, then forward. By the time they started up the pains in his chest were almost unbearable. He was fighting a reflex to open his mouth and breathe anything, even water, when they broke surface again.

There were three more of the lung-searing passages under water; when they broke water for the last time Matt saw that they were no longer outdoors.

The cave—if it was a cave—was about a hundred feet long and less than half as wide. In the center of it was the water entrance through which they had come. It was lighted from above, rather dimly, from some sort of glowing, orange clusters.

Most of this he noticed after he pulled himself up on the bank. His first impression was a crowd of Venerians surrounding the pool. They were obviously curious about their guests and chattered among themselves. Matt picked up a few words of it and heard a reference to "—*slime spawn*—" which annoyed him.

The three with Thurlow broke water. Matt pulled away from his custodians and helped drag him onto dry land. He was frantic for a moment when he could not find the lieutenant's pulse; then he located it. It was fast and fluttery.

Thurlow opened his eyes and looked at him. "Matt—the gyros . . ."

"It's all right, Lieutenant. Just take it easy."

Oscar was standing over him. "How is he Matt?"

"Coming out of it, it looks like."

"Maybe the immersion did him good."

"It didn't do me any good," asserted Tex. "I swallowed

about a gallon of water on that last one. Those little frogs are *careless*."

"They're more like seals," said Matt.

"They're neither one," Oscar cut in sharply. "They're *people*. Now," he went on, "to try to set up some friendly relations." He turned around, looking for the leader of the group.

The crowd separated, leaving an aisle to the pool. An amphibian, walking alone, but followed by three others, came slowly down this aisle toward them. Oscar faced her. *"Greetings, most worthy mother of many."*

She looked him slowly up and down, then spoke, but not to him. *"As I thought. Take them away."*

Oscar started to protest, but it did him no good. Four of the little people closed in around him. Tex yelled at him. "How about it, Oz? Let 'em have it?"

"No!" Oscar called back. "Don't resist."

Three minutes later they were herded into a small room that was almost completely dark, the gloom being broken only by a single sphere of the orange light. After depositing Thurlow on the floor the little people went away, closing the door after them by drawing across it a curtain. Tex looked around him, trying to adjust his eyes to the dim light, and said, "About as cozy as a grave. Oz, you should have let us put up a scrap. I'll bet we could have licked the whole caboodle of 'em."

"Don't be silly, Tex. Suppose we had managed it—a possibility which I doubt, but suppose we had: how would you like to try to swim your way out of here?"

"I wouldn't try it. We'd dig a tunnel up to the surface—we've got two knives."

"Maybe you would; I wouldn't attempt it. The Little People generally built their cities underneath lakes."

"I hadn't thought of that angle—say, that's bad." Tex studied the ceiling as if wondering when it would give way. "Look, Oz, I don't think we're under the lake, or the walls of this dungeon would be damp."

"Huh uh, they're good at this sort of thing."

"Well—okay, so they've got us. I'm not beefing, Oz—your

intentions were good—but it sure looks like we should 'a' taken our chances in the jungle."

"For Pete's sake, Tex!—haven't I got enough to worry about without you second-guessing me? If you're not beefing, then stop beefing."

There was a short silence, then Tex said, "Excuse me, Oscar. My big mouth."

"Sorry. I shouldn't have lost my temper. My arm hurts."

"Oh. How's it doing? Didn't I set it right?"

"I think you did a good job on it, but it aches. And it's beginning to itch, under the wrappings—makes me edgy. What are you doing, Matt?"

After checking on Thurlow's condition—unchanged—Matt had gone to the door and was investigating the closure. The curtain he found to be a thick, firm fabric of some sort, fastened around the edges. He was trying his knife on it when Oscar spoke to him.

"Nothing," he answered. "This stuff won't cut."

"Then quit trying to and relax. We don't want to get out of here—not yet, anyway."

" 'Speak for yourself, John.' Why don't we?"

"That's what I've been trying to tell Tex. I won't say this is a pleasure resort but we are about eight hundred per cent better off than we were a couple of hours ago, in every way."

"How?"

"Have you got any idea of what it means to spend a night in the jungle here, with nothing at all to shut it out? When it gets dark and the slime worms come up and start nibbling at your toes? Maybe we could live through a night of it, or even two nights, by being active and very, very lucky—but how about him?" Oscar gestured at Thurlow's still form. "That's why I made it our first business to find natives. We're safe, even if we are locked up."

Matt shivered. The slime worms have no teeth; instead they excrete an acid that dissolves what they wish to sample. They average about seven feet long. "You've sold me."

Tex said, "I wish my Uncle Bodie was here."

"So do I—he'd keep you shut up. I'm not anxious to

get out of here until we've had something to eat and some sleep. Then maybe the boss will be back on his feet and will know what to do next."

"What makes you think they'll feed us?"

"I don't know that they will, but I think they will. If they are anything like the same breed of cat as the natives around the polar colonies, they'll feed us. To keep another creature shut up without feeding it is a degree of orneriness they just wouldn't think of." Oscar groped for words. "You have to know them to understand what I mean, but the Little People don't have the cussedness in them that humans have."

Matt nodded. "I know that they are described as being a gentle, unwarlike race. I can't imagine becoming really fond of them, but the spools I studied showed them as friendly."

"That's just race prejudice. A Venerian is easier to like than a man."

"Oz, that's not fair," Tex protested. "Matt hasn't got any race prejudice and neither have I. Take Lieutenant Peters—did it make any difference to us that he's as black as the ace of spades?"

"That's not the same thing—a Venerian is *really* different. I guess you have to be brought up with them, like I have, to take them for granted. But everything about them is different—for instance, like the fact that you never lay eyes on anything but females."

"Say, how about that, Oz? Are there really male Venerians, or is it just a superstition?"

"Sure there are—the Little People are unquestionably bisexual. But I doubt if we'll ever get a picture of one or a chance to examine one. The guys who claim to have seen one are mostly liars," he added, "because their stories never add up."

"Why do you suppose they are so touchy about it?"

"Why won't a Hindu eat beef? There doesn't have to be any reason for it. I go for the standard theory; the males are little and helpless and have to be protected."

"I'm glad I'm not a Venerian," Matt commented.

"Might not be such a bad life," Tex asserted. "Me—I could use a little coddling right now."

"Don't go taking me for an authority on Venerians," warned Oscar. "I was born here, but I wasn't born *here*." He patted the floor. "I know the polar region natives, the sort around my own home town—and that's just about the only sort anybody knows."

"You think that makes such a difference?" Matt wanted to know.

"I think we're lucky to be able to talk with them at all—even if the accent does drive me wild. As for other differences—look, if the only humans you had ever met were Eskimos, how far would that get you in dealing with the mayor of a Mexican town? The local customs would all be different."

"Then maybe they won't feed us, after all," Tex said mournfully.

But they were fed, and shortly. The curtain was thrust back, something was deposited on the floor, and the door was closed again.

There was a platter of some lumpish substance, color and texture indeterminate in the dim light, and an object about the size and shape of an ostrich egg. Oscar took the platter and sniffed at it, then took a small piece and tasted it. "It's all right," he announced. "Go ahead and eat."

"What is it?" inquired Tex.

"It's . . . well, never mind. Eat it. It won't hurt you and it will keep you alive."

"But what is it? I want to know what I'm eating."

"Permit me to point out that you eat this or go hungry. I don't care which. If I told you, your local prejudices would get in your way. Just pretend it's garbage and learn to love it."

"Aw, quit horsing around, Oz."

But Oscar refused to be drawn into any further discussion. He ate rapidly until he had finished his share, glanced at Thurlow and said reluctantly, "I suppose we ought to leave some for him."

Matt tried the stuff. "What's it like?" asked Tex.

"Not bad. Reminds me of mashed soybeans. Salty—it makes me thirsty."

"Help yourself," suggested Oscar.

"Huh? Where? How?"

"The drinking bladder, of course." Oscar handed him the "ostrich egg." It was soft to Matt's touch, despite its appearance. He held it, looking puzzled.

"Don't know how to use it? Here—" Oscar took it, looked at the ends, and selected one, which he placed to his lips.

"There!" he said, wiping his lips. "Try it. Don't squeeze too hard, or you'll get it all over you." Matt tried it and got a drink of water. It was a bit like using a nursing bottle.

"It's a sort of a fish's gizzard," explained Oscar, "and spongy inside. Oh, don't look squeamish, Tex! It's sterile."

Tex tried it gingerly, then gave in and tackled the food. After a while they all sat back, feeling considerably better. "Not bad," admitted Tex, "but do you know what I'd like? A stack of steaming hotcakes, tender and golden brown—"

"Oh, shut up!" said Matt.

"—with melted butter and just swimming in maple syrup. Okay, I'll shut up." He unzipped his pouch and took out his harmonica. "Well, what d'yuh know! Still dry." He tried a couple of notes, then broke into a brilliant execution of *The Cross-Eyed Pilot.*

"Hey, stop that," said Oscar. "This is a sort of a sick room, you know."

Tex turned a troubled glance at the patient. "You think he can hear it?"

Thurlow turned and muttered in his sleep. Matt bent over him. "*J'ai soif,*" the lieutenant mumbled, then repeated distinctly, "*J'ai soif.*"

"What did he say?"

"I don't know."

"It sounded like French to me. Either of you guys savvy French?"

"Not me."

"Nor me," Matt concurred. "Why would he talk French?

I always thought he was North American; he spoke Basic like one."

"Maybe he was French-Canadian." Tex knelt beside him and felt his forehead. "He seems sort of feverish. Maybe we should give him some water."

"Okay." Oscar took the bladder and put it to Thurlow's lips; he squeezed gently so that a little welled out. The injured man worked his lips and then began to suck on it, without appearing to wake up. Presently he let it fall from his mouth. "There," said Oscar, "maybe he'll feel better now."

"Are we going to save that for him?" asked Tex, eyeing the remainder of the food.

"Go ahead and eat it, if you want it. It turns rancid a few hours after it's . . . well, it turns rancid."

"I don't believe I want any more," Tex decided.

They had been sleeping an undetermined length of time when a noise awakened them—a voice, unquestionably human. "Hey!" it demanded, *where art thou taking me? I insist that thou take me to see thy mother!*"

The noise was right at their door. "*Quell thy tongue!*" answered a native accent; the curtain was shoved aside and someone was pushed into the room before the door was again closed.

"Hello there!" called out Oscar.

The figure spun around. "Men . . ." he said, as if he could not believe it. "Men!" He began to sob.

"Hello, Stinky," said Tex. "What are you doing here?"

It was Girard Burke.

There was considerable confusion for the next several moments. Burke alternated between tears and uncontrollable shaking. Matt, who had awakened last, had trouble sorting out what was going on from the fantasy he had been dreaming, and everybody talked at once, all asking questions and none of them answering.

"Quiet!" commanded Oscar. "Let's get this straight. Burke, as I understand it, you were in the *Gary?*"

"I'm skipper of the *Gary.*"

"Huh? Well, I'll be switched. Come to think of it, we

174

knew the captain of the *Gary* was named Burke, but it never occurred to anybody that it could be Stinky Burke. Who would be crazy enough to trust you with a crate, Stinky?"

"It's my own ship—or, anyhow, my father's. And I'll thank you to call me Captain Burke, not 'Stinky.' "

"Okay, Captain Stinky."

"But how did he get here?" Matt wanted to know, still trying to catch up.

"He's just explained that," said Tex. "He's the guy that yelled for help. But what beats me is that it should happen to be us—it's like dealing out a bridge hand and getting thirteen spades."

"Oh, I don't know," objected Oscar. "It's a coincidence, but not a very startling one. He's a spaceman, he hollers for help, and naturally the Patrol responds. It happened to be us. It's about as likely, or as unlikely, as running across your piano teacher on the downtown streets of your home town."

"I don't have a piano teacher," objected Tex.

"Skip it. Neither do I. Now I think—"

"Wait a minute," broke in Burke, "do I gather that you were sent here, in answer to my message?"

"Certainly."

"Well, thank heaven for that—even if you guys were stupid enough to stumble right into it. Now tell me—how many are there in the expedition and how are they equipped? This is going to be a tough nut to crack."

"Huh? What are you talking about, Stinky? This *is* the expedition, right in front of you."

"*What?* This is no time to joke. I sent for a regiment of marines, equipped for amphibious operations."

"Maybe you did, but this is what you got—total. Lieutenant Thurlow is in command, but he got a crack on the skull so I'm temporarily filling in for him. You can talk to me—what's the situation?"

Burke seemed dazed by the knowledge. He stared without speaking. Oscar went on, "Snap out of it, Stinky. Give us the data, so we can work out an operation plan."

175

"Huh? Oh, it's no use. It's utterly hopeless."

"What's so hopeless? The natives seem friendly, on the whole. Tell us what the difficulty was, so we can work it out with them."

"Friendly!" Burke gave a bitter laugh. "They killed all of my men. They're going to kill me. And they'll kill you."

XV

PIE WITH A FORK

"OKAY," agreed Oscar. "Now that that's settled, I still want to know the score. Suppose you pull yourself together, Burke, and tell us what happened?"

The merchant rocketship *Gary*, built by "Reactors Ltd." and transferred to the family corporation "System Enterprises," was a winged rocket especially fitted for point-to-point operations on Venus. The elder Mr. Burke had placed his son in command, backing him up with an experienced crew; the purpose of the trip was to investigate a tip concerning ores of the trans-uranic elements.

The tip had been good; the ores were present in abundance. Young Burke had then undertaken to negotiate exploitation rights with the local Venerian authorities in order to hold the valuable claim against other exploiters who were sure to follow.

He had not been able to interest the local "mother of many" in his wishes; the swamp he wanted, she gave Burke to understand, was tabu. However, he was able to intrigue her into visiting the *Gary*. Once aboard the ship he again tried to get her to change her mind. When she turned him down again he had refused to allow her to leave the rocket ship.

"You mean you kidnapped her," said Matt.

"Nothing of the sort. She came aboard of her own free will. I just didn't get up and open the door for her and went on arguing."

"Oh, yeah?" commented Oscar. "How long did this go on?"

"Not very long."

"Exactly how long? You might as well tell me; I'll find out from the natives."

"Oh, well! Overnight—what's so criminal about that?"

"I don't know just how criminal it is here. On Mars, as I learned in school and as I'm sure you did too, the punishment would be to stake you out on the desert, unprotected, for exactly the same length of time."

"Hell's bells—I didn't hurt her. I'm not that silly. I wanted her co-operation."

"So you twisted her arm to get it. You held her prisoner, in effect kidnapped her by enticement and held her for ransom. Okay—you kept her overnight. What happened when you let her go?"

"That's what I'm trying to tell you. I never got a chance to turn her loose. I was going to, of course, but—"

"Sez you!"

"Don't get sarcastic. The next morning they attacked the ship. There must have been thousands of the beasts."

"So you turned her loose?"

"I was afraid to. I figured as long as we held her nothing much could happen to us. But I was wrong—they poured something on the door that ate it right away and they were in the ship before we could stop them. They killed my crew, just overran them—but we must have gotten at least twice as many of them, the brutes!"

"How come you're still breathing?"

"I locked myself in the comm room and sent out the call for help that got you here. They didn't find me there until they went through the ship, compartment by compartment. I must have passed out from the fumes when they melted their way in—anyhow I woke up while they were bringing me here."

"I see." Oscar sat a while and thought, his knees pulled up under his chin. "This is your first time on Venus, Stinky?"

"Well, yes."

"I thought so. It's apparent that you didn't know just how stubborn and difficult the Little People can be if you start pushing them around."

Burke looked wry. "I know now. That's why I distinctly called for a regiment of marines. I can't imagine what the Department was thinking about, to send three cadets and a watch officer. Of all the brass-hatted stupidity! My old man will raise plenty of Cain about it when I get back."

Tex gave a snort of disgust. "Did you think the Patrol was invented to keep a jughead like you from having to pay for his fun?"

"Why, you—"

"Quiet, Burke. And never mind the side remarks, Tex. This is an investigation, not a debate. You know the Patrol never sends marines until they've tried negotiation, Burke."

"Sure, that's why I specified marines. I wanted them to cut the red tape and get some action."

"You were kidding yourself. And there's no point in talking about what you'll do when you get back. We don't know yet that we can get back."

"That's true." Burke chewed his lip and thought about it. "Look here, Jensen, you and I were never very chummy in school, but that's unimportant now; we're in the same boat and we've got to stick together. I've got a proposition. You know these frogs better than I do—"

"People, not 'frogs.'"

"Okay, you know the natives. If you can manage to square this and get me out of here, I can cut you in on—"

"Careful there, Burke!"

"Don't get on your high horse. Just hear me out, will you? Just listen. Do I have free speech or don't I?"

"Let him talk, Oz," advised Tex. "I like to watch his tonsils."

Oscar held his tongue, Burke went on, "I wasn't going to suggest anything that would smirch your alabaster character. After all, you're here to get me out of this; it's my business if I want to offer a reward. Now this swamp we staked out is loaded with the stuff—trans-uranics, all the way from element 97 through 104. I don't have to tell you what that means—101 and 103 for jet-lining alloys; 100 for cancer therapy—not to mention the catalyzing uses. Why, there's millions in catalysts alone. I'm no hog; I'll cut you *all* in . . . say for ten per cent apiece."

"Is that all you have to say?"

"Not quite. If you can work it so that they'll let us go and leave us alone while we jury-rig some repairs on the *Gary* so that we can get away with a load this trip, I'll make it twenty per cent. You'll like the *Gary;* she's the sweetest job in the System. But if that won't work and you can get me back in your ship it's still worth ten per cent."

"Are you through?"

"Yes."

"I can answer for all of us. If I didn't consider the source, I'd be insulted."

"Fifteen per cent. There's no need to get shirty; after all, it's absolutely free just for doing what you were ordered down here to do anyhow."

"Oz," said Matt, "do we have to listen to this tripe?"

"Not any more of it," decided Jensen. "He's had his say. Burke, I'll keep this factual and leave my personal opinions out of it. You can't hire the Parol, you know that. In—"

"I wasn't offering to hire you, I was just trying to do you a favor, show my appreciation."

"I've got the floor. In the second place, we haven't got a ship, not at present."

"Huh? What's that?" Burke seemed startled.

Oscar gave him a quick resumé of the fate of the jeep. Burke looked both amazed and terribly, bitterly disappointed. "Well, of all the gang of stupes! Just forget that offer; you haven't got anything to sell."

"I've already forgotten it and you had better be glad I have. Let me point out that we wouldn't have been making a jet-landing in a jungle if you hadn't made an ass of yourself and then called for help. However, we hope to recover the jeep if I can manage to smooth out the trouble you've caused—and that's no small job."

"Well, of course if you can square things and get your ship back, the offer stands."

"Stop talking about that clumsy piece of bribery! We can't possibly promise you anything, even if we wanted to. We've got our mission to carry out."

"Okay—your mission is to get me out of here. It comes to the same thing; I was just being generous."

"Our mission isn't anything of the sort. Our prime mission is what the prime mission of the Patrol always is: to keep the peace. Our orders read to investigate a reported native uprising—there isn't any—and 'keep the peace.' There's not a word about springing Girard Burke from the local jail and giving him a free ride home."

"But—"

"I'm not through. You know how the Patrol works as well as I do. It acts in remote places and a Patrol officer has to use his own judgment, being guided by the Tradition—"

"Well, if it's precedent you're looking for, you've got to—"

"Shut up! Precedent is merely the assumption that somebody else, in the past with less information, nevertheless knows better than the man on the spot. If you had gotten any use out of the time you spent as a cadet, you'd know that the Tradition is something very different. To follow a tradition means to do things in the same grand style as your predecessors; it does not mean to do the same things."

"Okay, okay—you can skip the lecture."

"I need some information from you. Had the Little People here ever seen a man before you came along?"

"Uh . . . why, they knew about men, a little anyhow. Of course there was Stevens."

"Who was Stevens?"

"Mineralogist, working for my old man. He did the quickie survey that caused us to bring the *Gary* in. Oh, there was his pilot, too."

"And those are the only men these natives have encountered, aside from the crew of the *Gary?*"

"So far as I know, yes."

"Have they ever heard of the Patrol?"

"I doubt it—yes, they have, too. At least the boss mother seemed to know the native word for it."

"Hmm . . . that rather surprises me. So far as I know the Patrol has never had any occasion to land this near the equator—and if it had I think Captain Yancey would have briefed us about it."

Burke shrugged. Oscar went on, "It affects what we're to do. You've stirred up a mess, Burke. With the discovery of valuable minerals here, there will be more men coming along. The way you've started things off there could be more and more trouble, until there was nothing but guerrilla warfare between the natives and the men, everywhere you looked. It might even spread to the poles. It's the Patrol's business to stamp out such things before they get started and that's what I construe our mission here to be. I've got to apologize and smooth it over and do my darndest to correct a first bad impression. Can you give me any more information, anything at all, that might help me when I try it?"

"I don't think so. But go ahead—soft-soap the old girl any way you can. You can even pretend to take me away from here under arrest if it will do any good. Say, that might be a good idea! I'll be agreeable to it just as long as I get out."

Oscar shook his head. "I might take you out under arrest, if she wants it that way. But as far as I can see you are a perfectly legal prisoner here for a crime under the local customs."

"What in the world are you talking about?"

"I might point out that what you've admitted doing is a crime anywhere. You can be tried for it on Terra if she wants it that way. But it really doesn't matter to me, one way or the other. It's no business of the Patrol."

"But you can't leave me here!"

Oscar shrugged. "That's the way I see it. Lieutenant Thurlow might snap out of it at any time, then you could take it up with him. As long as I'm in charge I'm not going to jeopardize the Patrol's mission to try to help you get away with murder—and I do mean murder!"

"But—" Burke looked wildly around him. "Tex! Matt! Are you going to let him side up with those frog-people against a man?"

Matt gave him a stony-eyed stare. Tex said, "Button your lip, Stinky."

Oscar added, "Yes, do. And go to sleep. My arm hurts and I don't want to be bothered any more with you tonight."

The room quieted down at once, even though none of them got to sleep quickly. Matt lay awake a long time, worrying out their predicament, wondering whether or not Oscar could convince the frog mother—he thought of her as such—of the innocence of their intentions, and repeatedly blaming himself for the disaster to the jeep. Presently he fell into an exhausted sleep.

He was awakened by a moaning sound. It brought him wide awake at once and to the lieutenant's side. He found Tex already awake with him. "What is it?" he asked. "Is he worse?"

"He keeps trying to say something," Tex answered.

Thurlow's eyes came open and he looked up at Matt. *"Maman,"* he said querulously. *"Maman—pourquoi fait-il nuit ainsi?"*

Oscar joined them. "What's he saying?"

"Sounds like he's calling for his momma," said Tex. "The rest is just gibberish."

"Where did that bladder get to? We could give him a drink." It was found and again the patient drank, then seemed to drop at once to sleep. "You guys go back to sleep," said Oscar. "I want to snag a word with the guard that brings us our next meal and try to get to see the big mother. He's got to have some medical attention, somehow."

"I'll take the watch, Oz," Matt offered.

"No, I can't sleep very well anyhow. This darn thing itches." He held up his damaged arm.

"Well—all right."

Matt was still awake when the curtain opened. Oscar

had been sitting cross-legged at the door, waiting; as the native shoved inside a platter of food, he thrust his arm into the opening.

"Remove thy arm," said the native emphatically.

"Attend thou me," insisted Oscar. "I must have speech with thy mother."

"Remove thy arm."

"Thou wilt carry my message?"

"Remove thy arm!"

Oscar did so and the curtain was hurriedly secured. Matt said, "Doesn't look as if they intended to powwow with us, does it, Oz?"

"Keep your shirt on," Oscar answered. "Breakfast. Wake up the others."

It was the same dull fodder as before. "Split it five ways, Tex," Oscar directed. "The lieutenant may snap out of it and be hungry."

Burke looked at it and sniffed. "I'm sick of that stuff. I don't want any."

"Okay, split it four ways." Tex nodded and did so.

They ate; presently Matt sat back, burped reflectively, and said, "You know, while I could use some orange juice and coffee, that stuff's not bad."

"Did I ever tell you," asked Tex, "about the time my Uncle Bodie got incarcerated in the jail at Juarez?—by mistake, of course."

"Of course," agreed Oscar. "What happened?"

"Well, they fed him nothing but Mexican jumping beans. He—"

"Didn't they upset him?"

"Not a bit. He ate as many as he could and a week later he jumped over a twelve foot wall and bounced home."

"Having met your Uncle Bodie, I can well believe it. What do you suppose he would do under these circumstances?"

"Obvious. He'd make love to the old girl and inside of three days he'd be head man around here."

"I think I'll have some breakfast after all," announced Burke.

"You'll leave that chow for the lieutenant," Oscar said firmly. "You had your chance."

"You've got no authority over me."

"There are two reasons why you are wrong."

"So? What are they?"

"Matt and Tex."

Tex stood up. "Shall I clip him, boss?"

"Not yet."

"Oh, shucks!"

"Anyhow," objected Matt. "I get first crack—I'm senior to you, Tex."

"Pulling rank on me, eh? Why you unspeakable rat!"

"Mister Rat, if you please. Yep, in this instance I claim rank."

"But this is a social occasion."

"Shut up, you guys," instructed Oscar. "Neither of you is to clip him unless he gets to sniffing around that food dish."

There was a noise at the door, the curtain was pushed back and a native announced, "*My mother will see thee. Come.*"

"*Myself alone, or me and my sisters?*"

"*All of you. Come.*"

However, when Burke attempted to pass through the door two of the little creatures pushed him back inside. They continued to restrain him while four others picked up Lieutenant Thurlow and carried him outside. The numerous party set out down the passageway.

"I wish they would light these rabbit nests," Tex complained, after stumbling.

"It's light enough to their eyes," Oscar answered.

"Natch," agreed Tex, "but a fat lot of good that does me. *My* eyes don't see infra-red."

"Then pick up your big feet."

They were taken to another large room, not the entrance hall, for it contained no pool of water. An amphibian, the same who had viewed them and ordered them taken away on their arrival, sat on a raised platform at the far end of the room. Only Oscar recognized her as such; to the others she looked like the rest.

Oscar quickened his pace and drew ahead of his escort. *"Greetings, thou old and wise mother of many."*

She sat up and looked at him steadily. The room was very quiet. On every side the little folk waited, looking first from the earthlings to their chief executive, then back again. Matt felt that somehow the nature of her answer would show them their fate.

"Greetings." She had chucked the ball back to Oscar by refusing to assign him any title at all, good or bad. *"Thou sought speech with me. Thou may speak."*

"What manner of city is thine? Have I, perhaps, journeyed so far that manners are no longer observed?" The Venerian word meant much more than "manners"; it referred to the entire obligatory code of custom by which the older and stronger looked out for the weaker and younger.

The entire audience stirred. Matt wondered if Oscar had overplayed his hand. The expression of the leader changed but Matt had no way of reading it. *"My city and my daughters live ever by custom—"* She used a more inclusive term, embracing tabus and other required acts, as well as the law of assistance. *"—and I have never before heard it suggested that we fail in performance."*

"I hear thee, gracious mother of many, but thy words confuse me. We come, my 'sisters' and I, seeking shelter and help for ourselves and our 'mother,' who is gravely ill. I myself am injured and am unable to protect my younger 'sisters.' What have we received in thy house? Thou hast deprived us of our freedom; our 'mother' lies unattended and failing. Indeed we have not even been granted the common decency of personal rooms in which to eat."

A noise rose from the spectators which Matt correctly interpreted as the equivalent of a shocked gasp. Oscar had deliberately used the offensive word *"eat,"* instead of talking around it. Matt was sure now that Oscar had lost his judgment.

If so, Oscar went on to confirm it. *"Are we fish, that*

such should be done to us? Or are the customs such among thy daughters?"

"We follow the customs," she said shortly, and even Matt and Tex could interpret the anger in her voice. *"It was my understanding that thy breed had no decencies. It will be corrected."* She spoke sharply in an aside to one of her staff; the little creature trotted away. *"As to thy freedom, what I had done was lawful for it was to protect my daughters."*

"To protect thy daughters? From what? From my ailing 'mother'? Or from my injured arm?"

"Thy sister who knows no customs has forfeited thy freedom."

"I hear thy words, wise mother, but I understand them not."

The amphibian seemed nonplused. She inquired specifically about Burke, naming him by his terrestrial tag, calling it "Captain-Burke," as one word. Oscar assured her that Burke was no "daughter" of Oscar's "mother," nor of Oscar's "mother's mother."

The matriarch considered this. *"If we return you to the upper waters will you leave us?"*

"What of my 'mother'?" asked Oscar. *"Wouldst thou cast 'her' forth thus ailing, to die and to be destroyed by the creatures of the slime?"* On this occasion he carefully avoided the Venerian expression for "to be eaten."

The mother-of-many had Thurlow carried up to the dais on which she sat. Several of the little folk gathered around him and examined him, speaking to each other in high, lisping whispers. Presently the matriarch herself joined the consultation, then spoke again. *"Thy mother sleeps."*

"It is a sickly sleep. 'Her' head was injured by a blow." Oscar joined the group and showed them the lump on the back of Thurlow's head. They compared it with Oscar's own head, running gentle, inquisitive little hands through his blond hair. There was more lisping chatter; Matt found himself unable to follow even what he could hear; most of the words were strange.

"My learned sisters tell me that they dare not take thy

mother's head apart for fear that they could not get it back together," announced the mother-of-many.

"Well, that's a relief!" Tex said out of the corner of his mouth.

"Old Oz wouldn't let them anyhow," Matt whispered.

The leader gave instructions and four of her "daughters" picked up the unconscious officer and started carrying him out of the room. Tex called out, "Hey, Oz—do you think that's safe?"

"It's all right," Oscar called back, then explained to the matriarch, *"My 'sister' feared for the safety of our 'mother.'"*

The creature made a gesture that reminded Matt suddenly of his great-aunt Dora—she positively sniffed. *"Tell her that her nose need not twitch!"*

"She says not to get in an uproar, Tex."

"I heard her. Okay, you're the boss," Tex answered, and then muttered, "My nose, indeed!"

When Thurlow had been removed the leader turned toward them again. *"May thy dreams be of daughters."*

"May thy dreams be as pleasant, gracious mother."

"We will speak again." She gathered herself up to a lordly four feet and left the chamber. When she was gone the group of escorts conducted the cadets out of the council hall but by a different passageway than that from which they had come. The group stopped presently at another doorway. The guide in charge wished them farewell with the same formula as the matriarch. A curtain was drawn but it was not fastened, a point that Matt immediately checked. He turned to Oscar.

"I've got to hand it to you, Oz. Anytime you get tired of the Patrol and don't want to run for prime minister of the System, I can book you for a swell job, selling snow to Eskimos. For you it would be a cinch."

"Matt's not just fanning the air," agreed Tex. "Oscar, you were wonderful. Uncle Bodie couldn't have handled the old gal any slicker."

"That's high praise, Tex. I'll admit to being relieved. If the Little People weren't so downright decent it wouldn't have worked."

The living room of their apartment—there were two rooms —was about the size of the room they had been in, but was more comfortable. There was a softly padded, wide couch running around the wall. In the center of the room was a pool of water, black under the dim light. "Oz, do you suppose that bathtub connects with the outside?" Tex wanted to know.

"They almost always do."

Matt became interested. "Maybe we could swim out."

"Go ahead and try it. Don't get lost in the dark and remember not to swim under water more than half the distance you can hold your breath." Oscar smiled cynically.

"I see your point."

"Anyhow, we want to stay until we've gotten over the last hurdle."

Tex wandered on into the second room. "Hey, Oz—come look at this."

Matt and Oscar joined him. There were rows of little closets down each side, ten in all, each with its own curtain. "Oh, yes, our eating booths."

"That reminds me," said Matt. "I thought you had wrecked everything, Oz, when you started talking about eating. But you pulled out of it beautifully."

"I didn't pull out of it; I did it on purpose."

"Why?"

"It was a squeeze play. I had to shock them with the idea that they were indecent, or looked that way to us. It established us as 'people,' from their point of view. After that it was easy." Oscar went on. "Now that we are accepted as people, we've got to be awfully careful not to undo it. I don't like to eat in one of these dark little cubbyholes any better than you do, but we don't dare take a chance of being seen eating—you don't dare even fail to draw the curtain, as one of them might come popping in. Remember, eating is the only sort of privacy they observe."

"I get you," agreed Tex. "Pie with a fork."

"Huh?"

"Never mind—it's a painful memory. But Matt and I won't slip."

XVI

P.R.S. *ASTARTE*

OSCAR WAS SUMMONED again the next day into the presence of the city's chief magistrate and started laying the foundation, in a leisurely, indirect fashion, for formal diplomatic relations in the future. He began by getting her story of the trouble with the *Gary* and its skipper. It was much as Burke had admitted it to be, although from a different viewpoint.

Oscar had inquired casually as to why the swamp Burke wanted was tabu. He was worried that he might be invading religious matters but he felt that he needed to know —it was a dead certainty that others would be along, in due course, to attempt to exploit the trans-uranic ores; if the Patrol was to prevent further breaches of the peace the matter must be investigated.

The matriarch answered without hesitation; the swamp was tabu because the ore muds were poisonous.

Oscar felt the relief of a man who has just been told that it will not be necessary to lose a leg, after all. The ores were understandably poisonous; it was a matter that the Patrol could undoubtedly negotiate—conditional or practical tabus had been overcome many times with natives. He tabled the matter, as something to be taken up at a later time by the appropriate experts.

In a later interview he sounded her out on the subject of the Patrol. She had heard of it, in a fashion, apparently —she used the native word given by the polar-region natives to all colonial government, a word meaning "guardians of the customs" or "keepers of the law."

189

The native meaning was quite useful to Oscar, for he found it impossible to get over to her the idea that the Patrol was intended to prevent war—"war" was a concept she had never heard of!

But her conservative mind was naturally prejudiced in favor of any organization tagged as "guardians of the customs." Oscar approached it from that viewpoint. He explained to her that more of his own kind would be arriving; therefore the "great mother of many" of his own people had sent them as messengers to propose that a "mother" from Oscar's people be sent to aid her in avoiding friction.

She was receptive to the idea as it fitted her own experience and concepts. The groups of natives near the polar colonies were in the habit of handling their foreign affairs by exchanging "mothers"—actually judges—who ruled on matters arising out of differences in custom; Oscar had presented the matter in the same terms.

He had thus laid the groundwork for a consulate, extraterritorial courts, and an Earthman police force; the mission, as he saw it, was complete—provided he could get back to base and report before other prospectors, mining engineers, and boomers of all sorts started showing up.

Only then had he spoken to her of getting back—to have her suggest that he remain permanently as "mother" for his people. (The root word translated as "mother" is used for every position of authority in the Venerian speech; the modifiers and the context give the word its current meaning.)

The proposal left Oscar temporarily speechless. "I didn't know what to say next," he confessed later. "From her point of view she was honoring me. If I turned it down, it might offend her and crab the whole deal."

"Well, how did you talk your way out of it?" Tex wanted to know. "Or did you?"

"I think so. I explained as diplomatically as possible that I was too young for the honor and that I was acting as 'mother' only because Thurlow was laid up and that, in any case, my 'great mother of many' had other work which I was obliged, by custom, to carry out."

"I guess that held her."

"I think she just filed it away as a point to negotiate. The Little People are great negotiators; you'll have to come to New Auckland some time and listen to the proceedings of a mixed court."

"Keep to the point," suggested Matt.

"That *is* to the point—they don't fight; they just argue until somebody gives in. Anyhow, I told her that we had to get Thurlow back where he could get surgical attention. She understood that all right and expressed regret for the steenth time that her own little girls couldn't do the trick. But she had a suggestion for curing the boss."

"Yes?" demanded Matt. "What was it?" Matt had appointed himself Thurlow's caretaker, working with the amphibian healers who now had him as a professional responsibility. He had taught them to take his pulse and to watch his respiration; now there was always one of the gentle creatures squatting on the end of Thurlow's couch, watching him with grave eyes. They seemed genuinely distressed at not being able to help him; the lieutenant had remained in a semi-coma, coming out of it enough occasionally that it had been possible to feed him and give him water, but never saying anything that the cadets could understand. Matt found that the little nurses were quite unsqueamish about feeding a helpless person; they accepted offensive necessities with the same gallantry as a human nurse.

But Thurlow, while he did not die, did not get any better.

"The old girl's suggestion was sort of radical, but logical. She suggested that her healers take Burke's head apart first, to see how it was made. Then they could operate on the boss and fix him."

"*What?*" said Matt.

Tex was having trouble controlling himself. He laughed so hard he strangled, then got hiccoughs and had to be pounded on the back. "Oh, boy!" he finally exploded, tears streaming down his cheeks, "this is wonderful. I can't wait to see Stinky's face. You haven't told him, have you?"

"No."

"Then let me. Dibs on the job."

"I don't think we ought to tell him," objected Oscar. "Why kick him when he's down?"

"Oh, don't be so noble! It won't hurt any to let him know that his social rating is 'guinea pig.'"

"She really hates him, doesn't she?" Matt commented.

"Why shouldn't she?" Tex answered. "A dozen or more of her people dead—do you expect her to regard it as a schoolboy prank?"

"You've both got her wrong," Oscar objected. "She doesn't hate him."

"Huh?"

"Could you hate a dog? Or a cat—"

"Sure could," said Tex. "There was an old tomcat we had once—"

"Pipe down and let me finish. Conceding your point, you can hate a cat only by placing it on your own social level. She doesn't regard Burke as . . . well, as *people* at all, because he doesn't follow the customs. We're 'people' to her, because we do, even though we look like him. But Burke in her mind is just a dangerous animal, like a wolf or a shark, to be penned up or destroyed—but not hated or punished.

"Anyhow," he went on, "I told her it wouldn't do, because we had an esoteric and unexplainable but unbreakable religious tabu that interfered—that blocked her off from pressing the point. But I told her we'd like to use Burke's ship to get the lieutenant back. She gave it to me. We go out tomorrow to look at it."

"Well, for crying out loud—why didn't you say so, instead of giving all this build-up?"

They had made much the same underwater trip as on entering the city, to be followed by a longish swim and a short trip overland. The city mother herself honored them with her company.

The *Gary* was everything Burke had claimed for her, modern, atomic-powered, expensively outfitted and beautiful, with sharp wings as graceful as a swallow's.

She was also a hopeless wreck.

Her hull was intact except the ruined door, which appeared to have been subjected to great heat, or an incredible corrosive, or both. Matt wondered how it had been done and noted it as still another indication that the Venerians were not the frog-seal-beaver creatures his Earth-side prejudices had led him to think.

The inside of the ship had looked fairly well, too, until they started checking over the controls. In searching the ship the amphibians, to whom even a common door latch was a puzzle, had simply burned their way through impediments—including the access hatch to the ship's autopilot and gyro compartment. The circuits of the ship's nervous system were a mass of fused and melted junk.

Nevertheless they spent three hours convincing themselves that it would take the resources of a dockyard to make the ship fly again. They gave up reluctantly at last and started back, their spirits drooping.

Oscar had at once taken up with the city mother the project of recovering the jeep. He had not mentioned it before as the *Gary* seemed the better bet. Language difficulties would have hampered him considerably—their hostesses had no word for "vehicle," much less a word for "rocket ship"—but the *Gary* gave him something to point to wherewith to explain.

When she understood what he was driving at she gave orders which caused the party to swim to the point where the cadets had first been picked up. The cadets made sure of the spot by locating the abandoned litter and from there Oscar had led them back to the sinkhole that was the grave of the jeep. There he acted out what had happened, showing her the scar in the bank where the jeep had balanced and pacing off on the bank the dimensions of the ship.

The mother-of-many discussed the problem with her immediate staff while the cadets waited, ignored rather than excluded. Then she abruptly gave the order to leave; it was getting on in the late afternoon and even the Venerians do not voluntarily remain out in the jungle overnight.

That had ended the matter for several days. Oscar's attempts to find out what, if anything, was being done about the jeep were brushed off as one might snub a persistent brat. It left them with nothing to do. Tex played his harmonica until threatened with a ducking in the room's center pool. Oscar sat around, nursing his arm and brooding. Matt spent much of his time watching over Thurlow and became well acquainted with the nurses who never left him, expecially one bright-eyed cheerful little thing who called herself "Th'wing."

Th'wing changed his viewpoint about Venerians. At first he regarded her much as he might a good and faithful, and unusually intelligent dog. By degrees he began to think of her as a friend, an interesting companion—and as "people." He had tried to tell her about himself and his own kind and his own world. She had listened with alert interest, but without ever taking her eyes off Thurlow.

Matt was forced willy-nilly into the concepts of astronomy—and came up against a complete block. To Th'wing there was the world of water and swamp and occasional dry land; above that was the endless cloud. She knew the Sun, for her eyes, perceptive to infra-red, could see it, even though Matt could not, but she thought of it as a disc of light and warmth, not as a star.

As for other stars, none of her people had ever seen them and the idea did not exist. The notion of another planet was not ridiculous; it was simply incomprehensible—Matt got nowhere.

He told Oscar about it. "Well, what did you expect?" Oscar had wanted to know. "All the natives are like that. They're polite but they think you are talking about your religion."

"The natives around the colonies, too?"

"Same deal."

"But they've seen rocket ships, some of 'em, anyhow. Where do they think we come from? They must know we haven't been here always."

"Sure they know that—but the ones at South Pole think we came orignally from North Pole and the ones around

North Pole are sure we came from South Pole—and it's no use trying to tell them anything different."

The difficulty was not one-sided. Th'wing was continually using words and concepts which Matt could not understand and which could not be straightened out even with Oscar's help. He began to get hazily the idea that Th'wing was the sophisticated one and that he, Matt, was the ignorant outlander. "Sometimes I think," he told Tex, "that Th'wing thinks that I am an idiot studying hard to become a moron—but flunking the course."

"Well, don't let it throw you, kid. You'll be a moron, yet, if you just keep trying."

On the morning fifteen Venus days after their arrival the mother of the city sent for them and had them taken to the site of the jeep. They stood on the same bank where they had climbed ashore from the sinking ship, but the scene had changed. A great hole stretched out at their feet; in it the jeep lay, three-quarters exposed. A swarm of Venerians crawled over it and around it like workmen in a dockyard.

The amphibians had begun by adding something to the thin yellow mud of the sinkhole. Oscar had tried to get the formula for the additive, but even his command of the language was useless—the words were strange. Whatever it was, the effect was to turn the almost-liquid mud into a thick gel which became more and more stiff the longer it was exposed to air. The little folk had carved it away from the top as fast as it consolidated; the jeep was now surrounded by the sheer walls of a caisson-like pit. A ramp led up on the shoreward side and a stream of the apparently tireless little creatures trotted up it, bearing more jelled blocks of mud.

The cadets had climbed down into the pit to watch, talking in high spirits about the prospects of putting the jeep back into commission and jetting out again, until the Venerian in charge of the work had urged them emphatically to go up out of the pit and stay out of the way. They joined the city mother and waited.

"Ask her how she expects to get it up out of there, Oz," Tex suggested. Oscar did so.

"Tell thy impatient daughter to chase her fish and I will chase mine."

"No need for her to be rude about it," Tex complained.

"What did she say?" inquired the mother-of-many.

" 'She' thanks thee for the lesson," Oscar prevaricated.

The Little People worked rapidly. It was evident that the ship would be entirely free before the day was far advanced—and clean as well; the outside shone now and a steady procession of them had been pouring in and out of the door of the ship, bearing cakes of jellied mud. In the last hour the routine had changed; the little workers came out bearing distended bladders. The clean-up squad was at work.

Oscar watched them approvingly. "I told you they would lick it clean."

Matt looked thoughtful. "I'm worried, Oz, about the possibility that they will mess with something on the control board and get into trouble."

"Why? The leads are all sealed away. They can't hurt anything. You locked the board when you left it, didn't you?"

"Yes, of course."

"Anyhow, they can't fire the jet when she's in that attitude even if you hadn't."

"That's true. Still, I'm worried."

"Well, let's take a look, then. I want to talk to the foreman in any case. I've got an idea."

"What idea?" asked Tex.

"Maybe they can get her upright in the pit. It seems to me we could take off from there and never have to drag her out. Might save several days." They went down the ramp and located the Venerian in charge, then Matt and Tex went inside the ship while Oscar stayed to talk over his idea.

It was hard to believe that the pilot room had lately been choked with filthy, yellow mud. A few amphibians were still working in the after end of the room; elsewhere the compartment was clean.

Matt climbed to the pilot's seat and started inspecting. He noticed first that the sponge-rubber eyeguards for the infra-red viewer were missing. This was not important, but he wondered what had happened to them—did the little folk have the vice of souvenir snitching? He filed away the suspicion, and attempted a dry run on the controls, without firing the jet.

Nothing operated—nothing at all.

He looked the board over more carefully. To a casual inspection it was clean, bright, in perfect order, but he now perceived many little pits and specks. He dug at one with a finger nail, something came away. He worked at it a bit more and produced a tiny hole into the interior of the control board. It gave him a sick feeling at the pit of his stomach. "Say, Tex—come here a minute. I've got something."

"You think you've got something," Tex answered in muffled tones. "Wait till you've seen this."

He found Tex with a wrench in his hand and a cover plate off the gyro compartment. "After what happened to the *Gary* I decided to check this first. Did you ever see such a mess?"

The mud had gotten in. The gyros, although shut down, were of course still spinning when the ship had gone into the sink-hole and normally would have coasted for days; they should still have been spinning when Tex removed the cover. Instead they had ground to a stop against the mud—burned to a stop.

"We had better call Oscar," Matt said dully.

With Oscar's help they surveyed the mess. Every instrument, every piece of electronic equipment had been invaded. Non-metallic materials were missing completely; thin metal sheets such as instrument cases were riddled with pinholes. "I can't understand what did it," Oscar protested, almost in tears.

Matt asked the Venerian in charge of the work. She did not understand him at first; he pointed out the pinholes, whereupon she took a lump of the jelled mud and mashed it flat. With a slender finger she carefully separated out what seemed to be a piece of white string, a couple of inches long. *"This is the source of thy troubles."*

"Know what it is, Oz?"

"Some sort of worm. I don't recognize it. But I wouldn't expect to; the polar regions are nothing like this, thank goodness."

"I suppose we might as well call off the working party."

"Let's don't jump the gun. There might be some way to salvage the mess. We've *got* to."

"Not a chance. The gyros alone are enough. You can't raise ship in a wingless job without gyros. It's impossible."

"Maybe we could clean them up and get them to working."

"Maybe you could—I can't. The mud got to the *bearings*, Oz."

Jensen agreed regretfully. The gyros, the finest precision equipment in a ship, were no better than their bearings. Even an instrument maker in a properly equipped shop would have thrown up his hands at gyros abused as these had been.

"We've at least got to salvage some electronic equipment and jury-rig some sort of a sending set. We've got to get a message through."

"You've seen it. What do you think?"

"Well—we'll pick out the stuff that seems in the best shape and take it back with us. They'll help us with the stuff."

"What sort of shape will it be in after an hour or so in the water? No, Oz, the thing to do is to lock up the door, once the last of the filth is out and come back and work here."

"Okay, we'll do that." Oscar called to Tex, who was still snooping around. He arrived swearing.

"What now, Tex?" Oscar asked wearily.

"I thought maybe we could at least take some civilized food back with us, but those confounded worms bored into the cans. Every ration in the ship is spoiled."

"Is that all?"

" 'Is that all? Is that all?' the man says! What do you want? Flood, pestilence, and earthquakes?"

But it was not all—further inspection showed another thing which would have dismayed them had they not already been as low in spirit as they could get. The jeep's jet ran on liquid hydrogen and liquid oxygen. The fuel tanks, insulated and protected from direct radiation, could retain fuel for long periods, but the warm mud had reached them and heated them; the expanding gases had bled out through relief valves. The jeep was out of fuel.

Oscar looked this situation over stonily. "I wish the *Gary* had been chemically powered," he finally commented.

"What of it?" Matt answered. "We couldn't raise ship if we had all the juice this side of Jupiter."

The mother-of-many had to be shown before she was convinced that there was anything wrong with the ship. Even then, she seemed only half convinced and somehow vexed with the cadets for being unsatisfied with the gift of their ship back. Oscar spent much of the return journey trying to repair his political fences with her.

Oscar ate no dinner that night. Even Tex only picked at his food and did not touch his harmonica afterwards. Matt spent the evening silently sitting out a watch in Thurlow's room.

The mother-of-many sent for all three of them the next morning. After formal exchange of greetings she commenced, *"Little mother, is it true that thy Gary is indeed dead, like the other Gary?"*

"It is true, gracious mother."

"Is it true that without a Gary thou canst not find thy way back to thine own people?"

"It is true, wise mother of many; the jungle would destroy us."

She stopped and gestured to one of her court. The "daughter" trotted to her with a bundle half as big as the bearer. The city mother took it and invited, or commanded, the cadets to join her on the dais. She commenced unwrapping. The object inside seemed to have more bandages than a mummy. At long last she had it uncovered and held it out to them. "Is this thine?"

It was a large book. On the cover, in large ornate letters, was:

LOG
of
the
Astarte

Tex looked at it and said, "Great leaping balls of fire! It can't be."

Matt stared and whispered, "It must be. The lost first expedition. They didn't fail—*they got here.*"

Oscar stared and said nothing at all until the city mother repeated her question impatiently. *"Is this thine?"*

"Huh? What? Oh, sure! *Wise and gracious mother, this thing belonged to my 'mother's mother's mother.' We are her 'daughters.'*"

"Then it is thine."

Oscar took it from her and gingerly opened the brittle pages. They stared at the original entry for "raise ship"— but most especially at the year entry in the date column— "1971." "Holy Moses!" breathed Tex. "Look at that—just look at it. More than a hundred years ago."

They thumbed through it. There was page after page of one line entries of "free fall, position according to plan" which they skipped over rapidly, except for one: "Christmas day. Carols were sung after the mid-day meal."

It was the entries after grounding they were after. They were forced to skim them as the mother-of-many was beginning to show impatience: "—climate no worse than the most extreme terrestrial tropics in the rainy season. The dominant life form seems to be a large amphibian. This planet is definitely possible of colonization."

"—the amphibians have considerable intelligence and seem to talk with each other. They are friendly and an attempt is being made to bridge the semantic gap."

"—Hargraves has contracted an infection, apparently fungoid, which is unpleasantly reminiscent of leprosy. The surgeon is treating it experimentally."

"—after the funeral muster Hargraves' room was sterilized at 400°."

The handwriting changed shortly thereafter. The city mother was growing so obviously discontented that they glanced only at the last two entries: "—Johnson continues to fail, but the natives are very helpful—"

"—my left hand is now useless. I have made up my mind to decommission the ship and take my chances in the hands of the natives. I shall take this log with me and add to it, if possible."

The handwriting was firm and clear; it was their own eyes that blurred it.

The mother-of-many immediately ordered up the party used to ferry the humans in and out of the city. She was not disposed to stop to talk and, once the journey began, there was no opportunity to until they reached dry land.

"Look here, Oz," Tex started in, as soon as he had shaken off the water, "do you really think she's taking us to the *Astarte?*"

"Could be. Probably is."

"Do you think there is a chance that we will find the ship intact?" asked Matt.

"Not a chance. Not a chance in this world. On one point alone, she couldn't possibly have any fuel left in her tanks. You saw what happened to the jeep. What do you think a century has done to the *Astarte?*" He paused and looked thoughtful. "Anyhow, I'm not going to get my hopes up, not again. I couldn't stand it, three times. That's too many."

"I guess you're right," agreed Matt. "It won't do to get excited. She's probably a mound of rust under a covering of vines."

"Who said anything about not getting excited?" Oscar answered. "I'm so excited I can hardly talk. But don't think of the *Astarte* as a possible way to get back; think of her historically."

"*You* think of it that way," said Tex. "I'm a believer and a hoper. I want to get out of this dump."

"Oh, you'll get out! They'll come find us some day—and then they'll finish the mission we flubbed."

"Look," answered Tex, "couldn't we go off duty and not think about the mission just for the next quarter of a mile? These insects are something fierce—you think about Oscar and I'll think about Mother Jarman's favorite son. I wish I was back in the good old *Triplex*."

"You were the guy that was always beefing that the *Triplex* was a madhouse."

"So I was wrong. I can be big about it."

They came to one of the rare rises in the level of the ground, all of ten feet above water level. The natives started to whisper and lisp excitedly among themselves. Matt caught the Venerian word for "*tabu.*" "Did you get that, Oz?" he said in Basic. "Tabu."

"Yes. I don't think she told them where she was taking them."

The column stopped and spread out; the three cadets moved forward, pushing rank growth aside and stepped in a clearing.

In front of them, her rakish wings festooned in vines and her entire hull sheathed in some translucent substance, was the Patrol Rocket Ship *Astarte*.

XVII

HOTCAKES FOR BREAKFAST

THE CITY MOTHER was standing near the door of the *Astarte*, underneath the starboard wing. Two of her people were working at the door, using bladders to squirt some liquid around the edges. The translucent layer over the hull melted away wherever the liquid touched it. They grasped a free edge of the skin stuff and began to peel it away. "Look at that," said Tex. "Do you see what they've done? The ship is *Venusized.*"

His use of the term was loose; an item that has been "planetized" is one that has been rendered stable against certain typical conditions of the planet concerned, as defined by tests of the Bureau of Standards—for example, an item listed in the colonial edition of the Sears & Montgomery catalog as "Venusized" is thereby warranted to resist the excessive humidity, the exotic fungi, and certain of the planet's pests. The *Astarte* was merely encased in a sheath.

"Looks like it," agreed Oscar, his voice carefully restrained. "Sort of a spray-gun job."

"Five gets you ten it never saw a spray gun. The Venerians did it." Tex slapped at an insect. "You know what this means, Oz?"

"I'm way ahead of you. Don't get your hopes up. And don't try to get mine up, either. A hundred years is a long time."

"Oz, you don't get any fun out of life."

The little workers were having difficulties. The top of the door was much higher than they could reach; they were now trying to form two-high pyramids, but, having no shoulders to speak of, they were hardly built for the job. Matt said to Oscar, "Couldn't we give them a hand with that?"

"I'll see." Oscar went forward and suggested that the cadets take over the job of squirting on the solvent. The mother person looked at him.

"Canst thou grow a new hand, if needed?"

Oscar admitted that he could not.

"Then do not tamper with that which thou dost not understand."

Using their own methods the natives soon had the door cleared. It was latched but not locked; the door refused to open for a moment, then gave suddenly. They scrambled up into the airlock. "Wait a minute," Matt whispered. "Hadn't we better go easy? We don't know that the infection that got them is necessarily dead."

"Don't be silly," Tex whispered back. "If your immunizations hadn't worked, you'd have been a sick chicken long ago."

"Tex is right, Matt. And there's no need to whisper. Ghosts can't hear."

"How do you know?" objected Tex. "Are you a doctor of ghostology?"

"I don't believe in ghosts."

"I do. Once my Uncle Bodie stayed overnight—"

"Let's get on inside," Matt insisted.

The passageway beyond the inner door was dark, save for the light that filtered in through the lock. The air had a strange odor, not precisely foul but lifeless—old.

The control room beyond was dimly but adequately lighted; the light from outside filtered softly through the sheathing that still covered the quartz pilot's port. The room was very cramped. The cadets were used to roomy modern ships; the *Astarte*'s wings gave her a false impression of great size. Inside she was smaller than the jeep.

Tex began humming something about "—stout-hearted men—," then broke off suddenly. "Look at the darned thing!" he said. "Just look at it. To think they actually made an interplanetary jump in it. Look at that control board. Why, she's as primitive as a rowboat. And yet they took the chance. Puts you in mind of Columbus and the *Santa Maria*."

"Or the Viking ships," suggested Matt.

"There were men in those days," agreed Oscar, not very originally but with great sincerity.

"You can say that louder," commented Tex. "There's no getting around it, fellows; we were born too late for the age of adventure. Why, they weren't even heading for a listed port; they just blasted off into the dark and trusted to luck that they could get back."

"They didn't get back," Oscar said softly.

"Let's talk about something else," Matt requested. "I'm covered with goose pimples as it is."

"Okay," Oscar concurred, "I'd better get back and see what her royal nibs is doing anyway." He left, to return almost at once, accompanied by the city mother. "She was just waiting to be invited," he called out ahead of them, in Basic, "and huffy at being forgotten. Help me butter her up." —

The native official turned out to be helpful; except for the control room the other spaces were dark, even to her. She stepped to the door, made known her wants, and returned with one of the glowing orange spheres they used for lighting. It was a poor excuse for a flashlight, but about as effective as a candle.

Everywhere the ship was orderly and clean, save for a faint film of dust. "Say what you like, Oscar," commented Matt, "I'm beginning to get my hopes up. I don't believe there is anything wrong with her. It looks as if the crew had just gone out for a walk. We may be able to put her in commission."

"I'm ready to throw in with Oscar," Tex objected. "I've lost my enthusiasm—I'd rather go over Niagara Falls in a barrel."

"*They* flew her," Matt pointed out.

"Sure they did—and my hat's off to them. But it takes heroes to fly a box as primitive as this and I'm not the hero type."

The mother-of-many lost interest presently and went outside. Tex borrowed the orange sphere and continued to look around while Matt and Oscar gave the control room a careful going over. Tex found a locker containing small, sealed packages marked "Personal effects of Roland Hargraves," "Personal effects of Rupert H. Schreiber," and other names. He put them back carefully.

Oscar shouted for him presently. "I think we had better get going. Her nibs hinted that when she left."

"Come see what I've found. Food!"

Matt and Oscar came to the door of the galley storeroom. "Do you suppose any of it is any good?" asked Matt.

"Why not? It's all canned. Jigger for me and we'll find

out." Tex operated with a can opener. "Pheweyl" he said presently. "Anybody want to sample some embalmed corned beef hash? Throw it outside, Matt, before it stinks up the place."

"It already has."

"But look at this!" Tex held up a can marked: *Old Plantation Hotcake Flour.* "This won't be spoiled—hotcakes for breakfast, troops. I can hardly wait."

"What good are flapjacks without syrup?"

"All the comforts of home—half a dozen cans of it." He produced one marked: *Genuine Vermont Maple Syrup, unadulterated.*

Tex wanted to take some back with them. Oscar vetoed it, on both practical and diplomatic grounds. Tex suggested that they remain in the ship, not go back. "Presently, Tex, presently," Oscar agreed. "You forgot about Lieutenant Thurlow."

"So I did. Close my big mouth."

"Speaking of Mr. Thurlow," put in Matt, "you've given me an idea. He won't touch much of that native hash, even when he seems to come pretty far out of it. How about that sugar syrup? I could feed it to him from a drinking bladder."

"It can't hurt him and it might help," decided Oscar. "We'll take half the syrup back with us." Tex picked the cans up, Matt tucked a can opener in his pouch, and they went outside.

Matt was pleased to find Th'wing on watch in Thurlow's room when they got back; she would be easier to deal with than the other nurses. He explained to her what he had in mind, in polite circumlocutions. She accepted a can Matt had opened and tasted, beforehand, and turned her back apologetically while she tasted it.

She spat it out. *"Art thou sure that this will not harm thy ailing mother?"*

Matt understood her hesitation, since Venerian diet runs to starch and protein, not to sugar. He assured her that Thurlow would be helped thereby. They transferred the contents to a bladder.

The cadets talked over what they should do about the *Astarte* after dinner that night. Matt insisted that she could be made to fly; Tex remained of the opinion that they would be silly to attempt it. "She might get high enough to crash—no higher."

Oscar listened, then said, "Matt, did you check the tanks?" Matt admitted that he had. "Then you know there isn't any fuel."

"Then why are you arguing?" Tex interrupted. "The matter is settled."

"No, it's not, announced Oscar. "We'll try to fly her."

"Huh?"

"She can't fly and we'll try anyhow," Oscar went on.

"But why?"

"Okay—here's why. If we just sit here long enough, the Patrol will come along and find us, won't they?"

"Probably," agreed Matt.

"Absolute certainty. That's the way the Patrol works. They won't let us down. Look at the search for the *Pathfinder* —four ships, month after month. If their mishap hadn't killed them, the Patrol would have brought them back alive. We're still alive and we are somewhere near our original destination. They'll find us—the delay simply means they aren't sure we are lost yet; we haven't been out of touch so very long. Anyhow, we knew there wasn't a ship ready at either North Pole or South Pole to attempt an equatorial search, or we wouldn't have gotten the mission in the first place, so it may take a while before they can come for us. But they'll come."

"Then why not wait?" insisted Tex.

"Two reasons. The first is the boss—we've got to get him to a proper hospital before he just fades away and dies."

"And kill him in the take off."

"Maybe. That wouldn't faze him, is my guess. The second reason is—*we* are the Patrol."

"Huh? Come again."

"It's agreed that the Patrol wouldn't give up looking for us. Okay, if that's the sort of an outfit the Patrol is and we are part of the Patrol, then when they find us, they'll find us doing our level best to pull out unassisted, not sitting on our fat fannies waiting for a lift."

"I get you," said Tex. "I was afraid your busy little brain would figure that out, given time. Very well—mark me down as a reluctant hero. I think I'll turn in; this hero business is going to be sweaty and wearing."

It was indeed sweaty. The Venerians continued to be helpful but the actual work of attempting to outfit a ship for space had to be done entirely by the humans. With the permission of the city mother Oscar transferred their headquarters to the *Astarte*. Thurlow was not moved, but arrangements were made for one cadet to be ferried each day back to the city, to report on Thurlow and to bring food back. There were few supplies left in the *Astarte* which were still edible.

However the pancake mix turned out to be usable. Tex had gadgeted together an oil burner of sorts—they had no electrical power as yet—and had charged the contraption with a fish oil obtained from the natives. Over this he baked his hotcakes. They were noticeably inferior to any that any of the three had ever tasted, for the flour had aged and changed flavor. They showed little tendency to rise.

But they were hotcakes and they were drowned in maple syrup. It was a ceremony, at the beginning of each working day, held on the sly behind a locked door, lest one of their puritanical friends be offended.

They embarked on a systematic campaign to vandalize each of the other ships for anything at all that might prove useful in outfitting the *Astarte*. In this, too, they were dependent on the natives; Matt or Tex could pick out what was wanted, but it took the little folk to move anything several miles through swamp and water and unmarked jungle.

They talked of the flight as if they really expected to make it. "You give me radar," Matt told Oscar, "any sort of approach radar, so that I've got a chance to land, and I'll set her down somewhere at South Pole. You can forget about the astrogational junk; it'll be dead reckoning."

They had settled on New Auckland, South Pole, as their

nominal destination. North Pole would have been equally reasonable, but Oscar was a southern colonial, which decided it.

Oscar had promised the radar, not knowing quite how he could manage it. The *Gary* was the only hope; her communications room had been wrecked but Oscar had hopes of salvaging her belly radar. He set about doing it, while swearing at the impossibility of doing delicate work with one arm in a sling.

Little from the jeep was worth salvaging and none of it was entirely intact. Oscar had tried at first to use the radar equipment of the *Astarte*, but had given up—a century of difference in technology baffled him. Not only were the electronic circuits of the *Astarte* vastly more complicated and equally less efficient than the gear he had been brought up with but the nomenclature was different—the markings, for example, on a simple resistor were Greek to him.

As for radio circuits the only sending installation actually fit to operate was a suit walky-talky from the *Gary*.

Nevertheless there came a morning when they had done what they could do. Tex was dealing out hotcakes. "It looks to me," he said, "as if we were ready to go, if we had some 'go' juice."

"How do you figure that," asked Matt. "The control board isn't even hooked to the jet."

"What of it? I'm going to have to throttle by hand anyhow. I'm going to take that big piece of tubing we pulled out of the *Gary* and string it from you back to me, at the jet throttle. You can shout down it and if I like it I'll do it."

"And if you don't like it?"

"Then I'll do something else. Easy on that syrup, Oz; it's the very last."

Oscar stopped himself, syrup can in midair. "Oh, I'm sorry, Tex. Here—let me slop some from my plate onto yours."

"Don't bother. It was just a reflex remark. To tell the truth, I'm sick of hotcakes. We've had them every day now for more than two weeks, with nothing to break the monotony but hash à la native."

"I'm sick of them, too, but it didn't seem polite to say so, with you doing the cooking." Oscar pushed back his plate. "I don't mind the syrup running out."

"But it hasn't—" Matt stopped.

"Something bite you, Matt?"

"No, I—nothing." He continued to look thoughtful.

"Close your mouth, then. Say, Oz, if we had some 'go' juice for the *Tart*, what would you pick?"

"Monatomic hydrogen."

"Why pick the one thing she can't burn? I'd settle for alcohol and oxygen."

"As long as you haven't got it, why not wish for the best?"

"Because we agreed to play this game for keeps. Now we've got to go through the motions of trying to make some fuel, from now till they find us. That's why I say alcohol and oxygen. I'll whomp up some sort of a still and start cooking alky while you and Matt figure out how to produce liquid oxygen with just your bare hands and a ship's equipment."

"How long do you figure it will take you to distil several tons of alcohol with what you can rig up?"

"That's the beauty of it. I'll still be working away at it, like a good little boy, busy as a moonshiner, when they come to rescue us. Say, did I ever tell you about Uncle Bodie and the moonshiners? It seems—"

"Look here," interrupted Matt, "how would you go about cooking up some maple syrup—here?"

"Huh? Why fret about it? We're sick of hotcakes."

"So am I, but I want to know how you can make maple syrup right here. Or, rather, how the natives can do it?"

"Are you nuts, or is this a riddle?"

"Neither one. I just remembered something I had overlooked. You said there wasn't any more maple syrup, and I was about to say that there was still plenty in Thurlow's room." Two days before, it had been Matt's turn to go into the city. As usual he had visited Thurlow's sickroom. His friend Th'wing had been on watch and had left him alone with the lieutenant for twenty minutes or so.

During the interval the patient had roused and Matt had wished to offer him a drink; there were several drinking bladders at hand.

The first one Matt picked up turned out to be charged with maple syrup, and so did the next and the next—the entire row, in fact. Then he found the one he wanted, lying on the couch. "I didn't think anything about it at the time—I was busy with the lieutenant. But this is what bothers me: He's been taking quite a lot of the syrup; you might say he's been living on nothing else. I opened the first can when we first took it to him, and I opened both the other cans myself, as needed—Th'wing couldn't cope with the can opener. So I know that the syrup was almost gone.

"Where did the rest of the syrup come from?"

"Why, I suppose the natives made it," answered Oscar. "It wouldn't be too hard to get sugar from some of the plants around here. There's a sort of grass somewhat like sugar cane, up near the Poles; they could find something of the sort."

"But, Oz, this was *maple* syrup!"

"Huh? It couldn't be. Your taster has gone haywire."

"It was maple, I tell you."

"Well, what if it was—mind you, I don't concede that you can get the true maple flavor this side of Vermont, but what difference does it make?"

"I think we've been overlooking a bet. You were talking about distilling alcohol; I'll bet the natives can supply alcohol in any quantities."

"Oh." Oscar thought about it. "You're probably right. They are clever about things like that—that gunk they use to jell mud and those solvents they cleaned the *Tart* with. Kitchen chemists."

"Maybe they aren't kitchen chemists. Maybe they are the real thing."

"Huh?" said Tex. "What do you mean, Matt?"

"Just what I said. We want 'go' juice for the *Tart*—maybe if we just had sense enough to ask the mother-of-many for it, we'd get it."

Oscar shook his head. "I wish you were right, Matt. Nobody has more respect for the Little People than I have, but there isn't a rocket fuel we can use that doesn't involve one or more liquefied gases. We might even make them understand what we needed but they wouldn't have the facilities for it."

"Why are you so sure?"

"Well, shucks, Matt, liquid oxygen—even liquid air—calls for high pressures and plenty of power, and high-pressure containers for the intermediate stages. The Little People make little use of power, they hardly use metal."

"They don't use power, eh? How about those orange lights?"

"Well, yes, but that can't involve much power."

"Can you make one? Do you know how they work?"

"No, but—"

"What I'm trying to get at is that there may be more ways of doing engineering than the big, muscley, noisy ways we've worked out. You've said yourself that we don't really know the natives, not even around the poles. Let's at least ask!"

"I think he's got something there, Oz," said Tex. "Let's ask."

Oscar was looking very thoughtful. "I've realized for some time that our friends here were more civilized than the ones around the colonies, but I couldn't quite put my finger on it."

"What *is* civilization?"

"Never mind the philosophy—let's get going." Oscar unlocked the ship's outer door and spoke to a figure, waiting in what was to her bright sunlight and busy looking at the pictures in a 1971 *Saturday Evening Post*. "Hey, girlie! *Wouldst thou graciously conduct us to the home of thy mother?*"

It *was* maple syrup. Both Tex and Oscar agreed. Th'wing explained quite readily that, when the supply ran low, they had made more, using the original terrestrial stuff as a sample.

Oscar went to see the city mother, taking with him a

bottle of grain alcohol salvaged from the medical supplies of the *Gary*. Matt and Tex had to sweat it out, for it had been agreed that Oscar did best with her nibs when not accompanied. He returned after more than two hours, looking stunned.

"What gives, Oz? What did you find out?" Matt demanded.

"It's bad news," said Tex. "I can tell from your face."

"No, it's not bad news."

"Then spill it, man, spill it—you mean they can do it?"

Oscar swore softly in Venerian. "They can do anything!"

"Back off and try again," advised Tex. "They can't play a harmonica. I know; I let one try. Now tell us."

"I started in by showing her the ethyl alcohol and tried to explain that we still had a problem and asked her if her people could make the stuff. She seemed to think it was a silly question—just sniffed it and said they could. Then I positively strained myself trying to act out liquid oxygen, first telling her that there were two different things in air, one inert and one active. The best I could do was to use their words for 'living' and 'dead.' I told her I wanted the living part to be like water. She cut me off and sent for one of her people. They talked back and forth for several minutes and I swear I could understand only every second or third word and could not even get the gist of it. It was a part of their language totally new to me. Then the other old girl leaves the room.

"We waited. She asked me if we would be leaving soon if we got what we wanted. I said, yes if— Then she asked me to do her the favor of taking Burke along; she was apologetic about it but firm. I said we would."

"I'm glad of that," said Matt. "I despise Stinky's insides, but it sticks in my craw to leave him to die here. He ought to have a trial."

"Keep quiet, Matt," said Tex. "Who cares about Stinky? Go on, Oscar."

"After quite a wait, the other old girl came back, with a bladder—just an ordinary bladder by the appearance, but darker than a drinking bladder. Her nibs hands it to me and asks me if this is what I wanted. I said sorry but I did not want water. She squeezed a few drops out on my hand." Oscar held out his hand. "See that? It burned me."

"It actually was liquid oxygen?"

"That or liquid air. I didn't have any way to test. I think it was oxygen. But get this—the bladder wasn't even cold. And it didn't fume until she squeezed out the drops. The other gal was carrying it around as casually as you'd carry a hot-water bottle."

Oscar stared off into space a moment. "It beats me," he said. "The only thing I can think of is catalyst chemistry —they must have catalyst chemistry down to the point where they can do things without fuss that we do with heat and pressure."

"Why try to figure it out?" asked Tex. "You'll probably get the wrong answer. Just let it go that they've forgotten more about chemistry than we'll ever learn. And we get the 'go' juice."

For two days a steady procession of little folk had formed a double line from the water's edge to the *Astarte*, bearing full bladders toward the ship and returning with empty ones. Thurlow was already abroad, still attended by his patient little nurses. Burke was brought to the ship under escort and turned loose. The cadets let him alone, which seemed to disconcert him. He looked the ship over—it was the first he had heard of it—and finally sought out Jensen.

"If you think I'm going to ride in that flying coffin you're greatly mistaken."

"Suit yourself."

"Well, what are you going to do about it?"

"Nothing. You can stay in the jungle, or try to persuade the city mother to take you back."

Burke considered it. "I think I'll stay with the frogs. If you get through, you can tell them where I am and have them come get me."

"I'll tell them where you are all right and all the rest of it, too."

"You needn't think you can scare me." Burke went away.

He returned shortly. "I've changed my mind. I'm coming with you."

"You mean they wouldn't have you."

"Well—yes."

"Very well," answered Cadet Jensen, "the local authorities having declined jurisdiction, I arrest you under the colonial code titled 'Relations with Aborigines,' charges and specifications to be made known to you at your arraignment and not necessarily limited to the code cited. You are warned that anything you say may be used in evidence against you."

"You can't do this!"

"Matt! Tex! Take him in and strap him down."

"With pleasure!" They strapped him to an acceleration rest mounted in the galley, where, they had agreed, he would be the least nuisance. Done, they reported it to Jensen."

"See here, Oz," Matt added, "do you think you can make any charges stick against him?"

"I rather doubt it, unless they allow our hearsay under a 'best evidence' rule. Of course he ought to be strung up higher than the Milky Way, but the best I expect is to get his license revoked and his passport lifted. The Patrol will believe our story and that's enough for those items."

Less than an hour later Thurlow's nurses left the ship and the cadets said good-by to the mother-of-many, a flowery, long-winded business in which Oscar let himself be trapped into promising to return some day. But at last he closed the outer door and Tex clamped it. "Are you sure they understand how to keep clear of our blast?" asked Matt.

"I paced off the safety line with her myself and heard her give the orders. Quit worrying and get to your station."

"Aye aye, sir."

Matt and Oscar went forward, Oscar with the ancient log tucked in his sling. Tex took station at the hand throttles. Oscar sat down in the co-pilot's chair and opened the log to the page of the last entry. He took a stub of pencil that he had found in the galley, wet it in his mouth, entered the date, and wrote in a large hand:

He paused and said to Matt, "I still think we ought to shift the command."

"Stow it," said Matt. "If Commodore Arkwright can command the *Randolph* with his lights gone, you can command the *Tart* with a busted wing."

"Okay, if that's the way you want it." He continued to write,

O. Jensen, acting captain
M. Dodson, pilot and astrogator
W. Jarman, chief engineer
Lt. R. Thurlow, passenger (sick list)
G. Burke, passenger, civilian (prisoner)

"Muster the crew, Mister."

"Aye aye, sir. Call your name, too, Oz?"

"Sure, it's a short list as it is."

"How about Stinky?"

"Of course not! I've got him billed as cargo."

Matt took a deep breath and, speaking close to the speaking tube so that Tex could hear, called out: "Lieutenant Thurlow!"

Oscar replied, "I answer for him." He glanced back at the lieutenant, strapped in the inspector's rest where they could keep an eye on him. Thurlow opened his eyes with the puzzled, questioning look he always showed on the rare occasions when he seemed to be aware of anything.

"Jensen!"

"Here."

"Jarman!"

"Here!" Tex called back, his voice muffled and hollow through the tube.

Matt said, "Dodson present," then wet his lips and hesitated.

"Dahlquist!"

Oscar was about to reply when Thurlow's voice came from behind them: "I answer for him."

"Martin!" Matt went on mechanically, too startled to stop.

"I answer for him," said Oscar, his eyes on Thurlow.

"Rivera!"

"I answer for him," came Tex's voice.

"Wheeler!"

"Wheeler's here too," Tex answered again. "They're all here, Matt. We're ready."

"Complement complete, Captain."

"Very well, sir."

"How is he, Oz?"

"He's closed his eyes again. Raise ship when ready."

"Aye aye, sir. According to plan—*raise ship!*" He grasped the wing controls and waited. The *Astarte* reared on her belly jets, drove up and forward and into the mists of Venus.

XVIII

IN THE COMMANDANT'S OFFICE

PASSED CADETS Dodson and Jarman, freshly detached from the P.R.S. *Pegasus*, at Terra Station out from New Auckland, climbed out of the *Randolph*'s scooter and into the *Randolph* herself. Cadet Jensen was not with them; Oscar, on despatch authorization from the Academy, had been granted six months for leave at home, with the understanding that he would be ordered to temporary duty in the course of it, to accompany the first consul to the equatorial regions to his station and assist in establishing liaison.

Matt and Tex showed their orders to the officer of the watch and left with him the inevitable copies. He gave them their rooming assignments—in Hog Alley, in a room with a different number but otherwise like the one they had had. "Seems like we never left it," remarked Tex, as he unpacked his jump bag.

"Except it seems funny not to have Oz and Pete around."

"Yeah, I keep expecting Oz to stick his head in and ask if we'd like to team up with him and Pete."

The room phone sounded, Tex answered.

"Cadet Jarman?"

"Speaking."

"The Commandant's compliments—you are to report to his office at once."

"Aye aye, sir." He switched off and continued to Matt. "They don't waste much time, do they?" He looked thoughtful and added, "You know what I think?"

"Maybe I can guess."

"Well, this quick service looks promising. And we *did* do quite a job, Matt. There's no getting around to it."

"I guess so. Bringing in the *Astarte*, a hundred and eight years overdue, was something—even if we had dragged it in on wheels it still would be something. I won't start calling you 'Lieutenant' just yet, but—he might commission us."

"Keep your fingers crossed. How do I look?"

"You aren't pretty, but you look nineteen times better than you did when we grounded at South Pole. Better get moving."

"Right." Tex left and Matt waited nervously. Presently the call he expected came in, telling him, too, to report to the Commandant.

He found that Tex was still inside. Rather than fidget under the eyes of others in the Commandant's outer office, he chose to wait in the passageway. After a while, Tex came out. Matt went up to him eagerly. "How about it?"

Tex gave him an odd look. "Just go on in."

"You can't talk?"

"We'll talk later. Go on in."

"Cadet Dodson!" someone called from the outer office.

"On deck," he called back. A couple of moments later he was in the presence of the Commandant.

"Cadet Dodson, reporting as ordered, sir."

The Commandant turned his face toward him and Matt felt again the eerie feeling that Commodore Arkwright could see him better than could an ordinary, sighted man. "Oh, yes, Mr. Dodson. At ease." The elder Patrolman reached unerringly for a clip on his desk. "I've been looking over your record. You've made up your deficiency in astrogation and supplemented it with a limited amount of practical work. Captain Yancey seems to approve of you, on the whole, but notes that you are sometimes absent-minded, with a tendency to become pre-occupied with one duty to the expense of others. I don't find that very serious—in a young man."

"Thank you, sir."

"It was not a compliment, just an observation. Now tell me, what would you do if—" Forty-five minutes later Matt caught his breath sufficiently to realize that he had been subjected to a very searching examination. He had come into the Commandant's office feeling nine feet tall, four feet wide, and completely covered with hair. The feeling had passed.

The Commandant paused for a moment as if thinking, then went on, "When will you be ready to be commissioned, Mr. Dodson?"

Matt strangled a bit, then managed to answer, "I don't know, sir. Three or four years, perhaps."

"I think a year should suffice, if you apply yourself. I'm sending you down to Hayworth Hall. You can catch the shuttle from the Station this afternoon.

"The usual delay for leave, of course," he added.

"That's fine, sir!"

"Enjoy yourself. I have an item here for you—" The blind man hesitated a split second, then reached for another clip. "—a copy of a letter from Lieutenant Thurlow's mother. Another copy has been placed in your record."

"Uh, how is the lieutenant, sir?"

"Completely recovered, they tell me. One more thing before you go—"

"Yes, sir."

"Let me have some notes on what troubles you ran into in recommissioning the *Astarte*, emphasizing what you had to learn as you went along—especially any mistakes you made."

"Uh, aye aye, sir."

"Your notes will be considered in revising the manual on obsolete equipment. No hurry about it—do it when you come back from leave."

Matt left the Commandant's presence feeling only a fraction the size he had when he had gone in, yet he felt curiously elated rather than depressed. He hurried to the room he shared with Tex and found him waiting. Tex looked him over. "I see you've had it."

"Check."

"Hayworth Hall?"

"That's it." Matt looked puzzled. "I don't understand it. I went in there honestly convinced that I was going to be commissioned. But I feel wonderful. Why is that?"

"Don't look at me. I feel the same way, and yet I can't remember that he had a kind word to say. The whole business on Venus he just tossed off."

Matt said, "That's it!"

"What's what?"

" 'He just tossed it off.' That's why we feel good. He didn't make anything of it because he didn't expect anything less—*because we are Patrolmen!*"

"Huh? Yes, that's it—that's exactly it! Like he was thirty-second degree and we were first degree, but members of the same lodge." Tex started to whistle.

"I feel better," said Matt. "I felt good before, but now I feel better, now that I understand why. Say—one other thing."

"What?"

"You didn't tell him about the fight I had with Burke in New Auckland, did you?"

"Of course not." Tex was indignant.

"That's funny. I didn't tell anybody but you, and I could have sworn that no one saw it. I planned it that way."

"He knew about it?"

"He sure did."

"Was he sore?"

"No. He said he realized that Burke was out on bond

and that I was on leave and he had no wish to invade my private life—but he wanted to give me a word of advice."

"Yeah? What was it?"

"Never lead with my left."

Tex looked amazed, then thoughtful. "I think he was telling you not to lead with your chin, too."

"Probably." Matt started repacking his jump bag. "When's the next scooter for the Station?"

"About thirty minutes. Say, Matt, you've got leave of course?"

"Check."

"How about picking up my invitation to spend a few weeks on the Jarman spread? I want you to meet my folks —and Uncle Bodie."

"Uncle Bodie, by all means. But Tex?"

"Yeah?"

"Hotcakes for breakfast?"

"No hotcakes."

"It's a deal."

"Shake."